GREETINGS FROM
PRINCE EDWARD ISLAND

Dear Lydia and Zoey,

I found him!

Tall, dark and handsome—yes, I suppose so, in a tough sort of way—but where's the boy I remember? This Liam Connery is nothing like my sister's friend at Dunwoody High, the one I fell in love with.

Plus, there's something mysterious about him that just...sets me on edge. He didn't know I existed back then, and I'd say he doesn't really know I exist now, even though I'm staying in the same house with him and his mother, who _is_ a sweetheart.

Just goes to show—you can't trust memory. How are you both doing? Find _your_ "first love" yet?

Love,

Charlotte

P.S. See you New Year's Eve!

Dear Reader,

Most women wonder what happened to that first love, the first boy they had a crush on, the one who made them ask what love was all about.

My "first love," the boy I first noticed in second grade and who was my "first date" in seventh grade and with whom I went to the prom at graduation, is happily married—to someone else!—and driving a taxi in a large Canadian city, last I heard. I haven't seen him since our tenth high school reunion, over twenty years ago, although we come from the same hometown and as in all small towns, "there ain't much to see, but what you hear sure makes up for it!"

Zoey, Charlotte and Lydia have all been on a quest to look up their "first loves" in my GIRLFRIENDS miniseries. In this story, Charlotte goes to Prince Edward Island on business and just *happens* to find Liam Connery, the lean, intense boy she'd lost her young, untried heart to at eleven. Of course, they'd never spoken back then, but that doesn't mean she hadn't suffered all the agonies of true love.

Charlotte gets a shock. Liam isn't anything like she remembers. But she soon finds that the man he is today holds an entirely different kind of appeal....

I hope you enjoy Charlotte's story.

Warmest regards,

Judith Bowen

P.S. I love to hear from readers. Please let me know what you think of GIRLFRIENDS. Write to me at: P.O. Box 2333, Point Roberts, WA 98281-2333, or visit me at my Web site at www.judithbowen.com.

Charlotte Moore
Judith Bowen

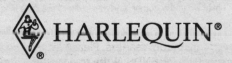

HARLEQUIN®

TORONTO • NEW YORK • LONDON
AMSTERDAM • PARIS • SYDNEY • HAMBURG
STOCKHOLM • ATHENS • TOKYO • MILAN • MADRID
PRAGUE • WARSAW • BUDAPEST • AUCKLAND

ISBN 0-373-71026-7

CHARLOTTE MOORE

Copyright © 2001 by J.E. Corser.

All rights reserved. Except for use in any review, the reproduction or
utilization of this work in whole or in part in any form by any electronic,
mechanical or other means, now known or hereafter invented, including
xerography, photocopying and recording, or in any information storage
or retrieval system, is forbidden without the written permission of the
publisher, Harlequin Enterprises Limited, 225 Duncan Mill Road,
Don Mills, Ontario, Canada M3B 3K9.

All characters in this book have no existence outside the imagination of
the author and have no relation whatsoever to anyone bearing the same
name or names. They are not even distantly inspired by any individual
known or unknown to the author, and all incidents are pure invention.

This edition published by arrangement with Harlequin Books S.A.

® and TM are trademarks of the publisher. Trademarks indicated with
® are registered in the United States Patent and Trademark Office, the
Canadian Trade Marks Office and in other countries.

Visit us at www.eHarlequin.com

Printed in U.S.A.

For Delia McCrae,
longtime friend

CHAPTER ONE

HARDWOODS, MOSTLY MAPLES, blazed on the hill-sides, elbowing aside, if only for a few weeks, the darker tones of gnarly cedar, abundant spruce, towering white pine. At the turn of the road, poplar or birch gleamed—rags of flat gold, tatters of amber, set against the brilliance of the blue October sky.

Wood smoke from kitchen fires hung in the trees, in the dips and gullies. Every hour at least, before turning onto the highway that afternoon, Charlotte had to slow for a farmer drawing a cart loaded with firewood or turnips, sometimes late potatoes, behind his tractor.

This was the best time of year, still weeks away from the winds of winter blowing down from Labrador. It still offered picnicking weather on a good day and, a bonus, the peace and expectant quiet of a tourist area between seasons—the summer travelers, families seeking sun, sea and lobster suppers, had all gone home now, and the color "peepers," the buses full of second-honeymooners and seniors up from Boston and New York or down from central Canada to gaze at all this autumnal glory, were only just beginning to arrive.

Charlotte loved everything about the Maritimes.

She was a city girl through and through, but she always felt completely at home on her annual trips east to the Gaspe, to Nova Scotia and New Brunswick, attending village auctions, winkling out estate sales, sometimes just plain exploring back roads and country lanes, as she'd done this time. She never tired of the scenery, but right now, fall colors and pastoral landscapes were far from her mind.

She couldn't stop thinking about Liam. *Liam Connery.*

The first boy she'd ever had a crush on. She'd been in grade five at Snowden Elementary, and he'd been a friend of her sister's, in grade eleven, at A.E. Dunwoody High in Toronto. He'd never even known Charlotte existed, of course, but that hadn't stopped her young heart from going pitter-patter whenever he showed up at their house with Laurel and her gang, and happened to glance her way.

What a laugh. She hadn't thought of him in years and years, just assumed he'd gone on and followed his dreams, as everyone tried to do after high school. As she had done. He'd talked of flying, so maybe he was Captain Connery now, piloting 747s for Air Canada, a handsome, sexy first officer married to a beautiful, sexy flight attendant.

Last spring, she'd started thinking about him again—and now, six months later, he was still on her mind. The idea of looking up first loves had arisen at last April's reunion of the summer staff of Jasper Park Lodge. Her curiosity had been aroused by the challenge—what *had* happened to Liam Connery?

She'd said as much to Zoey Phillips and Lydia Lane, her best friends, whom she'd first met working at the lodge when they were all eighteen. The summer they met, they'd traveled east together in Lydia's beat-up Toyota minivan and become partners for a few years in the now-defunct Call-a-Girl Company, the little odd-job and catering business they'd formed to earn money for college.

The three of them were still best friends. Both Zoey and Lydia were in Toronto now, but Zoey intended to head to British Columbia soon to attend a friend's wedding—and, Charlotte suspected, to look for her first love in the wilds of the Cariboo-Chilcotin. Sure, Zoey had scoffed at the initial suggestion, but Charlotte knew her friend was as intrigued as she and Lydia had been. Zoey was the pragmatist of the group. Lydia was the world's biggest romantic; maybe she was doing a little scouting of her own back home. Wouldn't it be fun to find out, when she got back, that her two friends had done the same thing, looked up their first loves? Charlotte smiled at the thought. They could compare stories when they got together at New Years.

A definite doggy snore rose from the back seat of her ten-year-old Suburban and Charlotte glanced over her shoulder at Maggie, her sister's Labrador retriever, snoozing on the back seat. Maggie. *That* was another piece of good fortune, the kind of luck she couldn't help thinking was fate.

Naturally, when she'd decided to try and track down Liam Connery, she'd asked her sister. Pay dirt. Laurel, who'd always been the archetype of the annoying, superior, bossy big sister, had lit right up and told her that, yes, she knew *exactly* where Liam Connery was and just leave it to her, she'd make arrangements for Charlotte to meet him.

That had seemed a little…weird. Laurel had never been terribly helpful before, preoccupied as she was with her new second husband and the horses and dogs she raised at their farm north of Toronto. But Charlotte got a phone call from Laurel two weeks later, telling her that everything was arranged, she could take Maggie, one of Laurel's three Labs, to Prince Edward Island to be bred at a retriever kennel owned by none other than the elusive Liam Connery. Charlotte's immediate reaction had been *hey, don't look a gift horse in the mouth!*

Everything had turned out perfectly. Of course, Charlotte was making the trip, anyway, not only to replenish the antiques, folk art and other stock for her one-woman decorative arts supply business, which served a small clientele in the design and decor trade, but to carry out a very special estate appraisal on Prince Edward Island. Now, thanks to her sister, she also had an excellent excuse to meet her first love again, face-to-face—she had a dog to deliver to his kennel. He raised and trained retrievers and hunting dogs, it turned out. So much for being a pilot.

Charlotte studied the highway signs. She was on Route 104, near the exit to Pictou, where she planned to get something to eat, and Caribou, Nova Scotia, the ferry terminal. She slowed as she entered the Pictou municipal limits, watching for a fast-food outlet, preferably with a strip of grass where she could let Maggie out for a pee. She'd miss Maggie. Maggie had been wonderful company on the long drive, plus a Labrador retriever was a dog with a very large bark and, well, you never knew what could happen, a woman traveling alone...

According to Laurel's plan she'd leave Maggie at Connery's kennel to be bred to one of his dogs, and then, when the deed was done, Maggie would be crated and put on a plane back to Toronto. Connery would take care of all that, while Charlotte went about the rest of her business on the island.

"Nearly there, Maggie, my girl," Charlotte murmured, slowing to inspect a seedy-looking fish-and-chip joint on Water Street. It was well past the supper hour and a gang of teens hung around the door, hooting at cars that drove by. She drove on, finally stopping for take-out at Amy's Pizzeria in a residential area on the way out of town—a medium, all-dressed, a can of Pepsi, a tin of Altoid mints, which she was addicted to and a liter of water.

There were six cars at the dock when she arrived, an hour before the ferry sailed at ten o'clock. Charlotte got out of the Suburban and pulled on a heavy wool sweater. She flipped her hair over the collar, stretched and shivered, clasping her arms around herself. It was dark already, just after nine in the evening and past the fall equinox by two weeks, but the causeway was well-lit.

She took a deep breath. It was good to smell the sea air again, to hear the surf sucking at the shoreline. The waves were never very high in the Northumberland Strait, protected as the waterway was by the large mass of Prince Edward Island to the north, and Cape Breton to the northeast, shielding the Gulf of St. Lawrence from the wilder action of the north Atlantic. But sea air was sea air.

She ate her pizza, which was cold by now, sitting on a log that marked the edge of the parking lot, while Maggie explored. Then she snapped on Maggie's leash for a walk down by the water—and was glad she had, when a cocker spaniel, also leashed, practically pulled his owner over trying to get near them. He began sniffing avidly at Maggie's back end. The leash was a precaution; Maggie wasn't supposed to come into estrus for another couple of weeks, according to Laurel, who knew about these things. Charlotte, who knew nothing about these things, didn't want to take any chances. Laurel would kill her if Maggie ended up having the wrong dog's puppies.

"Just trying to make friends." The older woman who owned the spaniel apologized. She seemed a little discomfited at her dog's determination to try again, oblivious to Maggie's low growl. "Come here, Freddy! Stop that now!"

"Yes," Charlotte said noncommittally, smiling. They moved away, down the rocky beach. She'd come across the comment many times. It was true; dogs were more interested in checking out each other's rear ends than anything else, it seemed. She'd gotten over the embarrassment long ago.

"Come on, Maggs." Charlotte led her back to the vehicle, where she shared the last two pieces of pizza with her beside the truck. Charlotte rubbed the retriever's ears and bent down to kiss the top of her glossy black head. "Good girl! What would I do without you?"

And she meant it.

THIS TRIP to Prince Edward Island was a lot more important than just trying to finagle a meeting with her lost first love, Charlotte mused as she gazed over the dark water the ferry ploughed through on its way across Northumberland Strait. Or doing her sister a favor. The bid she'd won—to appraise one of the country's fabled and nearly unknown collections of Canadiana furniture and folk art—was a definite coup for Charlotte Moore FolkArt Specialties. The extra option to help oversee the dispersal sale, together with the representative from Busby's, the Halifax auction firm in charge, was icing on the cake.

Good money and a three- or four-week job. Then she'd continue with her annual fall tour of small sales and estate auctions throughout the Maritimes and New England, during which she'd stuff the Suburban to the roof with lamps, quilts, baskets, mats and folk art treasures—spending maybe another leisurely three or four weeks. She'd enjoy the fall colors along with the tourists, and arrive back in Toronto in time for the pre-Christmas rush. Her buyers were always eager for anything she brought back, to supply decorators or to sell to the public in their own retail outlets. Charlotte's shop, which wasn't really a shop since she just rented warehouse space and ran her business from a home office with the occasional help of a part-time assistant, was basically closed until she returned.

As she drove off the boat at midnight, she decided taking the last ferry hadn't been one of her better ideas. She'd seen nothing during the ninety-minute crossing in the dark, and here, at the other terminal, Wood Island, there was no hotel, no motel, no bed-and-breakfast, nothing. Which meant a drive to Montague, another half hour, where she'd have to try and find accommodations that would take both her and Maggie. After enquiring at two that didn't allow dogs, no matter how well-behaved, she said the hell with it and checked into a rather shabby motel a few miles out of town, leaving Maggie in the Suburban overnight. She'd done it before.

By the time Charlotte drove back into Montague for breakfast the next day, deciding on a place called Mackenzie's Lunch, it was nearly ten o'clock. The diner was typical of the sort you'd find in any small town—lino floors, a counter with eight or ten stools, and booths lining the opposite wall with several For-mica-topped tables between. A motherly looking waitress with swollen ankles came over to take her order. There was only one other customer, a man wearing a Husqvarna cap at the counter, with a newspaper spread out in front of him.

"Clam rolls for breakfast?" Charlotte asked, after a quick glance at the typed, grease-spotted menu.

"Some like it," the waitress replied. "What'll you have, hon?"

"Two poached eggs, brown toast on the side and a glass of tomato juice."

"Coffee?" The waitress held the pot high, over the cup.

Charlotte covered the top with an open hand. "Tea, please."

"Comin' up!" The waitress waddled cheerfully back to the counter and poised her pot of coffee over the other customer's mug. "Refill, Sid?"

He nodded and glanced toward Charlotte. "Traveling through, miss?"

"Not really," Charlotte admitted, clasping her hands in front of her. How did people know, no matter where she went, that she wasn't a local? "I'm doing some work at the Rathbone estate at Cardigan River."

The man whistled and exchanged a meaningful look with the waitress. "Old Man Rathbone's dead. Couple months ago. I guess you heard?"

"Yes. Actually, I'm here to do an appraisal for the heirs. Furniture, art, that sort of thing."

Sid whistled again. "Now, there's a job and a half, ain't it, Gladys?"

"I would say," the waitress replied, pouring boiling water into a stainless steel teapot that Charlotte assumed was hers.

"Oh? Why's that?"

"The old man wasn't in his proper mind the last couple years. They say the place is a fearful mess."

"Oh my, yes. Old fool, wouldn't take no help from nobody." The waitress brought her tea. "They say when he ran out of wood he busted up good furniture to put in the stove—"

"No!" Charlotte put her hand over her mouth.

"He's supposed to have a wonderful collection. Surely he didn't put it in—in the fire?"

The waitress set Charlotte's breakfast in front of her. "Just firewood to him. They say the place has been cleaned up some now. There's a grandson there, I heard, lookin' after things. One of Bertie's boys, ain't he, Sid?"

The man at the counter nodded. "Nick Deacon, Bertie's youngest."

"Anyways. Young fella from Massachusetts or Connecticut or somewheres down there in the Boston States— You want anything else, honey, you just holler." The waitress clumped her way back toward the kitchen.

Charlotte poured the tea before it got too strong and added milk. The Rathbone collection—most of it dating back to the turn of the twentieth century—had been assembled mainly by the father and uncle of this Old Man Rathbone, brothers who'd settled the area just north of Montague, in Cardigan River, and accumulated a fortune from shipping and mercantile interests in the first half of the century. The late owner had been a widower for many years. Charlotte knew nothing about any family, but then, that wasn't her area. The heirs, the estate, the will— lawyers took care of things like that. Her job was to catalog and estimate a fair price for the art and furniture collection.

"Anything else, dear?" The waitress called from behind the counter. Sid put his paper to one side and swung around, too.

Charlotte took a big breath. Why not? "You know of Petty Cove Retrievers?"

"You bet. That's out there close by the estate you're a-goin' to." Sid frowned.

"You know a Mr. Connery?"

"A Mr. Connery?" Sid and the waitress looked at each other again. "Which one, that's the question," he continued, smiling. "Connerys is thick as fleas on a dog's back around here. Why Gladys here's mother was a Connery, wasn't she, Gladys. And there's Connerys out at Princess Point and some west of town here and plenty up north, all the way to Bay Fortune, ain't that right, Gladys? That's where Amos Connery is, married to your cousin, ain't he?"

Gladys topped up Sid's coffee again. "That's right. Amos married Ruthie, my second cousin."

"I suppose you'd be lookin' for a particular Connery, miss?" Sid's face became suspicious, as though he'd remembered he was talking to an outsider, someone From Away, not an Islander.

Charlotte nodded and picked up her windbreaker, then moved toward the cash register. "Someone my sister went to school with years ago in Toronto."

"Oh?" Sid shot another glance at the waitress.

Charlotte handed over a ten-dollar bill and received change, with the two of them regarding her curiously the whole time. "Liam Connery. You know him?" Charlotte left a two-dollar tip and pocketed her remaining change.

"Oh, we know him, all right—don't we, Gladys?" The waitress nodded, her cheerful face

suddenly worried looking. "Ah, no, miss," Sid
added, shaking his head. "You don't want to look
up *that* Mr. Connery. He's an ornery bugger. Keeps
to himself and he don't like strangers snooping
around."

"But he has the kennel, right?" Charlotte persisted.

"That he does. Over to Petty Cove, next to Cardigan River, right near where you're headed." Sid
rattled his newspaper loudly and snapped it against
the counter, as though dismissing both her and her
foolishness. "You might ask at Bristol's Store.
They'll give you directions, if you've got your mind
made up."

"I do. I'm delivering a dog to him, you see."

"Oh?" Sid's expression was skeptical. "Well, I
suppose that's all right, then."

"Thanks for the lovely breakfast," Charlotte said,
smiling at the waitress, who beamed back. "I'll be
on my way."

Charlotte needed gas and then she had to find a
place where she and Maggie could get out and
stretch. Maggie had been patient with the limited exercise she'd had over the past four days. She was
due for a good run; so was Charlotte. The gas attendant at the Irving station gave her directions to a
beach usually deserted at this time of year, a few
miles north of town.

Maggie whined as Charlotte put the vehicle into
gear and turned onto the highway. The sign mentioned Georgetown and Cardigan River, as well as
Annandale, Souris and East Point farther along.

Petty Cove, where Liam Connery had his kennel, was just a speck on the road map, but the beach she'd been directed to had to be pretty close to the cove. Maybe she'd run across him accidentally. What, sunning himself on the sand? Now, there was a ridiculous idea!

Sure, the place was small and everybody knew everybody—the entire island, Canada's smallest province, had only 130,000 people—but how likely was it that she'd meet Liam Connery before she was ready to meet him? Not very. She had two free days until Monday, when she was due to deliver Maggie, according to her sister's arrangements, and meet Mr. Busby from the Halifax auction house. Charlotte was looking forward to spending the weekend touring around with Maggie, maybe taking a drive up north, right to the end of the Island, at East Point. Or going to the province's capital, Charlottetown, for the day.

She was in no real hurry to meet her first-ever crush again, now that she was actually here. Besides, what had they said at the diner? That Liam Connery was an ornery bugger who didn't take to strangers?

Of course, she wasn't *really* a stranger, was she? She was a—ta-dum! Charlotte imagined thirties' radio music—"Voice from the Past." Not that Liam Connery would give a tinker's damn.

And what past? she reminded herself. She was the one who'd been in love with him, the lean, intense boy with the funny accent in her sister's class. He might remember Laurel, but he sure wasn't going to remember Laurel's little sister, a scrawny kid with a pixie cut and a head full of dreams.

That didn't matter; the idea back at the lodge re-union was just to see what had happened to the boy you'd had your first crush on. It was an exercise in curiosity, pure and simple. Had he turned out the way you'd imagined he would—wonderful, sexy, sensitive? Or was he paunchy and balding with a bad golf game and half-a-dozen kids? Was he the CEO of the local duct-cleaning service? Was he married? In jail? Dead?

That was all. Liam Connery, she remembered, had dreamed of flying. Turned out he'd become a dog breeder, of all things. *C'est la vie.*

No one, she was sure, not even her—and Charlotte knew she was definitely a romantic—expected this little exercise to be anything more than that. They'd have a coffee together, maybe, talk over old times—not that they had many in common—and move on. Their lives might have overlapped briefly once, but they didn't overlap now.

She had to admit, though, she was genuinely cu-rious. "Ornery bugger" didn't scare her. Not unless it was shotgun-slinging ornery, and she doubted that.

Charlotte slowed, peering at the narrow road that had suddenly materialized to the left. Okay. This had to be the beach road—exactly one mile from the turnoff. That was what the man had said—exactly one mile, which meant 1.2 kilometers. Distance in Canada was measured in kilometers now, not that they seemed to have noticed that little detail on Prince Edward Island.

The rutted dirt lane led across an open field stud-ded with frozen, rotted potatoes left after harvest, and wound downward toward the beach. Charlotte bumped along slowly. And happily.

The sun was high in the sky—it was noon—and there was no one, absolutely no one, on this deserted red sand beach. The scene before her was straight out of a travel brochure, except that there were no tourists here now and probably weren't even in the summer. This was rural, isolated P.E.I., the way it had been a century before.

Several hundred yards from the hummocks of dune grass that edged the high tide line, waves broke, a line of white foam that spun smoothly, over and over, from one distant shore to the other, between the headlands. A flock of shore birds swooped and dived high above, their cries wild and beautiful.

How peaceful. How serene.

Charlotte sighed at the silence as she shut off the ignition. What could *possibly* be more wonderful?

CHAPTER TWO

"MAGGIE!" Charlotte shaded her eyes and stared at the rocky headland several hundred yards in front of her.

Then she turned and gazed back down the long curve of the bay, toward where she'd left her vehicle, almost hidden in the tall grass. Each individual footprint she'd made in the cool, firm sand as she'd rounded the bay was in sharp focus. A third of the way back to the Suburban, she could see the windbreaker and sweater she'd discarded, along with her socks and shoes. She was still hot, even though clouds had scudded in from somewhere to partially block the sun and a steady breeze had sprung up.

Charlotte frowned. Maybe Maggie had backtracked behind her while she was running? They'd played at the edge of the water for a while and then shared lunch—an apple, a bag of Doritos and some beef jerky, plus kibble for Maggie, sitting on the grass beside the truck. Then Charlotte had decided to go for a run. She was in no hurry to leave, although she'd considered going on to Charlottetown that afternoon.

"Maggie!" No answering bark. Annoyed, Charlotte tried whistling—a faint, ineffective sound whipped away by the rising wind. The tide had turned when they'd arrived but was still a long way out on the shallow sandy tidal flats. Charlotte had spent a good hour tossing a stick in the surf, laughing as the retriever leaped into the rolling waves time and again, before they'd returned to the shore for their lunch.

She gazed back toward the sea. The tide had come in considerably. No sign of a dog, but that was to be expected. Maggie wouldn't have gone out to the water by herself. Maggie never wandered—*never*.

But there was no big black dog now. Charlotte broke into a slow, cool-down lope. She wasn't really worried. Ten more minutes and she'd make her goal, the rocks that marked the headland, then go back. Maggie was bound to show up by the time she reached the Suburban.

Whoa. Charlotte stopped dead. She tilted her head slightly, listening. A dog? On the land side? Toward that straggle of trees on the other side of the dunes? She remained still, aware of her heavy breathing and the pounding of her pulse. Now that she wasn't running, she felt chilled in her loose cotton cargo pants and perspiration-soaked T-shirt.

There! A chorus of barking followed by a single, excited bark. More like a yip. *Maggie?*

"Maggie!" Charlotte tried the whistle again, but her lips were so stiff that no sound emerged. Her teeth chattered.

Damn that dog, anyway! So much for blue ribbons in obedience. Charlotte veered toward the dunes, which blocked her view of the land, toward the steep hill that rose from the shore. This was totally unlike Maggie! It wasn't as though she was a terrier, following her nose after mice. Or a spaniel, snuffling around in the underbrush for birds. She was a retriever. So what was she doing in the woods, barking after squirrels or chasing rabbits?

Charlotte reached the top of the dune and peered toward the copse of trees where she'd heard the barking. "Maggie! Yoo-hoo! Come, Mag-gie, *come!*"

No sign of Maggie, but Charlotte heard something that alarmed her. Another dog? The deeper tones didn't sound right. She squinted at the dark trees, eyes shaded, willing Maggie to appear. The prospect of having to go after her, to navigate clumps of saw-edged grass and broken sticks and dead sea things did not appeal.

"Ma'am?"

Charlotte shrieked and felt the goosebumps double in size all over her shivering body. "Omigosh! I didn't hear you coming!"

"I'm sorry, ma'am." A boy of thirteen or fourteen had emerged over the side of the dune from the north. He turned red as a beet. "You lookin' for something, ma'am?"

"My dog. She's—" Charlotte waved in the general direction of the woods "—in there somewhere."

"*Your* dog?" The boy seemed puzzled. He put two fingers to his mouth and let fly a piercing whistle, one long and two short.

To Charlotte's amazement, a dog shot out of the trees. Maggie! Oh, no—there was *another* black dog, right behind the first one. They ran together, occasionally turning to nip playfully and to paw each other with their front feet, then run side by side again. Neither animal headed their way.

"Y-yours?" Charlotte was befuddled.

"Liam's." The boy looked over his shoulder, then glanced at her again. He seemed worried. "My dad's cousin."

Liam *Connery?* No. She wasn't ready to meet him; she wasn't dressed properly. She hadn't thought of what she was going to say yet. She had a definite, much-tweaked plan for their first meeting, and this wasn't it. But it *had* to be him—how many Liams could there be in this tiny corner of the island?

The boy sent her another look. He was handsome, with fair skin and piercing blue eyes and a few freckles still left from childhood. "Liam's right mad about Scout going over the side like that...."

He stared toward the two dogs, now running in a madcap manner along the line where the grass met the trees, his expression about as helpless as Charlotte felt. Then she saw him glance over his shoulder.

"Scout's here, Liam, just like you figured," he said. "He's goin' after another dog. I called him but he's a bad old boy and he won't come."

To her horror, Charlotte saw a man striding toward them up the same side of the dune the boy had taken, dressed in a camouflage jacket and carrying a—a big gun! He had another dog with him, a large brown dog with a coarse-looking coat, wavy along the back.

The ominous comments she'd heard at the diner, about Liam Connery not taking to strangers, skipped through her mind.

This was Liam Connery? The man approaching didn't resemble the boy of her memories. He was tall and powerful looking. Dark hair—that was as she remembered—dark eyes, what she could see of them. What color *had* his eyes been—brown? Green? She couldn't recall. A three-day growth of beard gave him a dangerous, lawless air. Scuffed lace-up work boots, a faded plaid shirt under the open jacket. The gun slung over his shoulder. Hair in need of a trim.

He stood beside the boy—ignoring her completely—and gazed out at the dogs frolicking halfway up the side of the hill.

"Well, Goddammit. Would you look at that."

That was all he said, in a low, forceful tone that made her skin crawl. Charlotte was shivering uncontrollably. She wished she'd tied her windbreaker around her waist instead of dropping it on the sand several hundred yards back. The brown dog sat attentively at the man's side, ears alert, but showing no sign of joining the other two dogs.

"Your bitch, ma'am?" He finally glanced her way. The drawled query shocked her. She wasn't used to calling Maggie a bitch, even though she knew that was the proper name for a female dog.

"Y-yes," she managed to say. "M-my sister's, actually." She turned to him, but his attention was back on the hillside.

"She wouldn't be in heat, would she?"

He looked directly at her without a trace of recognition in his eyes. They were brown—a very dark brown—shot with gold and green. She shook her head. "No—at least, I don't think so."

"Good," he continued flatly. "Most people would have the sense not to let loose a bitch in heat."

"It's my sister's dog," Charlotte answered, her voice small. She decided this definitely wasn't the time to tell him she was delivering Maggie to his kennel.

Liam frowned, put his fingers to his mouth, as the boy had, and let loose an ear-splitting whistle, gazing intently toward the hill. Then he swore again.

"I have no idea why she won't listen. She's usually obedient," Charlotte said, then, irked by the man's disdain, added proudly, "She's a champion, after all."

He threw her a quick glance, eyes narrowed, interested—the first time, Charlotte suspected, that her presence had actually registered with him.

"Champion?"

"Show champ. Many times over." Maybe she *ought* to sing Maggie's praises a little. The Lab had not made a good first impression by running off and not coming back when she was called. "Lots of ribbons. Obedience trophies, too."

Liam Connery made a nasty noise in his throat, and the boy glanced at him. "You want me to go get 'em, Liam?"

"Better do that, Jamie. Scout's got one thing on his mind right now, and it isn't his dinner."

He turned and stared at her finally, sizing her up— a little rudely, in Charlotte's opinion. In the past five minutes, she'd had second thoughts about everything. First love! This man was a lout. A *hunter,* from the looks of the gun, even though she didn't

see any ducks or anything. But the gun had to be for
something. He wasn't even polite. He was rude, he
was bossy—and she didn't like the way he referred
to Maggie as a bitch in heat, even if she was.

Charlotte was doing some serious readjusting. So
much for the romantic first-crush reunion story—
Zoey and Lydia would die laughing when they heard
about *this*.

The boy began to slide down the hummock toward
the dogs. She stepped forward, anxious to take some
kind of action, too. "Wait! I'll go with you."

"Ma'am—?"

Charlotte glanced back. Liam stood silhouetted
against the sky, holding out his jacket, which he'd
taken off.

"Better wear this." He hitched one shoulder toward the beach, and Charlotte automatically looked
that way.

Her clothes! The tide had inched in far enough
now that the water had reached her sweater and
jacket. As she watched, an incoming wave slurped
up the sand, smoothly covered her clothes, released
them and then slipped back down the sand into the
sea. Charlotte could have wept. Everything—everything!—was going wrong.

She might as well accept his offer. Her teeth were
chattering. As she walked toward him, his eyes narrowed again, focusing on her face. Recognition? A
hint? No way. She'd never have known him if the
boy hadn't mentioned his name, and fifteen years
ago he hadn't even been aware she existed.

He held the garment, and she slipped her arms into

the sleeves. Without a word, he pulled it up on her shoulders and around her neck. She avoided his eyes. The dog by his side never missed a move, watching everything Charlotte did, every gesture. He had yellow eyes—kind of creepy.

"Th-thanks," she said, wrapping her arms around herself in the cozy flannel lining. It was an oddly intimate thing to do: give her his coat, which was huge on her and still warm from his body. A very generous gesture. She took back her first impression.

Okay. Still rude, maybe. But generous.

"You stay here. I'll go get your stuff."

Still bossy, too. Charlotte opened her mouth to say she'd go get her clothes herself, but he started toward the beach before she could speak. The brown dog followed him. She clamped her lips shut and stared miserably in the direction the boy had taken. Jamie reached down and grasped Scout by the scruff of the neck. He snapped on a leash and made a grab for Maggie, who danced around them both, tail high. Scout shook himself vigorously then barked, straining to get free again. Jamie hung on tightly, thank heavens.

"Maggie!" She thought she'd try again, to no effect. *"Come!"* Maggie didn't even look her way.

Charlotte noticed that Liam had picked up her clothes but, instead of walking back to join her, was heading toward the boy. The wind had come up. She couldn't hear anything they said but saw Liam dig into the pocket of her jacket and extract something shiny, which he handed over.

Her car keys!

He talked to Jamie for another minute or so, then strode toward her, while his young cousin began to drag Scout down the beach in the direction of her vehicle, with Maggie happily cavorting behind, showing off for her new boyfriend, who tugged enthusiastically at his leash. Both dogs were yipping and whining with excitement.

Charlotte felt faint. Maggie had abandoned her without even a backward glance. Where was Jamie taking them?

She was freezing, but she felt she had to make *some* kind of move. She took a few steps forward and nearly fell down. Her legs were stiff, her lips numb.

Liam hiked the gun he still carried higher on his shoulder and tossed something up the dune toward her. Ugh, her wet sneakers. She stuck her sandy feet in them, grimacing at the unpleasant sensation.

"This way," he called, and veered to the north, gesturing to her to follow him. The brown dog fell into step at his left side.

She planted her feet firmly. She wasn't going anywhere, not until she knew what was happening.

He glanced over his shoulder and with an expression of pure annoyance turned around and walked back.

"Problems?" he asked from a distance of about twenty feet, at the base of the dune.

She gazed down at him, thinking he looked like he'd stepped out of an outfitter's catalog, with his hunting clothes, his sturdy boots, his gun, his windblown hair. "Uh, what did you do with my car keys? And where's my dog? Where are we—?"

"You can warm up at my place." He waved an impatient hand in the direction he'd been walking. "Ten minutes on the other side of this headland. It's cold, and your clothes are wet," he went on, frowning. "Okay? Jamie will drive. He knows a shortcut that—"

"Does he have a driver's license?"

Liam sighed loudly. "He's been driving since he was twelve. He's taking a back lane through the fields," he explained slowly, as though he were dealing with a simpleton. "A private road. Perfectly legal. He'll meet us at the house. Now, are you coming?"

What choice did she have? She could have stayed where she was and—and what? She had no dog, no keys, no car, and her sopping wet windbreaker and sweater were still in his hand. What was she going to do—wrestle them away from him and run? Run where? And why? She was wearing his jacket. He was just being hospitable, offering her a place to warm up out of the wind and the cold, maybe even a cup of tea. Jamie would be there in a few minutes; it wasn't as though she'd be alone with this rather intimidating man and...what if she was? She was twenty-eight years old, well able to take care of herself.

For pity's sake, what did she *think* might happen?

"Okay. I—I'm coming," she called out, hoping it sounded fairly ordinary, or at least as though she'd just had a cramp in her foot or a stone in her shoe or there'd been some equally good reason that had prevented her from following him immediately.

She stumbled down the dune, keeping her arms around herself to hold the jacket, which reached past her hips, against her skin. The wind had increased, whipping her hair across her face, and the clouds had darkened. A serious storm coming? She was chilled to the bone.

Liam, as expected, was no gentleman. He strode ahead, his dog at his side, obviously familiar with the lay of the dunes and, when they entered the woods, each twist and turn of the path. Only occasionally did he glance back.

She did her best to keep up. She had a sudden giddy vision of Hansel, with her as Gretel scurrying behind him, two children lost in the magical dark woods, scattering bread to mark their way, crumbs that were immediately gobbled up by the birds.

She might well be Gretel, blindly stumbling along, but the analogy stopped there: Liam Connery knew exactly where he was headed. All she had to do was follow him.

CHAPTER THREE

IT WAS HARD TO BELIEVE they'd walked less than ten minutes by the time the gloomy path through the sea-stunted forest gave way to a more open area of dull dry grass dotted with scrub alders and willows. Liam stopped once, to supervise her scramble over a derelict wooden fence, which she managed—gracefully, she thought—then forged ahead with her close behind him.

Charlotte heard dogs barking before she saw the house, a two-story cedar-shingled frame building with a big wraparound veranda and a darling cupola on top, complete with battered widow's walk. The style, more commonly without the cupola, was popular along the coast. Supposedly, a seafarer's wife could stand on the tiny balcony and gaze out to sea to spy her spouse as he sailed into harbor.

Whether that was so she could put a cake in the oven or chase the gardener out of her bed, Charlotte didn't know, but cupolas were a charming addition to any dwelling, and she'd always wanted to sit in one, maybe take up a book to read.

Liam's house was much grander than she'd expected it to be, even needing a coat of paint as it did and some attention to the landscaping. There were trees and bushes—a crab apple, two lilacs and several escallonias—that looked as though they'd once been productive but had been allowed to grow wild and unpruned. Everything seemed a bit run-down, a bit neglected.

"How many more dogs do you have?" she asked as she hurried to catch up to him.

"Twelve right now, not counting a new litter a month ago," he replied, reaching for the latch that opened the wooden gate. An ancient sumac, its branches laden with candelabras of scarlet cone-shaped fruit, guarded the entrance path.

"Puppies! How lovely," Charlotte said, trying to be conversational. Liam didn't respond. He was a singularly uncommunicative man. Thank goodness she had Maggie with her, as a pretext for conversation once they sorted out the introductions. She could hardly imagine what she'd have come up with if she'd just located him in the phone book and called. Knowing her, she'd have blurted out something about the crush she'd had on him when she was eleven and when could they get together to discuss it.

A waist-high white picket fence surrounded the house, each post surmounted by ornamental wood-carvings in a last-century style. Charlotte noted the detail avidly. Folk art of all kinds, from architecture to furniture and the decorative arts: these were the passions she'd turned into a livelihood over the past few years.

Completing the quaint domestic picture—forest to one side, open shore and sea to the other, with the sun suddenly breaking through—wood smoke poured from a brick chimney. Of course! Liam Connery didn't live alone. Twelve dogs. Plus puppies. What was that—another five or six? And no doubt a wife, kids, mortgage and a big feed bill. After all, if Charlotte was twenty-eight, he had to be at least thirty-three or -four by now.

A family man. What an unsettling thought. So far, Charlotte had not factored a wife and children into the mental picture she'd formed. He seemed so…remote. Detached. Self-sufficient. So—how had Sid put it?—*ornery.*

They entered a small linoleum-floored anteroom full of coats and boots, and smelling slightly of dog. The dog with him—she still hadn't heard Liam call it by name—settled with a sigh into a blanket-lined wicker basket. She didn't know whether or not to slip off her sneakers, deciding, in the end, that she'd keep them on, considering she wasn't wearing any socks. She wiped the soles carefully on the mat beside the door, noting that she was desecrating a traditional hooked mat, faded but sturdy, that would probably bring seventy-five dollars at an auction in Toronto. Collectors snapped up mats like these.

Liam, she was relieved to see, walked to a glass-fronted cabinet that contained several guns and deposited the one he'd had slung over his shoulder, locking the door and pocketing the key.

"Why do you have the gun?" she asked, unable to resist.

"To shoot ducks," he said. "You want to keep the coat on for now?"

He moved to the door that separated the vestibule from the rest of the house and paused, less than a yard away from her, waiting for her response.

Charlotte searched his gaze for a clue as to the situation—and saw nothing but an odd wariness. Beneath that scruffy beard, he'd grown up to be a handsome man, in his rough way. And yet he struck her as...almost scary. She decided to stay wrapped up in the jacket, if for no other reason than that she was suddenly embarrassed at the prospect of exposing herself in her damp, no doubt revealing, T-shirt. She nodded.

Modesty, thy name is Woman, she thought, mangling the half-remembered phrase.

He opened the door and gestured her forward into a kitchen. There were no lights on in the room, and it seemed a little gloomy, if delightfully warm.

Liam flipped a wall switch to turn on a light.

"Liam? That you?" came a thin voice from one corner of the room. Charlotte's gaze settled on an elderly woman, probably in her early seventies, her hands occupied with yarn and knitting needles, and accompanied by a cat that perched on the upholstered back of her chair. The woman looked toward them but there was something unusual in her flat gaze.

"I'm home, Ma. Brought company. She got her clothes wet down at the shore and she could use a cup of tea and a warm-up."

"Oh? Any luck?"

Liam, who'd taken off his boots, picked up a teakettle that was sitting on a gleaming modern commercial range and went to the sink. "Nope. Scout wasn't in the mood. He had other things on his mind." He glanced at Charlotte and she felt herself flush.

The whole kitchen was furnished in a surprisingly up-to-date fashion, with a large refrigerator, a dishwasher and double stainless steel sinks. The appliances appeared to be about ten years old. Somehow, she hadn't expected a modern kitchen. An older woodstove was in one corner, near the woman's chair, and was probably the source of the wood smoke she'd noticed. That suited the room.

"Stay there, Ma," he said, although the woman had made no effort to get up. "I'll make the tea." He ran some water into the kettle.

"Where's Davy's boy?"

Liam looked toward his mother. "He'll be along shortly. He's got Scout."

The woman chuckled and put her knitting aside. "That Scout is quite a rapscallion." She shook her head, smiling. Charlotte got the impression that she was pleased to hear about Scout's hijinks. "He sure doesn't take after his daddy, does he? Old Jimbo. Now, there's a dog who's all business. Did you say you'd brought someone, Liam?"

Charlotte stared at the older woman, shocked. *Hadn't she seen her?* She glanced at Liam. He had set the kettle on the stove. He shot her a warning look that she couldn't quite decipher.

"Yes. This is—I never did ask your name, ma'am." He actually smiled slightly It made a huge difference to what Charlotte had come to believe was a perpetually grim expression.

"Charlotte," she said, stepping forward and rather foolishly holding out her hand. "Charlotte Moore. From Toronto."

He frowned. "I'm Liam Connery—"

"I know who you are." She desperately wanted to set the record straight. About Maggie. About Laurel. About herself.

"You do?"

"Actually, believe it or not, I was more or less on my way here, to your place. To drop off a dog—"

"That Labrador?" He was still frowning.

"Yes." She took a deep breath. "I understand that you made some arrangements with my sister Laurel to have Maggie bred here...."

"You're Laurel Moore's sister?" He seemed completely taken aback.

"I am. Her younger sister. I remember you but—" she laughed nervously "—I don't suppose you remember me."

He shook his head. "No, I don't. And I think there's been a misunderstanding." He turned toward his mother again without explaining. "This is my mother, Ada Connery."

"How do you do, Mrs. Connery?" Charlotte said formally. "Thank you for letting me stop in to warm up."

The older woman nodded and smiled. "I'm sorry I didn't see you, dear. My eyes aren't what they used to be. It must be dark in here. Come in, sit yourself down. Liam, there's some of that date cake in the bread box. Cut a slice for our guest, Mrs. Moore—''

''Oh, I'm not married.''

''*Miss* Moore. Get her a cup of tea, Liam.''

''Please, call me Charlotte.'' She looked helplessly at Liam. He pointed at his own eyes with both forefingers, then gave her a thumbs-down gesture, both hands. Blind?

Her dismay must have been obvious. He nodded and walked toward her. ''That sweater okay to go in the dryer?'' It was on the kitchen table, along with her balled-up jacket.

Charlotte remembered why she was here—to dry her clothes.

''Sure, it's wool but it's washable. The jacket can go in, too.''

He held her clothes in one hand but didn't move away. ''So what's this about leaving your sister's bitch here? Didn't she get my message?''

''Message?''

''I left her a message, let's see—'' he ran one hand through his already dishevelled hair ''—just about a week ago.''

''My sister and her husband are in Belize on holiday. A week ago?'' Charlotte paused, trying to think back. So much had happened in a week!

''Whatever. Your sister called here quite a few times, tried to talk me into breeding her bitch, but I told her I wouldn't consider it.''

''You're *joking*.'' Charlotte didn't mean that at all—joking. She was shocked to her core. ''Laurel said she had it all arranged!''

"She lied." He glanced toward the stove, where the kettle had just begun to boil.

"My sister doesn't lie," Charlotte said stiffly. She had to defend her own sister, for heaven's sake! But she'd been suspicious of Laurel's sudden enthusiasm at discovering that Charlotte was not only traveling to Prince Edward Island on business, but wanted to meet Liam Connery. Had Laurel set her up?

Liam cracked a smile, which frayed Charlotte's jittery nerves even more. "Must've changed, then," he said easily, taking a step toward the stove. He put her sweater on the counter. "She sure knew how to tell a tall tale at Dunwoody High."

"But I *have* to leave Maggie here. I have other things I have to—"

"Sit down." He indicated a chair at the kitchen table, then poured water over the tea bags and put the teapot back on the stove. He deposited a thick ceramic mug unceremoniously on the table, before picking up her clothes again and disappearing into another doorway that led off the kitchen. She wondered why he hadn't offered his mother tea. She heard the slam of a door—the dryer—and then the sound of the machine starting.

"Psst!" Startled, Charlotte looked toward the corner where Liam's mother was gesturing. "Don't pay him no mind. He's awful particular about who he breeds his dogs to, the Labs and the Chessies both."

"But—" Charlotte began, then thought better of it. The tea was starting to simmer. She got up to take it off the stove and bring it to the table. It was already black as tar. Honestly! Didn't he even know how to make a pot of tea?

"So, in the area tourin', are you?" Ada Connery asked in a friendly tone, resuming her knitting.

"Actually, I'm here for a few weeks. I'll be doing some work on the Rathbone estate. I'll need to find a place for Maggie first, though, now that there's been a mix-up." *Now that Laurel had screwed up royally!* "I understand the estate is nearby." The tea was hot and welcome. She wrapped her cold fingers around the mug, then took some sugar from a graniteware bowl that stood on the table, and stirred it in.

"Yes, indeed. Matter-of-fact, it's right next door, just through the woods. You can't miss it. There's not much around here but the post office and the store. There's the lobster supper in summer, over at Cardigan River. That's all closed now."

"I see," Charlotte murmured. She sat down gingerly on a kitchen chair. The soles of her sneakers squeaked on the linoleum floor, and the woman across the room looked up.

Ada Connery shook her head. "Old Mr. Rathbone was always quite a gentleman, you know. Until he took his turn, that is. He became fairly hard to handle then, from what I've been told, always skulking about, springing up on people to surprise them. Boo!" She waved one hand quickly, as though imitating her deceased neighbor. "Couldn't be trusted with a match in the end. Dementia, they say."

She glanced in Charlotte's direction with her sightless eyes and pulled another strand of yarn from

the wicker basket by her side. Charlotte could count
at least four completed mittens from where she sat,
and wondered how many were in the basket and why
Ada Connery kept knitting more.

"My late husband did odd jobs over there sometimes—gardening and what not. The old gentleman
was very fond of huntin' dogs. Liam has a couple of
'em now. But I do believe the neighborhood has im-
proved since the old fellow has passed on. He was
what they called a *philanderer* in my day—Miss
Charlotte will be working at Gerard Rathbone's
place, did you know that, Liam?"

Liam had returned from disposing of her clothes
and was carrying a sweater—not hers. "No, I didn't,
Ma." He didn't sound that interested. "Here— If
this fits, you're welcome to it."

"Thanks." Charlotte took the sweater and removed his jacket. "I'm assisting with the estate appraisal for the heirs," she explained. "Art, furniture,
that sort of thing."

He raised one eyebrow briefly as though to un-
derline his indifference. Her damp T-shirt was stuck
to her breasts and belly, as she'd suspected. She was
seized with an enormous shiver, the kind you felt
right down to your shins, and quickly tugged on the
garment he'd handed her, a Nordic-patterned sweater
in greens and blues.

He'd turned away the instant she pulled off the
jacket. Her earlier fit of modesty hadn't been necessary. This man clearly had no interest—whatsoever—in her as a female. As a shapely woman wear-

ing a revealing garment. He hadn't even sneaked a peek, from what she could tell.

"I believe Bertie's boy, Nick, is taking care of things over there for the family. I saved your dinner in the oven, Liam." It took Charlotte a few seconds to realize that the family Ada was talking about was the Rathbones.

"I'll have it later, Ma." Liam went to the window that overlooked the path they'd taken to the house. "Here's Jamie now."

"What about my dog?" Charlotte stood quickly. Poor Maggie.

"I'll make sure she's all right."

Without another word, he left. Charlotte took a gulp of the sweet tea. What she'd meant, what she wished she'd said, was, *Aren't you going to take her off my hands, as my sister supposedly arranged?* Surely Laurel hadn't been so foolish as to think that if Charlotte just showed up with Maggie, she'd be able to convince this man to breed the dog to one of his prize animals....

Frankly, Charlotte didn't give a damn. It was Laurel's problem, not hers. What she cared about was finding a place to board Maggie until her sister and brother-in-law got back from their holiday.

"You'll want to have a look at the puppies before you go. Liam says they're the best litter he's had from Bear, and that's sayin' something."

"Bear is—?"

"His Chesapeake Bay retriever daddy dog. Scout's daddy is Old Jimbo, Liam's Labrador daddy dog. He's gettin' on, poor fella."

Charlotte's head was spinning with dog details.

"Darn that old Scout! He's quite a scamp." The older woman chuckled again. "Yes, my son gets near a thousand dollars for one of Bear's pups and he won't sell to just anyone. He's very particular. Very particular, indeed."

Indeed. Her sister—or perhaps Maggie—obviously had not passed the test.

"You go on out, miss. Take any one of those jackets hanging there in the mudroom."

"You're sure you'll be all right? You want some tea?" That was a silly thing to say, obviously Liam's mother did just fine on her own. She'd been alone when they arrived.

Ada Connery laughed. "Of course I'll be all right. If I want tea, I'll get it. I'm not crippled up or anything, you know—it's just that my eyesight is poorly these days."

According to Liam, his mother was stone-blind.

Charlotte went out. Her Suburban was safely parked in the driveway. The wind caught her hair in cold gusts and the sunshine that had broken through the clouds earlier had vanished. The sky was very dark.

Jamie emerged from a shed at the back of the property, where there were several barn-red outbuildings. "Want to see the new litter?"

Everyone here was pup-crazy! That was okay by Charlotte. She liked pups, too. Who didn't? "Sure." She made her way over to the boy. "Where's Maggie?"

Charlotte could see several chain-link runs out behind the sheds. Four or five dogs stood at attention behind the fence, regarding her alertly. They were all shades of brown. Some were black. One barked, but the rest were silent and watchful. Labradors and Chesapeake Bay retrievers, Ada had said.

Jamie gestured toward the driveway. "Liam told me to leave her in your truck, since you'd be going soon, anyway."

She walked beside him as he led her into the closest building.

"This here is Sammy," the boy said proudly. "She's one of Liam's top bitches." Charlotte couldn't help wincing. She just wasn't used to hearing that *word* all the time.

"Oh, wow," she said softly, kneeling down. Five chocolate-brown pups with the bluest eyes she'd ever seen poked their noses out between the slats of their pen and sniffed at her ankles.

"Want to hold one?" Jamie held the pen door wide open and a tan-colored dog—obviously the mother—came toward them, wagging her tail. Jamie scratched her ears.

"Look at their blue eyes!" Charlotte said. She'd never seen pups with eyes like that before.

Jamie gave her an indulgent look. "All Chessies have blue eyes when they're babies. Then they turn green and then finally yellow, when they grow up. Amber, Liam calls it."

Liam, Liam, Liam. A major case of hero worship here. Where was he?

Charlotte bent to study the pups. They'd clustered around her feet, and one had its tiny teeth in her shoelace. She picked it up. The puppy had tons more skin than it needed, which gave its face a dozy, wrinkly look. Just like a little bear. Its little candy-pink tongue came out for a few seconds when it yawned. How adorable. A thousand dollars!

"So, this Sammy—the mom—is this her first litter?"

"Her fourth. Sammy's the best. I helped train her," he added proudly.

"I'll bet that's quite a job," she said, tickling the pup under its chin.

"Not really. Liam says I'm a natural. I got a talent for it. But you don't have to do much with these little fellas," he said modestly. "They got the instinct. Liam trains gun dogs for other folk—Labradors, weimaraners, goldens, you name it. He's got five boarders now, but mostly he trains his own Labs and Chessies and sells them started."

"Started?"

"Partly trained. I've got a pup of my own," Jamie went on enthusiastically, his blue eyes meeting hers. "Buster. Liam gave 'im to me. One of Old Jimbo's pups. A brother to Scout. Liam says I can set up with my own dogs now, but my ma says I got to finish school first."

"How old are you, Jamie?"

"Fourteen."

"Shouldn't you, uh—" Charlotte paused and winked "—be in school today?"

"Yeah," he said, with a jaunty shrug. "I can catch up." Then he sighed and stood. "Man, I hope there's some dinner left. I'm starving, and that damn old Scout knocked our dinner into the bay.''

Charlotte walked slowly back to the house—no sign of Liam—gradually piecing together the events of the afternoon. Liam had taken out his dog and his cousin's son for a training session. Where was the boat? Scout had caught scent of Maggie—must have, what else?—and thrown himself over the side, knocking their lunch into the water, and then struck out for shore, either to defend his territory or to make a new friend. Maybe both. Jamie had been sent to get him back. Liam had secured the boat and then followed to see what was going on, accompanied by the far more obedient Bear.

None of this was quite how she'd planned it—not dropping off Maggie as supposedly arranged by her sister, not meeting her first crush after all these years. She'd meant to be cool, collected, hair perfect, looking her best. The day was a complete mess all around.

Jamie took his meal out of the oven and sat down at the table. He seemed completely comfortable in the kitchen, as though he spent a lot of time there.

"Do you mind if I check on my clothes, Mrs. Connery?'' Charlotte asked. Ada was contentedly knitting in the corner, the radio beside her turned on low.

"You go right ahead, dear.''

"Where's Liam?'' Charlotte asked nonchalantly on her way through to the room that housed the washer and dryer. She hadn't expected him to disappear without a word.

"Probably went down to bring back the launch," Jamie said with his mouth full. He chewed for a few seconds and forked up a lump of potato, which he held midway to his mouth. "We ditched the boat when Scout bailed, and now with this storm blowin' up, Liam no doubt went to bring it in. Could blow away."

No doubt. Well, it would've been nice to thank him in person. But then, he didn't seem like the kind of man who would care all that much. She would've liked the opportunity to talk to him a little more about boarding Maggie. She'd be back in the area on Monday; maybe if she didn't find another kennel, she could approach him then.

Her clothes were dry. She whipped off the borrowed sweater in the laundry room, folded it neatly and set it on top of the dryer, wondering whose it was. It was a youthful, Icelandic style, not the sort of garment an older woman like Ada Connery would wear. Her own sweater felt wonderfully warm. She was feeling a lot better.

"Jamie, when you see Liam, will you thank him for me?"

"Sure." The boy continued plowing through his meal, which looked pretty complete—meat, potatoes, gravy, green beans.

"Thank you, Mrs. Connery, for letting me use your dryer. Plus the tea was very nice."

"Oh, don't mention it, girl! I love having company. Don't get so much of it, now that we don't have regular guests anymore...."

"Regular guests?" Charlotte slowly pulled on her windbreaker.

The older woman waved one hand at the ceiling—painted tongue-and-groove, Charlotte noted. "My late husband and I ran this place as a bed-and-breakfast for a short time, along with my brother, Clement. Then, well—" She frowned and bent her face toward her knitting again. "Fergus passed away and Clement died a couple of years later, and my eyes began to bother me, so Liam came home to take over. He's got no patience for visitors, so I just let it go. You didn't think we needed this whole big house for just the two of us, did you, Charlotte? My land, no!"

A bed-and-breakfast. That made sense. The house was definitely perfect for it, size-wise. The modernized kitchen made sense now, too. And, no, she couldn't quite see Liam Connery in the hospitality business. The fact that Ada's husband had died and her son had no interest would account for the generally run-down air. The house and yard, anyway, if not the dog kennels.

"Well, I'll be on my way."

Ada waved cheerfully but made no attempt to get up. Charlotte wondered if she wasn't bothered by more than poor vision. Arthritis?

It had started to rain. By the time she reached the highway over the muddy, rutted red-earth road, the rain was coming down in sheets and Maggie was whining piteously. She smelled like wet dog.

"Miss Maggs, what *are* we going to do with you until that rotten sister of mine gets back?" Charlotte muttered, peering through the windshield when she came to the end of the lane.

Charlotte spotted a sign on the road, waving in the wind, lashed by the rain: Petty Cove Retrievers. A painted head-and-shoulders picture of two dogs, one brown, one black. Bear and Old Jimbo? And another sign, very faded, above it: Petty Cove Bed-and-Breakfast. With a crudely lettered Closed sign nailed over it. How depressing.

First things first. Find a nice, cozy place to stay for the night. Next, consider calling Laurel to give her a piece of her mind. At the Belize Hilton, if necessary.

"All arranged," was it? Not according to Liam Connery.

CHAPTER FOUR

Dear Lydia,

P.E.I. greetings from us both! Yes, Maggie is still with me and I'm writing this from the Bluefish Inn at Souris, up in the northeast corner of the Island. It's raining here and I'm sick of traveling. And, yes, I've already met the man I used to dream about in grade five and have put that particular little fantasy to rest. He's not at all the way I remembered him—so cold, so standoffish. Scary, almost. Still handsome, though, if you like rough and rugged.

There's worse news. Wait until I see that sister of mine! Laurel set me up. Turns out there was no arrangement to have Maggie bred at Liam Connery's kennel, after all, so now I'm faced with having to talk that terrible man into taking her on as a boarder, at least until Laurel and Frank get back. I can't ship her home yet and I can't keep her with me while I'm working. Speaking of which, guess what? I'm going to the Rathbone mansion tomorrow afternoon to get started. Really looking forward to it....

Love, Charlotte

P.S. Has Zoey gone west to British Columbia yet?

P.P.S. Will send an address when I rent a room somewhere. B&Bs are mostly closed already for the winter.

THAT'S RIGHT, Charlotte thought as she rounded the corner at Poplar Point on the return trip. I'm going to have to convince that unfriendly, annoying, unpleasant man to keep Maggie for a few weeks. Simple, really. He ran a kennel. He had boarders. Five of them; Jamie had said so. Well, here was another one. She was happy to pay whatever he charged. And she'd make damn sure Laurel paid her back.

The sky was clearing—an omen?—as she drove into Cardigan River, which was a tiny knot of buildings at the narrowest part of the small bay that opened to the east, to Northumberland Strait. As Ada Connery had said, there wasn't much to it.

Bristol's Store, with a faded Firestone banner draped in the window and one gas pump outside on the graveled lot, looked as promising as anything. The interior was dark and cluttered and smelled of cigarette smoke and hot dogs. A four-stool lunch bar ran along one side of the L-shaped counter. A large, dull-looking man, his tongue squashed pinkly between fleshy lips, occupied a wooden chair by the cash register. He wore a name badge that read Abner. A woman with her hair tied up in a kerchief and an apron around her thin waist scrubbed the counter with a rag.

She raised her head. "Help ya?"

Charlotte took off her sunglasses. "I'm looking for a room to rent. Do you know of anything around here?"

The woman left her cloth on the counter and stood straight, staring at Charlotte. "Room to rent? What for?"

"I'll be working at the Rathbone estate for a few weeks. I need a place to stay."

The cloth got picked up, slopped into a sink full of soapy water, pulled out, wrung and vigorously applied again to the cracked Formica. "Uh-huh. Round here, eh? Petty Cove? Nothing much there. Cardigan River?"

"Yes." Charlotte waited through the long silence that followed, looking around a little desperately. The boy-man hadn't changed expression and was twirling the dials on a transistor radio near the cash register. Electronic squawks filled the air.

"You could try Clara Jenkins. She takes tourists in the summer. Don't know if she's got any rooms free now. Quit fiddlin' and put down that radio, Abe, y'hear!" She turned back to Charlotte. "You want me to call?"

"That would be very kind."

"Oh, don't mention it. Anything else for ya?"

"Bottled water?"

"Over by the pop cooler. Bottom shelf. Should be a few left from the summer folk. We don't get much call for bought water from the reg'lars."

As she spoke, the woman dialed an old-fashioned rotary wall phone. "Clara? Listen here, I got somebody in the store says she wants a room—what's that? Okay, I'll send her up. How's John? Uh-huh. Oh, that's a shame. Hope he's feelin' better soon. 'Bye, dear.'' She hung up and turned to Charlotte without missing a breath. ''You find your water all right?''

''Yes, thanks.'' Charlotte opened her wallet. The bell over the door jangled and two men entered— young, handsome fisherman types, with longish hair and creased ball caps pushed back from their tanned foreheads. They both paused when they saw her, and Charlotte recognized the familiar, lightning-swift male appraisal. All men did it—*almost* all men, she corrected, remembering Liam Connery's indifference. Then they swung themselves up onto stools at the lunch counter.

''Coffee, boys?'' The store lady already had her hand on the coffeepot.

The cashier, Abe, took Charlotte's money and made change slowly and accurately, counting under his breath. He wasn't as young as she'd thought at first, with deep lines around his eyes and a little gray in his brown hair. She smiled encouragement and he smiled back, which seemed to amuse the newcomers.

''Coffee, Bonnie. And you can fill up my thermos jug, too. Say, got yourself a gal there, Abe?''

Abe shook his head. ''Nope. She's new. I don't know her.''

''And of course you wouldn't take a date with anybody you didn't know, right, Abe?'' The two men laughed again, but Charlotte could see it was all in good fun.

"Now, you go on up the hill and bear right at the first corner," the woman called Bonnie said to her. "Second house on the left after you make the turn. Buff-colored, ya can't miss it. Big lilac bush out front. Clara says she'll be watchin' out for you."

"Oh!" Charlotte rapidly rearranged her plans. "I was going to go over to the kennel and then—oh, never mind, I'll go up and see about the room."

The two men exchanged glances. "Got a dog, have you? What kind?"

Charlotte nodded. It amazed her how perfect strangers here thought nothing of taking part in a conversation, but she was beginning to get used to it. There were no strangers on Prince Edward Island, she realized. There were only Islanders and People From Away, the "summer folk."

"A Labrador retriever. It's my sister's, actually. I want to make arrangements to board her at the kennel."

"That'd be Liam Connery's place?" one drawled, his blue eyes interested.

"Yes."

"Uh-huh." He took a sip of his coffee, eyes narrowed.

The other shook his head. "Good luck to you, miss. Liam can be right tough to get along with. Especially when it comes to them fancy huntin' dogs of his." He smiled pleasantly.

"Thank you." Charlotte headed back out into the sunshine.

So. Liam Connery definitely had a reputation, everywhere she mentioned his name. *Ornery. Particular. Right tough.*

Well, she could handle him. *Begin as you mean to go on,* she mused. She meant to board Maggie at Petty Cove Retrievers, which was, after all, a commercial kennel business—wasn't it?—then get straight to work checking out the Rathbone estate. She was flexible, she was reasonable, she was sweet-tempered…and she was stubborn.

In the end, one way or another, she usually got what she wanted.

IT WAS A BIT DISAPPOINTING after all that, to discover Liam Connery wasn't even home. Dogs barked from the direction of the kennels as she drove up, and Maggie started to whine in response.

Charlotte didn't dare let her out of the truck.

"Yes?" Ada came to the door, her sightless eyes focusing somewhere over Charlotte's head. "Can I help you?"

"Good morning, Ada. It's Charlotte—remember me from last week? Charlotte Moore?"

"Surely I do! Come in, dear." The older woman held the door open wide. "I'll put on the kettle."

"Thanks, but I can't stay. I wanted to speak to Liam, if I could."

"He's not here. He's, uh…" His mother had a confused look on her face, as though trying to remember just where her son was. "Let's see, it's Monday, isn't it? He's away this morning, miss."

"I see." Charlotte frowned. That was disappointing. "I wanted to talk to him about boarding my sister's dog for a few weeks."

"Oh, heavens yes, of course you can leave your puppy here. I haven't even met her, have I? Why don't you bring the little sweetheart in for a few minutes?"

Maggie obliged, leaping gracefully out of the Suburban and following Charlotte back to the door of the house, where she gently nosed Ada's knee. "Oh, my. Isn't she a dear little thing?" Liam's mother bent to pat Maggie's glossy black coat. At nearly seventy-five pounds and fully grown, Maggie wasn't exactly a "little thing."

"You bring her on into the kitchen, why don't you. I'll get Jamie to see to her when he comes home from school, if Liam's delayed."

"Are you sure?" This was a break! She couldn't do an end run around the absent son to get what she wanted—an agreement to board Maggie—from the mother, but it was a start. Charlotte had no doubt that Ada would fall in love with Maggie once she was on the premises, and so would Liam if he gave the dog half a chance. Charlotte would come back later and discuss the details.

"Oh, yes!" Ada waved her hand in a throwaway gesture that was becoming familiar. "Don't give it a thought. My son's growl is worse than his bite, you know. This is a lovely dog, Charlotte. A lovely, lovely girl!" She smoothed Maggie's broad head, and Maggie responded with that happy confident Labrador look Charlotte knew so well. "She can stay right here by the fire with me and Chip!"

Chip must be the cat. Luckily, Maggie tolerated cats well. Laurel's horse barn was always full of them.

"If your son objects, I'll have to make some other arrangement." Charlotte closed her eyes in silent prayer. *Please, let that not happen!*

"Nonsense! This is the perfect place, next door to where you'll be working. Why didn't I think of it the other day? You can visit her anytime you want. Have you been over to the estate yet, dear?"

"I'm planning to do that this afternoon or maybe tomorrow," Charlotte said, taking a step backward toward the path that led to the house. "I've been busy. I just found somewhere to live and—"

"Where's that?"

"A place they mentioned at the store—"

"Not Clara Jenkins's!"

"Yes, as a matter-of-fact."

"Oh, that won't be suitable, not at all. She just has bachelors staying there, folks who aren't a bit fussy. She's certainly no cook. Why, I hear all she puts out for breakfast is a pot of porridge and a spoon."

Charlotte had noticed that the room she'd taken for the week was very sparsely and boringly furnished, with a worn lino floor, sagging single bed and a monstrous television in the corner, which she had no intention of using. Lucky she'd only be in Petty Cove a month, because she didn't think she could stand the color of the walls for too long, either. They weren't periwinkle or aqua or even last year's seafoam but a plain all-out fifties-or-bust turquoise.

She hadn't enquired about the meals, which were included.

"I've taken the room for a week," she said. "I'll give it a try." If worse came to worst, she could always find something in Charlottetown, although a commute of an hour everyday, both ways, didn't appeal.

"If only I'd known," Ada said fretfully, looking rather lost again.

Perhaps it was the empty stare of her sightless eyes, but Ada's expression often took on a vague, bewildered look.

"I just hope you're comfortable there, dear. And you put your foot down about the breakfast. You can always come to us if you're not happy."

"You mean—" *Come to us?*

"We've got all kinds of rooms upstairs," the older woman said, brightening. "Nice rooms, too, all with their own plumbin' and lovely sea views. It'd be like old times!"

It was rather sad, really, Charlotte thought as she drove back down the lane. Ada had obviously loved playing hostess in her own little guest house. With her sight gone and her husband dead, those days were past. And with a son who didn't seem to care about anything but his dogs, they would most likely never return.

"I WON'T HAVE that damn dog here." Liam poured milk over the cornflakes in his bowl, his regular evening snack, and carried it to the table. Ladling sugar onto the crisp cereal, he looked up. "You hear me, Ma?"

There was no answer from the corner, where his mother sat knitting, her needles clicking noisily. The Labrador at her feet gazed at him, sighed and put her big head down on her paws again.

"Look, will you, Liam? Even Maggie thinks you're rude. Of course I hear you!" She leaned down and patted the Labrador's shoulder. "There's a sweet girl."

Liam began eating. The sound of the spoon hitting the bowl added to the *click-click* of knitting needles, the *tick-tick* of the kitchen clock on the wall and the occasional crisp *snap-snap* of the wood fire in the parlor stove.

"I don't have a good feeling about it, that's all. Plus, that bitch is bound to come into heat while she's here, according to Laurel Moore's reckoning, and I'm not prepared to deal with that. It's nothing but trouble. Her sister should've left her home."

"But she's no trouble at all. She's beautifully trained—look at her! She hasn't moved a muscle all afternoon, just stayed by my chair, good as gold. Liam, I want to do that poor girl a favor," his mother said stubbornly. "Travelin' all that way, arriving here plumb tired out, and then nowhere to leave her puppy while she works? Even Chip gets along with our visitor, don't you, Chippy?" The cat, sleeping in a basket by the stove, didn't move.

Liam stood and took the bowl to the sink, where he rinsed and dried it and put it back in the cupboard. He was in jeans and a plaid work shirt and stocking feet. The pendulum clock on the wall struck eight chimes.

"Damn sneaky, if you ask me, coming around this morning when I was away."

"She has a name, you know. It's Maggie. And the girl's name is Charlotte. And you weren't home. How was she to know? And besides, the sign out there on the road does say *boarding kennel,* doesn't it?"

"Matter-of-fact, it doesn't, Ma. It says, Training and Boarding."

"Well, there you go—"

"That means the only dogs I board are dogs I'm being paid to train. This dog isn't here to be trained." He glanced over at the Labrador, who had raised her noble head again to give him an injured look. "She probably wouldn't know a pheasant from a stick of firewood. Labs like this have had all the starch bred out of them. They're show dogs!"

"Old Jimbo's a Labrador," his mother shot back. "And a darn fine one, too. One of the best dogs you've ever had—you've said so many times yourself."

"Jimbo's different. He's a working dog. There's not a show animal in his pedigree, not one. Folks like Laurel Moore, and there's plenty more like her, have ruined the breed, as far as I'm concerned. I'm not having that bitch of Laurel's around, and that's that." He headed toward the outer door of the kitchen.

"Davy get his boat out of the water?" Ada enquired mildly.

Liam stared at his mother. "He did. And don't you go changing the subject, either—"

"Changing the subject! The subject is closed, that's what. Maggie is staying right here with me. I need a companion, don't I? Home alone all day with you here and there and people coming to the door and what not—"

"You've got Chippy, Ma." Liam smiled slightly.

"Oh, pooh! Chippy's just a cat."

"And Bear."

"Bear's always with *you*. He's stuck to you like a piece of lint."

Liam signed and reached for his jacket. "You haven't convinced me, Ma, but I guess she's here now, like it or not. If you say you want her, I'll keep her. When did you mention the woman was coming back?"

"She said she'd come to talk to you this evening. Arrange the particulars, if you were agreeable." Ada picked up speed with her needles. "Oh, and Liam?"

He stopped, his hand on the doorknob. "What's that, Ma?"

"Thank you, son."

Liam sighed again and went out, closing the door quietly behind him. He started his rounds in what he and Jamie always called the Maternity Ward, where Sammy and her five pups were housed. He had another bitch ready to whelp in a couple more weeks— Sunny, a young Labrador with her second litter on the way. He'd move her in soon.

Liam handled each puppy and checked it over carefully, as he did every evening before observing them for ten or fifteen minutes. He liked to get to know each animal's personality, keep an eye on every stage of a pup's development. These little guys were just four weeks old but the chase-and-fetch instincts came early, and it was important to find out which pups were go-getters and which ones liked to snooze an extra five minutes if they could.

Then he went over to the kennel where Old Jimbo was housed with his pal, a neutered male called Spindle. Spindle was a mixed-breed, a weird-looking animal, the result of a Labrador mating with a weimaraner, a visitor he'd had one fall who got mixed-up with one of his best bitches when no one was looking. Spindle and Old Jimbo—who'd been called that since he was two years old—were inseparable. If they weren't such close friends, Liam would have retired Jimbo to the house and a life of ease by the fire. The dog was getting too arthritic to go out in the boat the way he once had, but Liam knew it'd break his heart to be sent to the house. He seemed to know that house dogs weren't real dogs—and Old Jimbo was a real dog, through and through.

If Liam hadn't decided not to breed Jimbo any more and if he hadn't made up his mind long ago to draw the line at breeding any kind of show animal, he'd have used Old Jimbo on Laurel's bitch.

He had to admit Maggie was a good-looking specimen—like the woman who brought her. It was just that she was useless. An animal bred to be trotted around the ring in front of a judge. He had no interest in breeding useless dogs. There were already enough of them in the world.

Lights approached from the lane, and Liam paused on his way to the boarding kennels. The white older-model Suburban, Laurel's sister drove, broke through the trees.

He watched her drive slowly into the yard and then jerk to a sudden stop. He shook his head. What he'd told his mother was true: he didn't have a good feeling about this woman.

He drew in a deep breath, squared his shoulders and took a step toward the vehicle, as she opened the driver's door. Might as well get it over with. She could thank his mother for the good news he was about to hand her. If it'd been strictly up to him, they'd both—she and the dog—be hitting the road.

CHAPTER FIVE

BY HALF PAST EIGHT, it was dark. Charlotte had already slowed, when she spotted Liam standing in the yard, in the glare of her headlights. She hit the brake hard, an automatic reaction.

Oops. She got out and zipped up her jacket. Well, never mind. Begin as you mean to go on with this man, she reminded herself. She jammed her hands deep into her jacket pockets. "Oh, hello! I didn't see you there."

Naturally, he said nothing. *Don't let him rattle you.* "I guess you know about Maggie being here."

He nodded.

"Is that going to be okay? I mean, can you take her as a boarder for a few weeks?" she rushed on. "Your mother says it's all right."

She stopped about ten feet from him. He was dressed very much as he had been the first time she'd seen him. Very casually, in working man's clothes—jeans, boots, jacket.

"My mother doesn't run the kennel."

"Oh." Charlotte knew her sudden blush wouldn't show up in the deepening gloom. The yard lights were on, but at this time of night they made little difference. "Well, I'm sorry about that. You weren't here when I came around or I would have spoken to you—"

He made a movement, as though to walk in the direction of one of the kennels. "I'm checking on the dogs. Maybe we can discuss this while I finish my rounds."

Oh, definitely, Charlotte thought, hurrying toward him. Why waste time talking to a customer when you could be doing two things at once?

He held open the door to an outbuilding and waited for her to enter, then followed her in, flicking on a light as he closed the door behind him. The raucous sound of barking assaulted her eardrums. He whistled loudly, and the noise stopped.

"They don't know you. That's why they're barking. It's the Chessies, mainly. They're natural guard dogs."

She followed him as he walked along the length of the kennel, stopping to speak softly to each individual dog and to fondle its ears and run his hand down its sides. The dogs responded with big "grins" and wagging tails. Charlotte noted that the kennels were very clean, with raised sleeping platforms and cement runs that led to a door that opened to the outside. The scent of a mild disinfectant hung in the air. Along the wall were miniature brass harness hooks, with a collar and a lead hanging from each and a neatly printed card inset into a plastic sleeve with the animal's name. *Chester. Minnie. Kate. Scout. Sunny. Hunter. Ben.* Two runs were empty.

"Are these all yours?"

"The two at the other end are young dogs I'm

training, Chester and Minnie. Hunter's mine, and so are Scout and Sunny. They're brother and sister from two different litters. Kate's mine. I got George and Spinner, those two Chessies over there, from next door."

"Oh?" Charlotte noted the two light brown dogs, standing stiff-legged in one of the kennels, each on high alert, watching the humans.

"When the old man died, there was no one to look after them, so I brought them here."

"I see. I notice they're a different color than Bear."

"He's what they call a 'dark brown.' The breed comes in any color, as long as it's brown," he said. Charlotte expected a smile, but there wasn't one. His gaze was steady on the two Rathbone dogs. "They're what is called sedge. The color of dry grass."

"What kind is that one?" She pointed to a spaniellike dog, quite different from the others. She was pleased to hear Liam so voluble. At least this was one subject he didn't seem to mind talking about.

"A Clumber. A very old spaniel-type hunting dog, although the exact origin of the breed is unknown. Some think they're French, originally. Whatever they are, they're great gun dogs. Very calm. Belongs to a buddy of mine."

Charlotte looked significantly at the two empty runs at the end of the building. "So, it looks like you've got room for Maggie, then?"

He straightened from where he'd bent to fondle

Hunter's ears and stared directly into her eyes. She felt a funny little shudder inside.

"Not really," he said slowly. "I've never got room for dogs I don't want on the place. This is a special case, I guess."

"What's that supposed to mean?" She tried to keep her tone even. Conciliatory. Friendly. After all, she was the one who needed the favor here.

"I raise and train retrievers. Working dogs. Hunters' companions. I don't have time for show dogs, which is what your sister raises. And I especially don't have time for show bitches that might be going into heat. Do you understand?"

He gave her a hard look and she nodded automatically. She had to admit that was a reasonable excuse for refusing to take Laurel's dog. "It'd only be until my sister gets home and I can ship Maggie back. A couple of weeks."

"As it happens, my mother's taken a fancy to your sister's bitch so I'll keep her while you're in the area." He glanced over at the runs again, then continued softly. "But it's strictly a favor for my mother, so don't thank me."

"Oh, I didn't plan to!" Charlotte retorted, stung. "I'd like to know what you've got against me and Maggie, anyway. You don't even know us!"

"You?" His eyes were wary on hers, then abruptly he looked away again. "Nothing. Your big sister needs her ass kicked, but that's hardly your fault."

"Laurel couldn't possibly have known anything about this mix-up!"

"She knew. She'd contacted me before on this subject. She knew very well that I wouldn't agree to breed a show bitch. I considered it briefly, as a favor to an old friend, but in the end I decided against any exceptions to my rule." He began to walk slowly toward the door at the other end of the building, and Charlotte fell into stride beside him.

"And why is that?" Charlotte hurried to match her pace to his.

"Because the dog world is small. Because if other breeders heard I was breeding my top gun dogs to show bitches, they'd be after me to do the same with theirs. I don't need the aggravation."

"Maybe Laurel didn't realize you'd changed your mind. Maybe she thought it was still on," Charlotte persisted. Annoyed as she was about Laurel's duplicity—and she *was* quite certain Laurel had misled her—she still felt a need to defend her sister.

"She knew," he said again. He glanced at her. "I have a feeling your sister thought you might be able to sweet-talk me into changing my mind, once you showed up here with her bitch."

"Laurel would *never* do that!" Charlotte was furious with the turn this conversation had taken—after all, her sister!—but she couldn't resist the thought: *could* she sweet-talk him into it? She could be pretty persuasive when she put her mind to it. Would serve him right, Mr. Know-Everything Dog Guy!

He turned to face her. "Don't even think about it. The answer is no. You can pay me for board by the week. Eighty dollars is what I charge without any training, in advance. Take it or leave it."

"Oh, I'll take it. What choice do I have?" She was sure the irony was completely lost on him. "Can I go see Maggie now?"

Anything to get out of his company, since she was obviously so unwelcome! To think she'd been looking forward to meeting Liam Connery again, to seeing what had become of him. To think she'd actually *dreamed* about him more than once. She was annoyed with herself for the time she'd wasted, for all the tender thoughts and recollections she'd allowed herself to indulge in about her happy childhood years—especially her first feelings of attraction to a member of the opposite sex. The sappy sentimental fantasies she'd spun.... He was nothing at all like the boy she remembered.

"Maggie's up at the house."

Without another word, he disappeared into one of the outbuildings, and Charlotte went back to the truck to get her handbag, which contained her checkbook. With her appointment to meet Mr. Busby the next day and her need to get on with the job she'd come to do at the Rathbone estate, she didn't have time to find anything else for Maggie. If she had the time, she'd scour the Island to avoid dealing with *him*.

What a man! Lucky for him he worked with dogs. Lucky for him his business didn't depend on customer relations and people skills. He didn't have any.

THE RATHBONE HOUSE—a mansion, really—was a large three-story building in the Second Empire style, popularized in the late 1700s in the United

States. This house, built more than a hundred years later, had a mansard roof, slate in this case, and a huge wraparound veranda that didn't really belong to the style and may have been added later. Out back, a glass conservatory was attached to one half of the south elevation, with doors leading from both the conservatory and the house to the extensive gardens, probably well over two acres and, sadly, in a state of serious neglect. Even some of the windows in the conservatory were broken.

Charlotte shivered. Such a grand house, now looking empty and very much abandoned. Charlotte didn't know what the family intended, whether the house would be sold. She expected to learn all of that soon. Mr. Stanley Busby, owner of the Halifax auction house in charge of the appraisal and eventual sale of the contents—the man who had accepted her bid, in fact—was due to arrive any moment.

She'd called his office in Halifax the morning before, to discover that he'd be arriving the next day and driving out from Charlottetown in the afternoon to meet her at two o'clock.

She was half an hour early. Why not explore a little? The watchman who was supposed to be looking after the place, according to Mr. Busby, was nowhere in evidence, although she did see an older, rather beat up camper at the end of the long drive way, near the trees. The watchman's?

The grounds once must have been magnificent. Now, the gravel paths she walked along were overgrown with weeds. A huge hedge of lilacs, their leaves beginning to fall, ranged along one side of the property, to the southeast. What a stunning display

that would be in early June, she thought, imagining
the voluptuous heads of lilac and pink and white,
nodding in the salty spring breeze. A neglected herb
garden, quite formally laid out and complete with a
little teak garden seat tucked under a painted arbor,
showed only some creeping thyme still growing in
the beds and over the paths, and several shaggy overgrown sage bushes. Charlotte sat down on the garden
seat to get out of the wind.

Rathbone House fascinated her. Much money and
attention had been lavished on the landscaping at one
time, and she wondered who had designed the gardens and maintained them so carefully. Had there
been lawn parties here? Picnics on the banks of the
now debris-choked stream at the bottom of the garden? Ladies in white dresses, men in straw hats?
Tennis matches and teas?

Old Man Rathbone, as the locals referred to him,
had not kept things up. The neglect went back many
years. Yew trees, which marked the entrance to the
rose garden, had once been clipped into neat formal
shapes, but that shaping had been blurred by the ram-
pant growth of many seasons. The rose garden, with
its cast-iron filigree gate, was a garden in name only,
with two or three ancient stumps showing through
the soil here and there, and one vigorous climbing
rose, long past flowering, which clung to the stone
half-wall at the back of the garden. Wresting a garden of any kind from nature in this difficult climate
would not have been easy. Someone—once—must
have cared enough to try.

Charlotte heard a car approach and got to her feet. She shifted her bag higher on her shoulder and began to pick her way carefully to the front of the house.

Mr. Busby, a tall, slim man in his late sixties or early seventies, with a sunny smile and the most amazing eyebrows, was just getting out of his rental car.

"Charlotte Moore," she said, extending her hand. He shook it heartily.

"Delighted to meet you, Miss Moore. I'm looking forward to working with you." He gave a slight laugh, releasing her hand. "You're a very talented young lady and you come highly recommended." His eyebrows, which were silver-gray like his hair, resembled two butterflies that had alighted on his brow and were about to take flight at any second. As he talked, they trembled gently.

"Thank you." Charlotte liked Mr. Busby immediately.

"I do hope I'm not late," he added.

"Oh, no. I'm early." Charlotte waved an arm to encompass the grounds. "I wanted to take a look around."

"And do you like what you see?"

"It's a fascinating place!"

"Indeed." Mr. Busby had withdrawn a ring of keys from his pocket and was inspecting them carefully. He selected one. "Why don't we go in straight away and have a look around."

"I didn't see any sign of the watchman you mentioned yesterday," Charlotte said as they began to walk toward the house.

"No?" Mr. Busby frowned. "He's a most unreliable fellow. He's supposed to be living on the premises in his camper...."

"There's a camper at the end of the drive, beside those bushes." Charlotte pointed.

"Oh, good Lord! I suppose that's his. Luckily there isn't much in the way of crime out here, and a member of the family is due to arrive this week to take a look at things. Day after tomorrow, in fact. Nick Deacon, a very nice young fellow. I expect he'll settle in here for a few days, and then, of course, you'll be here on a daily basis yourself, so at least the house will be occupied. Are you staying in Montague?"

"No, I've found a boardinghouse in Cardigan River."

"Excellent!"

Charlotte hadn't realized a member of the family would be on the premises—not that it made any difference to the job for which she'd been hired. "What do they intend to do about the property?"

Mr. Busby carefully inserted a key into the lock on the massive walnut-paneled front door with the beveled-glass inset she'd admired earlier. "I believe they may sell. My advice was that it would need a good deal of fixing up if they want a decent price. I suppose that's what Nick is coming up to have a look at. And, of course, fall's the wrong time of year to put an estate like this on the market. Well, here we are!"

He gazed around admiringly. They were in a high-ceilinged entrance hall painted a rather drab mustard color. The cream-painted moldings were beautiful, though, clearly hand carved in another time. The carpet over the limestone tiles was Turkish, although Charlotte could hardly make out the pattern, it was so soiled. Sultanabad? What a shame!

"Rather run-down, but I'm hoping we can organize a room for you to work in, get it cleaned up and sorted out. Light a fire in a fireplace. Cheer things up a little. I wonder where that man is I hired?" He looked out the window, as if expecting to see him. "I'd like to get the furnace running."

Charlotte was glad she'd worn a warm fleece jacket. The house was cold and dank, with a musty smell that spoke of old plumbing, neglected cellars and leaky chimneys.

What the place needed was open windows and sunshine. Fresh air and heat would drive out the moisture and mustiness. Even dreary as it was, the house was absolutely magnificent. What wonders did it hold? Already she could see a landscape on the wall that she felt sure was by Mary Lee Simpson, the well-known New Brunswick painter who'd died in the 1930s.

"Didn't you say something about bringing a dog along?" Mr. Busby had opened the door that led to the kitchen at the end of the corridor. "Whew!"

"Yes, my sister's Labrador."

"Good. You'll want a friendly face around here." He smiled, went to the windows and pulled up the blinds to reveal panes of dirty glass, which shed a weak light on the kitchen, large and fitted in mid-century appliances. The refrigerator and stove, if sold, would fetch a good price from a collector. Nineteen-fifties stuff was all the rage, she'd discovered in her decorative arts business over the past few years.

"That's better." Mr. Busby rubbed his hands together and looked around. "I can't imagine that anyone would mind if you brought your dog in here. Of course, I'll check with Nick when he arrives. Nick Deacon, by the way, is the old man's great-nephew."

"I've already made arrangements with a kennel. But I'd be happy to bring Maggie with me some days." Charlotte hadn't thought much about the fact that she'd be working in a secluded rural place, a run-down old mansion, with no near neighbors and probably not even a phone. Of course, she had her cell phone. And the electricity was on.

"There are neighbors, of a sort, Miss Moore—"

"Oh, please! Call me Charlotte." Mr. Busby was so old-fashioned and gentlemanly, but she couldn't bear it if he called her "Miss" the whole time they were together.

"Charlotte," he repeated, nodding. "May I say you have a very pretty, old-fashioned name? I was rather fond of a girl named Charlotte, once. Well—" he colored slightly and cleared his throat "—ahem, as I was saying, there are neighbors, technically. A blind woman and her son live on the next cove. Apparently there's a footpath through the woods from here to there, about ten minutes away. Cyril—he's the watchman—told me the old woman's husband was hired on to take care of the place occasionally before he died. That's quite a few years ago, I believe. Anyway, Charlotte, you're not entirely alone out here.''

''I've met them, actually—the blind woman and her son.''

Mr. Busby's eyebrows threatened to take flight. ''You *have?*''

''Yes. The son runs a kennel and that's where I've put Maggie.''

''Oh, very good! Splendid! Now, let's just have a quick walk-through and see what we can see.''

CHARLOTTE SPENT the rest of the afternoon making notes and indulging herself in exploring. Stanley Busby stayed until late afternoon. He started by tracking down the watchman—who, it turned out, was whiling away the day at Bonnie Bristol's lunch counter. Then he made arrangements for a phone line to be put in so Charlotte could use a fax machine and have Internet access, as well as a working phone if she didn't want to rely on her battery-powered cell. He also saw to the furnace and various other jobs that he felt needed his attention.

Charlotte chose the dining room as a workroom, because it was spacious with large windows facing the southeast, overlooking the gardens, and because it was furnished with a large mahogany dining room table and sideboard. She could use them to lay out smaller items she was examining, or as a surface for her laptop and paperwork.

Before Mr. Busby left, he asked Charlotte's opinion on the grounds. ''I'm of two minds,'' he said, brow furrowed. ''The plans are to hold the sale here, whether it's soon or in the spring, and I do think it would be more appealing if the grounds were tidied up. What's your view?''

''I suppose that would be up to the family,'' Charlotte replied, busy imagining the lilacs in bud, the paths swept, the fountain running and the snowdrops and tulips poking through the earth. ''There'd be some expense. But it would be lovely....''

''Yes, yes. There'd have to be some money spent,'' Mr. Busby agreed. ''And it might be difficult to find someone to do the work. I'll tell you what, we'll let Mr. Deacon decide when he arrives, shall we? Good idea! Excellent!''

And off he went, leaving Charlotte with the pleasant sensation that she'd been very helpful.

It was nearly six by the time she left, and Clara Jenkins had been very firm: six o'clock was when she served the evening meal, not a minute sooner, not a minute later. Charlotte was hungry, or she wouldn't mind missing dinner. The meal served the previous evening, her first, had been overdone roast beef, mashed turnips, mashed potatoes and gravy, followed by an unidentifiable dessert, which she hadn't eaten. Her two fellow boarders kept inspecting her curiously throughout the meal, without addressing a single remark to her. The instant dinner was over, they disappeared to what the lady of the house called ''the lounge,'' and the television went on loudly. It was tuned to a sports channel and there it stayed.

Charlotte had wondered why they didn't watch television in their rooms and leave the common lounge for boarders who wanted to relax and read, perhaps. She'd trudged up the stairs to her room where she'd sat on her bed, trying to get interested in the novel she'd brought with her.

Her pillow was lumpy and she hadn't slept well. She didn't like the place. Maybe she'd get used to it. But if they had mashed turnips and stringy roast beef and no salad again tonight, she was leaving. She'd get a room in a nice hotel with a decent dining room in Charlottetown, if she had to, and drive the hour each way, morning and afternoon.

On the other hand, Mrs. Jenkins, who—she'd informed Charlotte—had been somewhat inconvenienced by taking in a third boarder at this time of year, seemed friendly enough and quite solicitous. Zoey would've called her nosy. And she *did* have a husband—John—who wasn't well, so one had to forgive her excesses. Possibly.

Charlotte sighed. She'd already learned more about John and his nonstop series of afflictions than she'd ever wanted to. She missed Maggie. The big black dog was better company than the two bachelor boarders who occupied the other rooms in the Jenkins boardinghouse. One leered and the other mumbled constantly to himself.

She was tempted to go to the Connerys tonight and spend an hour with Ada. Ada was blind but she was normal. Charlotte liked her very much, no matter what she thought of her son. And Maggie.... Maybe Liam wasn't home. How could she find out ahead of time, without driving there? She felt like such a coward! If she arrived unannounced and he

was there, she'd have to stay to be polite, and she
didn't think she could stand an hour or two with
Liam Connery in the same room. Not after the day
she'd had. She was sure to say something she'd regret.

Charlotte parked where Mrs. Jenkins had told her
to park and walked wearily toward the house. Her
back hurt and she suspected her hair was full of cobwebs. She opened the front door without knocking—
as she'd been instructed—to the smell of boiled turnip.

"You're late!" Mrs. Jenkins's thin smile took
some of the sting out of the reprimand as she carried
dessert into the dining room and plunked it at the
end of the table—three bowls of something bright
pink and wiggly. The two bachelors briefly gave her
their attention, eyes pale and curious, then returned
to their plates, heaped high.

Turnip again. And the same indigestible roast
beef, now sliced and warmed up in the leftover
gravy. But there was a salad, thank heaven, and this
time she actually recognized the dessert. Everyone
knew what Jell-O looked like.

CHAPTER SIX

THE RAIN LASHING DOWN had the chill of sleet in it. For all that it was only the second week of October, the wind reminded Charlotte that winters here could be long and bitter.

She paused before she got out of the truck, fingers gripping the wheel tightly, shoulders tense. Had she made the right decision, coming over to the Connerys? After that hideous meal and then spending an hour listening to the bloodthirst of the crowd and the screaming of the announcers coming up through the floor from the WWF bout on the lounge television, Charlotte decided facing Liam Connery's indifference, even rudeness, was preferable to the alternative.

She'd go mad if she had to spend her evenings in the Jenkins's household. It was too cold and dark to do anything outdoors, especially by herself. Liam knew she wanted to see Maggie from time to time and Ada was very friendly toward her, had been right from the start.

So, despite her less than satisfactory visit yesterday evening, here she was again.

Liam opened the door. He hesitated briefly— Charlotte wished she could read his expression but

the overhead light threw shadows onto his face—
then stepped back and gestured her in.

"Dirty weather," he said. She thought that must
be an attempt at small talk.

"Yes, isn't it!" She took off her jacket and
handed it to him. He turned to hang it on one of the
hooks that lined the wall nearest the kitchen door.
"I came over to see Maggie, if that's all right."

"I figured you might have," he replied. That was
that! What had she been worried about?

"Company, Ma," he announced as they entered
the warm, brightly lit kitchen. Jamie sat at the
kitchen table, a chunk of wood in front of him and
shavings on the floor. He grinned and waved with a
chisel he was holding. Maggie bounded toward
Charlotte, wagging her tail.

"Oh, Maggikins!" she whispered, burying her
face in the dog's ruff. Tears prickled at the back of
her eyes. She felt as though Maggie was her only
true friend on Prince Edward Island. Mr. Busby was
very nice, but he had gone back to Halifax. Ada liked
her, but Ada was pretty much housebound, plus she
had a son who didn't hide his dislike of Charlotte or
her dog, no matter what he said.

"Who's that, Liam?" Ada occupied her usual
chair, this time with Chippy in her lap, no knitting
needles in sight.

"It's Charlotte, Ma. Come over to visit us this
evening." He raised one eyebrow, as if to check on
the accuracy of his statement.

Charlotte nodded and smiled. "Hello, Ada."

"Come in, come in! Sit by me, dear. Take this

chair.'' She indicated the general direction of the wooden chair placed near her upholstered one. "Liam's just showing the boy a thing or two about carving ducks. He wants to learn for a school project or something. Is that it, Jamie?''

"Mr. Dickson's class, Auntie. And if I've got a turn for it and they come out real good, I could sell plenty next summer to the tourists....''

Liam grinned as he walked past the boy and reached out to muss his hair. Jamie ducked, grinning. "You said I could!''

"I did. If you're any good at it, Jamie. Of course you'd probably be able to sell them regardless, good or bad. Tourists will buy anything.''

Jamie laughed and shot an embarrassed sideways glance her way. Charlotte read the look: she was a tourist. If not a tourist, certainly someone From Away.

Charlotte took the chair that Ada indicated. Maggie sat down and pressed her big head against Charlotte's knee. "I thought maybe you'd have Maggie in a kennel outside,'' she began.

"Oh, no! The dear dog's staying right here with me, no matter—''

"Ma,'' Liam interrupted. "I told you she could be going into heat any day now, according to Charlotte's sister, and when that happens, she's got to be locked up for her own good.''

"Well, I suppose you're right,'' his mother said grudgingly. She patted Chippy so vigorously that the cat protested with a yowl and hopped off her lap.

Charlotte stared at Liam, willing her thoughts into

his head: *Of course, you could just have her bred, the way Laurel wanted, and that would be the end of the problem, you stubborn man.* If Laurel expected her to change this man's mind, well, she was working on it....

Liam didn't show any sign that he'd received her telepathic message, although he did look at her once, his face puzzled. It was almost as though he was wondering why she'd come over—and what his mother saw in her.

"How you gettin' on at Clara's?" Ada said. She got up and walked slowly but steadily to the stove. Reaching out, she picked up the teakettle and walked to the sink, where she filled it with water. Charlotte realized that Ada knew every object's exact placement in her domain, the kitchen.

"The room, you mean?"

Ada put the kettle on the stove and purposefully made her way back to her chair, her head high. "The room, the food, who else is lodging there. The Dunster man?"

"There *is* someone named Bert Dunster—"

"He's from up Three Corners way. Don't know why they don't keep him t' home. S'pose nobody'll have him. Can't shut him up. Who else?"

"I'm not sure of his last name, but Mrs. Jenkins calls him Freddie."

"Freddie?" Ada turned toward her son. "Could that be Freddie Burns, the one who left Tabby Wright's sister high and dry last winter?"

"Could be, Ma. I don't keep track of that stuff," Liam replied. He was watching Jamie's progress with the carving tools. The boy was concentrating on taking a long curl of wood off the side of the block.

"How's the food?"

"It's, uh, it's all right," Charlotte said weakly.

"Pah! I don't believe you. Clara Jenkins is no cook, never has been. What did you have for supper tonight?"

"Roast beef—"

"Probably overdone!"

"—potatoes—"

"She can hardly ruin a potato, can she? Mashed?"

"Yes. Gravy and turnips, too."

"Turnips!" Ada was silent for a few moments. Charlotte wondered what the consensus was on turnips. Could they be ruined? "You like turnips?"

"Yes. Um, sometimes," Charlotte answered truthfully.

"What about dessert? She put out a plate of squares? Fruit cobbler? Angel cake? Apple pie? Pudding?"

"Jell-O."

"Jell-O!"

Ada lapsed into shocked silence. Charlotte stifled a sudden desire to giggle. Liam's mother seemed to take Charlotte's experiences at the rival Clara Jenkins's house so seriously. She risked a glance at Liam, but he was intent on what Jamie was doing. Boy and man, both handsome, it was plain enough that they were related. Could well have been father and son. Dark heads close together, bending over the block of wood.... How strange that Liam hadn't married, that he lived with his mother and taught other men's sons instead of his own.

Charlotte took a deep breath. Well, sitting here

was certainly more interesting than listening to television noise back at her room. She wondered, briefly, what people really did for *fun* around Cardigan River and Petty Cove.

"Have you heard of any sales coming up in the area, Ada?" Might as well get the lay of the land on her favorite topic—rural auction sales.

"Sales?"

"You know, yard sales, auction sales, estate sales. I'm always interested in what I might find at sales like that."

"Why, it's mainly junk, girl! What would you want with old junk people want to get rid of?"

"I make my living buying and selling what you call 'junk,' Ada," she said wryly, shooting another glance toward the table. This time she met Liam's curious gaze. "That's what I do. I buy folk art of any kind, also paintings, quilts, weather vanes, old furniture and jewelry, stuff like that and then I sell it to my clients in Toronto."

"Folk art?"

"Paintings by amateurs, driftwood sculpture, those homemade whirligig things people have on their mailboxes—"

"Go on with you! Who'd want that?"

"My customers."

"What kind of customers?"

"Decorators. Interior designers. Collectors. You'd be surprised how people value old things for their own houses. Mats like that hooked one you have out in the porch area, for instance. How much do you think someone would pay for that in Toronto, Ada?"

"That faded old thing? Why, they'd be crazy if they gave you five dollars for it!"

"Five dollars!" Charlotte laughed. "I could easily get fifty dollars for it and probably twice that from the right customer."

"No!"

"It's true." She was delighted at Ada's dismay.

The older woman shook her head slowly several times. "Why, I knew they were different up there in Ontario, but I never figured them for fools! Charlotte, did you know we lived in Toronto for a few years? When my Fergus was alive. He had a good job there working for the city."

"I did know, Ada," Charlotte said softly, stealing another glance at Liam. "That's where I met your son. He knew my sister, Laurel." Charlotte paused, then couldn't resist continuing. "I had a big crush on him once, did you know that? When I was about eleven. Of course, he didn't know I even existed."

"Who—Liam?"

Liam shook his head slowly, as his mother had done, a smile hovering. "You're kidding, right?" He actually looked a little uncomfortable. Charlotte was glad she'd spilled the beans. It put the whole first love, first crush thing in perspective—a silly, girlish idea.

"It's true. You used to come over to our house. I remember you had a big brown dog that went everywhere with you and—"

"Why, that'd be Hector, Liam!" his mother broke in.

"And when my sister's gang would come over for pool parties, I'd hide in the bushes and spy on everyone. With my best friend, Rosie McDermott. You'd be surprised at what we saw."

"You did?"

Liam was actually smiling now, and it did wonderful things to Charlotte's middle. She'd come to believe he was such a severe humorless man.

"You and your friend hid out in the bushes?"

She nodded. Ada laughed and got up to attend to the kettle, which had begun to boil. "Kids! You'll have a cup of tea? It won't keep you awake, will it?"

"Tea would be lovely." Nothing would keep her awake tonight. Not even the lumpy pillow.

"Liam? Jamie?"

They both agreed and kept their attention on the decoy, which was starting to take on recognizable shape under Liam's guidance. Ada put some squares she said she'd made that day on a plate and muttered under her breath about Clara Jenkins's baking skills, something that included "biscuits" and "bullets" in the same sentence.

Charlotte was tired but happy, and so glad she'd decided to come to the Connerys. Tomorrow was her first big day on the job, sorting through the furniture, china and other items she'd seen at the Rathbone place. She'd peeked into one cupboard and discovered what she took—at first glance, anyway—to be an entire set of Meissen porcelain, a turn-of-the-century pattern, easily a hundred years old. She could hardly wait to dig through it.

And she'd apparently bridged some sort of gap here. Maggie seemed content and that was the main thing. Ada was delighted with her visit, and even Liam didn't seem quite as fierce as he had. Maybe he was no different now than he'd been yesterday and last week, when she'd first met him. Maybe she was just getting used to him, not letting him frighten her anymore with his silence and abruptness.

When she got up to leave, he accompanied her to the door. Maggie tried to follow, but she told the dog to stay. Maggie settled back by Ada's chair with a big sigh and soulful brown eyes.

"Well, thanks for everything," Charlotte said, when she'd put on her boots and jacket in the anteroom. No matter what she told herself, Liam still made her nervous. Very nervous. She just couldn't seem to figure him out—was he the doting son or the stubborn kennel owner? The rude man who'd ordered her to follow him on the beach, or the kind one who'd offered her his jacket? Basically, he had to be okay. Laurel always said dogs didn't like bad people.

The wind caught at the door when he opened it. "There's a sale at Three Corners next weekend. Farm sale."

"Oh!" She'd nearly forgotten her query. She paused halfway out the door. "Next weekend? Good, I'll try and get to it."

He acted as though he was going to say something else, but changed his mind. He nodded in response to her repeated thanks and closed the door.

Well, Charlotte thought as she picked her way across the muddy yard, he'd actually been helpful. Offered information instead of her having to pry it out of him.

It was a start, wasn't it?

"HALF-PAST NINE, JAMIE." Liam nodded at the wall clock. "I'd better run you home."

"School in the morning!" Liam's mother said.

Jamie sighed and put down his chisel. "Can I work on this tomorrow after chores?"

"Sure. Soon as we're finished with the dogs. Maybe you want to use my workshop."

"You figure?" He looked up at Liam eagerly. "The power tools and everything?"

"Why not? I'll talk to your dad."

"Dad'll let me." The boy replaced the chisels in their box and carefully lowered his half-carved decoy into a canvas sack sitting on the table. Then he began sweeping up the shavings. Liam watched him, hands jammed into his back pockets.

"I *like* that Charlotte!" his mother said with enthusiasm. "Don't you, Liam? She's a fine girl. I suppose she's pretty, too. I wish I could see her better. Is she pretty, Liam?"

"Pretty enough," he answered shortly.

"Oh, you! *Is* she, Jamie?"

"Yes, she is, Auntie. She's got dark hair, all shiny and bouncy, and the nicest blue eyes you ever saw, and she smiles all the time...."

"She wear glasses?" Ada was sitting forward in her chair, listening.

"Nope. No glasses." Jamie put the shavings into the kindling box beside the parlor stove. He glanced at Liam. "I'm ready. I'll just get my jacket and books." The boy came to the Connerys several days a week on the schoolbus. Liam employed him part-time, helping take care of the dogs—feeding, cleaning kennels, exercising. Those days he often stayed for supper with the Connerys and did his homework in peace and quiet at their kitchen table, before returning home.

"Don't get any bright ideas, Ma," Liam said softly, when Jamie disappeared into the anteroom.

"Bright ideas?" The older woman had a spot of color in each cheek. "What in the world could you be talkin' about?"

"You know, Ma. Bright ideas like inviting her to stay here with us."

"But look at what she has to put up with at Clara's! Jell-O! And that awful Freddie Burns looking her over at each meal—you know what he's like. We've got plenty of room, son. This is a big house. And she'd only be here a couple of weeks."

Liam frowned. "I'm quite sure she can handle herself with the likes of Freddie Burns."

"Why, Liam! I've never known you to be inhospitable. Is it—?" She clamped her lips shut. "Oh, never mind."

"What did you mean to say, Ma?"

"I just wondered, oh, you know, if it had anything to do with having a—well, having a woman in the house. A *young* woman." Ada turned away and reached in the pocket of her skirt for a tissue. She dabbed at her eyes.

"You thinking about Dorrie?"

"Well, yes, you know what I mean. Oh, forget I mentioned it. I just thought—well, I just thought it might be nice to have some company in the house, that's all. It'd only be for a short while."

Jamie stuck his head in the kitchen door. "Can I drive, Liam? I got my learner's now."

"Here." Liam tossed him the keys. "Get in the truck. I'll be right there."

He watched his mother closely. The older

woman's face was lined and tired. Since her blindness had come on five or six years ago, she'd aged twenty years.

"Could you turn on the radio for me, Liam? Before you go?" she said, adjusting the afghan on her lap with fretful fingers. "Where's that darn Chippy gone to?"

Liam walked over and turned on the radio. He knew she could reach it well enough. "I might be a while, Ma," he said, leaning over and putting his hand on her shoulder. "I may watch the end of the hockey game with Davy. You go off to bed, don't wait up for me."

She patted his hand. "Never mind about me, Liam. I know how hard it is for you here. Not much of a life, is it? Dorrie—"

"Don't say anything about Dorrie. Please."

"But it's true, son. It's been six years. I pray it'll be over soon...."

"Don't say that, Ma!"

"I'll say it if I like!" Ada went on stubbornly. "When will it end? You should be off somewhere, flying planes—"

"I've got my dogs."

"Pah! Dogs. This is no life for a man of your age. You should have children, a family—"

"I had a family," Liam said in a hard voice.

"You deserve a woman who loves you, a woman who's healthy and fit. Here you are stuck playing nursemaid to an old woman—"

"You're not an old woman," he interrupted. "You're my mother."

"Oh, Liam." Her voice was soft as she reached for her son's hand and squeezed it briefly.

Liam stood straight. "As for Dorrie—" His voice was harsh. "You know there's nothing that can be done, Ma."

When he'd gone, Ada rested her head on the upholstered back of the chair and closed her eyes. Chippy hopped onto her knee again, and she began stroking the cat, humming along with the radio.

An old Frank Sinatra tune, "My Way."

"Now, ain't that humorous, Chippy?" She leaned forward suddenly and moved her hand so she could scratch behind the cat's ears. "As if anyone ever gets to do things their way! That definitely ain't how things happen around Petty Cove, is it?"

The cat purred, eyes half-closed, head high, and dug its claws rhythmically into the afghan on the old woman's lap.

CHAPTER SEVEN

DAVY MACDONALD, Liam's cousin, was working on his old Ford truck. He was always working on something.

"He's out back," Alice said, one child on her hip, another clinging to her skirt. "In the shed. Why don't you take him this?" She opened the fridge and pulled out two cans of Alpine.

"Jamie get his homework done?" she asked as she handed Liam the beer. Alice was blond and pretty, almost as pretty as she'd been when Davy married her, straight out of high school, fifteen years before. Jamie had arrived with running shoes, as the old folks always said with a wink and a leer, and there'd been four more since then.

"Yes. He's doing well with his math," Liam replied. "He's a smart boy."

Alice beamed. "Well, we think so. But you've done wonders with him, Liam, you really have. We appreciate it, Davy and me, even if Davy don't say much. The time you spend with him, keeping him busy with the dogs, not running around the country with some of those boys. And the money he gets working for you—" she shook her head and continued softly "—it's a big help, Liam. It really is."

Liam nodded and walked past the small living room. Two children were lying on the floor in front of the television set. There were toys strewn across the floor and un-ironed clothes lying on the sofa. A radio blared from another room in the small bungalow.

"Jamie?" Liam paused, one hand on the doorknob.

"I think he's gone out already," Alice said, gently rocking the baby on her hip. "Probably saying good night to Buster." She laughed and threw back her head. "He's crazy about that dog you gave him."

Liam walked to the shed, a shingled frame building that Davy used as a combination garage and workshop. A series of shelves held his tools, his fishing gear, his spare parts, his welding torch. His fishboat, the *Alice B.,* was on blocks in the frozen grass to one side of the shed.

Liam opened the door, throwing a square of yellow light onto the dark grass. He blinked his eyes. "Davy?"

"Over here." Davy was wedged underneath the front part of his rusty Ford. "Trouble with the fuel pump."

"Need a hand?"

"No." Davy grunted, clanged at something under the vehicle, then began to come out from under the engine, sideways. "Just about got her licked. You bring Jamie home?"

"Yeah. Here—" He passed Davy a can of beer. "I'm surprised you aren't watching the hockey game."

"Come over to watch it with me?" Davy laughed, popped the tab and took a swallow of beer. "Man, that's good. I can't get near the set. It's otherwise engaged. You got time to go to Watson's?" He took another swallow of his beer and set it down on his workbench. "We could watch the last period over there."

"Not tonight."

"Okay, we'll go back and see if the girls' show is over. Hell of a note that you've got to ask your own kids if you can watch a game, ain't it?"

"I don't know. I'm not a father."

Davy squinted at his cousin. He finished unrolling his sleeves, pulled out his shirttail and tucked it into his jeans again. "Want to come back to the house, anyway?"

Liam shrugged. "Sure. I'm in no big hurry to go home."

"Hey." Davy stood and wiped his hands on an oily rag. He was thinner than Liam and a little shorter. A wiry, muscular man. "You know Alice. Coffee's always on. Say, Jamie tells me there's a visitor down there at Cardigan River."

"She's staying at the Jenkins place," Liam said shortly.

"I thought Ada might've offered her something. You know how she misses that old bed-and-breakfast thing."

Liam nodded.

"Jamie says she's working at the Rathbone house for a few weeks."

Liam nodded again. He picked up a wrench from Davy's workbench, hefted it, then put it down again.

"Jamie says she's real good-lookin'."

Liam stared straight at his cousin. "What is it you want to say, Davy? Why don't you come right out and say it?"

"Nothing." Davy held up both hands. "Nothing at all. I just figure, hey, new woman around. That's news. Single, too, Jamie tells me." He drained his beer, crumpled the can in one fist and tossed the metal wad in the direction of the corner. It landed in a cardboard box already half full of cans.

"You know how I feel about that, Davy."

"Yeah. But it's time you made a change in how you feel about—"

"Forget it!" Liam said angrily. He jammed his hands in his pockets and looked toward the black, grimy square of window over the workbench. "She doesn't do a thing for me, pal."

"No?" His cousin eyed him curiously. "Jamie says she's got a dog you're boardin' for her. Nice Lab."

"Her sister's dog. Show bitch." Liam smiled. "Your son sure talks a lot more here than he does at my place."

Davy laughed and slapped him on the shoulder. "Let's go see about that hockey game. See if we can pry the girls away from the TV."

They left the shed, Liam still carrying his beer, and Davy closed the door behind them. Several hundred yards away, the surf brushed against the shore. The moon was rising.

"Listen, Liam," Davy said as they walked, his breath a cloud in the cold air. "You know what they say about cuttin' bait or fishing? Well, that expression ain't just for fishermen, y'know. No one would hold it against you if you started seein' someone."

"Before I tell you it's none of your Goddamn business, even if we do go all the way back to eight-year-old kids cutting cod cheeks to buy our smokes from Abe down at Bonnie's store—"

Davy laughed and slapped Liam on the shoulder again. "Yeah. Remember that?"

"—what the hell's brought this on all of a sudden? Just because a single woman turns up in Petty Cove—"

"Cardigan River."

"Well, it'll be Petty Cove if Ada gets her way, I figure. The two of them hit it off. The point is, I've met her, I've talked to her, and—she's fine, she's okay, she's good-looking, but hell, that's it."

"That's it?"

"Yeah. That's it." He laughed but the sound was strained. "Now get off my back about this."

"Not your type, eh?"

"That's right."

"Just what *is* your type, pal?" Davy asked softly. "It's been a long, long time. Six years now."

Liam didn't say anything until Davy reached for the doorknob. They'd been standing outside talking, illuminated only by the single bulb in the yard light. In a sudden movement, Liam crushed the beer can he was holding, his face a mask. "I don't know, Davy. I honest to God don't know anymore."

UPHOLSTERED CHAIRS, two, poor condition. $20.

Carved mahogany side table, nineteenth-century English, fair condition—what a shame the top was scratched and there was a water mark on the polished surface. $800.

Antique sterling candlesticks, three, Gorham. $250 each.

Tapestry, eighteenth-century Flemish, good condition. ?

Charlotte had written a question mark in the value column because it was nearly impossible to put a price on something like the tapestry. The subject was popular—nymphs in the trees and ladies and gentleman walking together in a garden—but the size was rather daunting, more than ten feet square. Not a domestic piece, at least in today's homes. It was obviously part of a larger tapestry that had been cut to fit the end wall of this library. If you had a lot of buyers interested in this, it might go for a considerable amount. If not—

Charlotte marked down "$900 plus." A similar-size piece had sold at auction a year ago, according to her information, for $1,400. She didn't want to overestimate value on the estate, better that the owners be pleasantly surprised by a high bid on an item like this than to sell it at half the estimated price. And antique tapestries were definitely a specialized market.

The library. She didn't know what to do with the library. The room smelled mustier than most, which was not a good sign, but she'd need to consult Mr. Busby on the contents. Books were not her area. A perusal had turned up possibly rare first editions, as well as paperbacks by John D. MacDonald and Zane Grey. Perhaps the entire contents could be sold to a book dealer. She made a note of that in the journal she was keeping as she worked her way through the house.

This was her second day on the job and she'd already gone through the old gentleman's bed-room—not much there except some rather grand thirties-style satin curtains, all loops and swags, which the family might like to keep or sell with the house, two old-fashioned eiderdown comforters, cov-ered in plum-colored ruched satin, which might be of interest to a textile collector or a ''shabby chic'' decorator, and a nearly valueless queen-size bed and mattress purchased from a local department store. Distressed oak veneers, probably even fake, jostling for space in the same room with priceless antique Sevrès porcelain! The vases sat dusty and neglected on a beechwood chest that had probably been built in New Brunswick or Nova Scotia a hundred years before. She wanted to investigate the chest further, make some phone calls. Museums were interested in pieces like that.

She wondered what the old man had chopped up for firewood. The house appeared to be a total mish-mash of almost worthless pieces, like the stained and soiled upholstered chairs by the fireplace in the par-lor. Gerard Rathbone had obviously spent most of his time in these chairs, judging from the number of cigarette burn marks in the ruined marquetry floor near the fireplace. When he hadn't been lying in bed smoking, judging by the burn marks beside the oak veneer bed. It was a wonder the whole place hadn't gone up in flames.

Then she'd stumbled across something that would set her heart pounding—like the rare matched pair of Chinese painted mirrors hanging askew on a wall behind a door. The mirrors were in perfect condition, beautifully painted, and would probably fetch two to three thousand at auction, maybe more. That room had contained other Oriental collectibles—carved Chinese ivory figures, jade items, mother-of-pearl in-laid wooden boxes. A mahogany partner's desk in the library, plus a stunning example of the current rage, a small "fancy" furniture table, probably from the Baltimore area, about 1815! Something like that might sell for many thousands of dollars at the right auction.

Coming across pieces of such value made her nervous. Thank heavens the house hadn't been robbed in the three months or so it had stood empty. Mr. Busby must have said something to the so-called watchman, because he'd been on the job both days she'd been here. He parked himself in the kitchen in front of a roaring fire in the woodstove, sipped coffee from the pot he had going on the stove, and worked his way through a stack of old newspapers he'd found somewhere. Perhaps he'd brought them with him.

"I don't take the paper regular, so it's all news to me!" he'd said, when she'd asked why he was read-ing a month-old *Charlottetown Guardian*. One eye was patched and he didn't shave everyday, but despite the piratical look this gave him, Cyril Rush seemed cheerful and harmless enough. Charlotte was glad of another soul to speak to occasionally. She definitely planned to start bringing Maggie with her soon.

She was expecting the family representative any time. Nick Deacon. According to Clara Jenkins, he was a sailor, a gentleman yachtsman. She didn't know what he did for a living, if anything; all she knew was that he spent his time "dipsy-doodling around on a boat—not even a fishboat!" Charlotte decided she'd ask him what he wanted done with the contents of the library.

Charlotte had stopped at Bonnie Bristol's store that morning and bought her lunch. She'd thanked Mrs. Jenkins profusely for her lukewarm offer to do up a packed lunch everyday...but refused. Cold overcooked roast beef sandwiches with margarine and ballpark mustard on sliced white, and maybe a candy bar thrown in, or a piece of last week's gingerbread—what she predicted her landlady would produce—was not her idea of a noon meal.

Instead, yesterday she'd bought an apple, a pint of chocolate milk and a carton of peach yogurt and, now that Cyril had the kitchen running, she had bread, ham and cheese, which she planned to turn into a grilled sandwich. A cupboard held packaged pound cake and cookies for afternoon tea, there was milk and lemonade in the ancient refrigerator, and she'd put decent ground coffee and filters on her list of what to pick up when she went to Montague or Charlottetown.

And there were dog treats for Maggie, of course.

Half an hour later, Charlotte carried her lunch onto the south-facing veranda. The storm from two days before had blown itself out, leaving blue skies and a hint of summer warmth. Indian summer. Nearly all the leaves had turned their fall colors now.

Ah, life could be worse, she thought, biting into half of the grilled ham-and-cheese. Her hair was a mess; digging around in a longtime widower's old house had its cobwebby hazards. Her jeans and cotton-knit pullover—her working garb—had seen better days, but she was comfortable.

A radio. She needed some music while she—

A dog ran across the abandoned herb garden. A low-to-the-ground, floppy-eared white and pale tan dog that looked vaguely familiar.

Cruller!

Charlotte sat straight up. A black Labrador following the spaniel—Maggie?—lifted its nose into the air and then veered in her direction. Before she could say anything, the dog had bounded onto the veranda, licked her face with a big pink tongue and scarfed up a quarter of her sandwich.

"Scout!"

Stunned, Charlotte gazed at the western corner of the building, where Liam had just emerged. He whistled sharply, and Scout bounded back down the steps and toward him, the image of a faithful, obedient dog.

Burping as he went, Charlotte guessed.

"He hurt you?" Liam looked concerned. He must have seen Scout jump up and lick her.

"No." She could barely stop herself from laughing. "Don't you feed your dogs?"

"What do you mean?"

"He ate my sandwich."

Liam swore and turned to frown at the Labrador, who was oblivious to any censure, his pink tongue lolling, his brown eyes soft and loving. It was obvious his master could do no wrong. Charlotte was pretty sure that went for just about anybody else, too. Like all Labradors, Scout adored people and lived for an "attaboy" and a handout. No wonder they were such a popular family dog.

She leaned on the railing of the veranda. "Somehow, I don't think Scout's one of your star pupils, is he?"

Liam looked at his dog and shook his head ruefully. "Nope. Too damn much personality."

"Make someone a great family pet," she suggested slyly.

He glanced up. "Yeah, well, how are things going over here? Ma sent me to check on you."

Of course. He wouldn't have come on his own. She noticed he was carrying a brown paper bag.

"Come up," she said. "I've got a pot of tea, if you'd like some."

He climbed up the steps and plunked the paper bag down on the blistered and rusted wrought-iron table she was using. "Here's some dessert."

Charlotte peeked in the bag. "Oh! Cookies?"

"Oatmeal raisin."

"My favorite!" She pulled one out and bit into

one, savoring the crunchy, sweet texture. "Yummy. Sit down. Tea?"

He shook his head. "Ma's worried. Figures you're not getting enough to eat over at Clara's." His dark eyes regarded her briefly, then flicked away.

"My landlady is not the best cook," she admitted. "I'm not getting much sleep, either. Too noisy. Actually, after my week's up, I'm going to look around for something else."

"You are?"

Charlotte nodded, mouth full. She swallowed. "I'm going to check out Montague. Maybe even Charlottetown. You know any good places? *Quiet* places?"

"Nope." He cleared his throat. "Well, I'd better head back. I wondered if you want me to bring Maggie."

"Oh, I was just thinking about that! I'd love to have her with me here in the daytime."

"I'll bring her over, then."

"No, let me. I'll drive to your place tomorrow morning, on my way here. I don't want to put you to any trouble."

"It's no trouble. I can bring her through the woods. There's a path between this cove and the next."

"Your mother told me about it." Charlotte caught her breath suddenly. She realized he was watching her. Every time she glanced away, toward the dogs or the garden, his eyes were on her. Then, when her attention returned to him, or she said something, he looked away. She didn't know what to make of it.

He stood at the edge of the veranda and whistled. The heavyset, low-slung spaniel came trotting around the corner of the house, expression never changing, and made his way up the stairs toward them. If ever there was a dog that looked as though he had something important on his mind, it was Cruller.

"I've never seen a dog like that."

"Not too many Clumbers around. I'm working him for a friend in Wolfville."

"Is he any good?"

"The best. Plenty of focus, like a Chesapeake, but without the intensity. Slow and steady. He never gives up, do you, old fella?" Liam bent down to scratch the dog's ears. The spaniel gazed up with his perpetual sad look, panted a little, glanced respectfully at Charlotte, then trundled back down the stairs on some new, desperately important mission.

"Why do they call him Cruller?"

Liam paused. "What, you don't think that's a good name for a hunting dog?"

Charlotte laughed. "It's a ridiculous name for *any* dog! *Cruller?*"

"My buddy's girlfriend named him. It's his color. That light tan is called 'lemon' in the breed. So he's a lemon-and-white. Lemon? Cruller?" He sent her a glance and shrugged. "I don't know. She thought it went together. *Scout!*"

Liam started down the steps. The Labrador had perked up his ears and then dashed around the house again. "Damn dog!"

Charlotte smiled. Then she realized what Scout must have heard. A car engine.

"You expecting somebody?" Liam called up to her.

"That might be Nick Deacon. Do you know him?"

Liam didn't acknowledge her question, but Charlotte had the distinct impression that he knew Rathbone's great-nephew. She walked down the steps with the intention of circling around to the front of the house.

"Scout! Cruller!" Liam called the dogs.

"Coming?" Charlotte paused at the edge of the house. She wasn't quite sure why she wanted him with her. Cyril Rush was in the house; no doubt, he was expecting Deacon, too. After a few seconds' hesitation, Liam walked slowly in her direction. The dogs followed.

The great-nephew—and that was certainly who it appeared to be—drove a rental SUV, a green Blazer. He was wearing jeans, a Gore-Tex jacket and sunglasses.

"Hi!" He walked toward her, hand outstretched. "You must be Charlotte. Busby told me you were here."

Charlotte took his hand. He was younger than she'd realized—about her age, maybe a little older—and handsome, in a tanned, blond, preppy kind of way. His handshake was firm. "Charlotte Moore. Yes, I'm trying to work my way through your uncle's stuff."

"Not a task for the fainthearted. Connery?" Nick

Deacon took a step toward Liam; the two men shook hands briefly. "I didn't know you were back here! I thought you were still out slaying dragons and shooting down bad guys."

Charlotte frowned. *Slaying dragons?*

"Hey!" Nick turned, smiling at her. "You knew Liam here was a hotshot fighter pilot, didn't—"

"That was quite a while ago, Nick," Liam interrupted. "Years ago."

"You still fly, though?" Nick sounded surprised.

Liam shook his head. "I train gun dogs now. Fish with my cousin. Do some carpentry work. A little of this, a little of that."

Charlotte was puzzled. She knew that Liam Connery, as a boy, had dreamed of flying. She'd had no idea he'd actually become a pilot. A fighter pilot in the air force? So what was he doing here? Surely he hadn't left the air force just to look after his mother full-time? There were people you could hire to do that—friends, relations to depend on, neighbors. Ada Connery could live in a nice retirement place somewhere. She wasn't running the bed-and-breakfast, anyway. Her husband was dead; why wouldn't she move closer to her son, not the other way around?

Nick whistled through his teeth and shook his head as he surveyed the house and the gardens. "Man, the old place is getting pretty run down, isn't it."

Charlotte looked from him to Liam. This wasn't the time to discuss fixing the place up, exploring what plans the family had, finding a handyman, maybe, to spruce up the grounds.

"Well, I'd better be on my way," Liam said, taking a step back. "I'll bring Maggie over later."

"Maggie?" Nick glanced from Charlotte to Liam and back again, a smile on his handsome face. He'd pushed his sunglasses onto his forehead, and he had the bluest eyes Charlotte had ever seen. "Let me guess, your little girl? You two are married, right?"

He laughed, and Charlotte blushed hotly. She knew it was only a joke, but— "Heavens no!" She attempted a laugh, not daring to look Liam's way. "Maggie's my dog. My sister's, actually. Liam's keeping her for me, until I can ship her back to Toronto. It's a long, complicated story, believe me! You don't want to know."

Nick grinned and held up both hands. "O-kay."

Liam had already started to walk toward the woods that separated the Rathbone property from his place. Charlotte hurried to catch up with him.

"Liam!"

He swung around. He seemed as remote and distant as she'd ever seen him. The weak attempts at joking about Cruller's name, Scout's misbehavior, Clara Jenkins's cooking, seemed a million miles away. Had he taken offense at Nick Deacon's stupid remark? Surely not.

"I'll drive over this evening and let you know. I want to see your mother, anyway. And—and we'll decide about Maggie then. I'll have to ask Nick for permission. It's his family's place. Maybe they don't want a dog here."

He nodded briefly, his eyes barely meeting hers. She felt as if she'd been slapped. What had hap-

pened? What had thrown this chill into the middle
of things? Was it Nick's arrival? His comment about
Liam's flying career? They'd seemed cordial enough
when they'd shaken hands. Who could tell with men!

She didn't have time to think about that now. She
hurried back to where Nick was waiting, leaning
against the hood of his vehicle.

"Okay. Let's go in, shall we?" She wanted to
apologize for being such a mess, but decided it
wasn't professional to draw attention to her looks,
no matter what her feminine instincts were—and
then realized she hadn't felt the need to apologize to
Liam. "I've got a lot to show you."

"I'll just bet you do!" He tucked her arm through
his in a friendly manner and they moved toward the
broad steps that led to the front door. Charlotte
glanced over her shoulder, but Liam had disappeared. Into the deep, dark woods, from which he'd
emerged in the first place.

No sign of the well-paid Cyril Rush, either. In
Charlotte's opinion, he was about as much of a
watchman as a stick of gum. So much for security!

Another very good reason to have Maggie on the
premises.

CHAPTER EIGHT

"I CAN'T BELIEVE IT—Liam Connery!" Nick drummed well-manicured nails on the granite tabletop. He and Charlotte were in the lounge at the Confederation Hotel, which was part of the city's conference complex and a building that could have been situated in any modern city anywhere. There was nothing particularly charming about it, except the location on Charlottetown's quaint inner harbor.

Nick Deacon had insisted Charlotte join him for dinner and, in the end, they'd decided to go all the way to the capital city, where Nick was staying for the week. Contrary to Mr. Busby's prediction, Nick had no intention of moving into his great-uncle's house, not as long as there was a luxury hotel room within reasonable driving distance.

Charlotte had left a message with Ada for Liam not to expect her that evening, after all, and she'd driven her Suburban so she could return on her own and save Nick the additional trip back to Cardigan River. She relaxed in her comfortable upholstered chair, savoring the service, the quiet, the view outside the twenty-foot windows.

"You knew Liam Connery before, I gather?"

"Years ago. Him and his cousin, Davy Macdonald. And they had another sidekick I don't remember as well. I think his name was McEachern. I spent a few weeks here each summer and they were my heroes." Nick smiled. "They were terrors, Liam and Davy. Hell-raisers, fighters—stuck together like glue. They were five or six years older than me, so of course I idolized them. Haven't seen either one in years." He shook his head.

"Did you know the family?" Charlotte was curious. Liam's cousin, Davy Macdonald, had to be Jamie's father. She'd been curious about Liam Connery ever since she'd arrived and had had very little opportunity to ask anyone questions. Anyway, *who* could she ask? It seemed disloyal to quiz her landlady or Bonnie Bristol about their neighbor.

Nick glanced up at the waitress and signaled for another drink. Charlotte was nursing her rye and water, since she'd be driving later.

"No. Although the family didn't live far from my uncle. Story was, Fergus Connery drank and wasn't around much." Nick laughed. "You'll notice, Charlotte, that Islanders either drink or they don't drink. The Connerys, most of 'em, are drinkers."

Charlotte merely smiled.

"Old Gerard had a different kind of rep. He was known for keeping the ladies company when their men were away, even when my great-aunt was alive." Nick winked at her. "Hell, I even heard rumors that Liam was his kid."

Charlotte stared, openmouthed. "His son!"

"Yeah. Which would make us related, huh?" Nick picked up his glass and grinned. "Hey, him and half the other kids at Cardigan River." He waved his glass. "Hell, it's just gossip. People always talk a lot in small places like that."

"Or don't talk at all," Charlotte put in, thinking of how little anyone had said about Liam Connery, except that he was particular. Ornery. Nothing personal had ever been offered.

"That's true. The rumor probably got started because Liam spent a lot of time with my uncle—fishing and hunting. They were both strong, silent types. Cut from the same cloth. His own father was usually away fishing. Or drunk, I heard. Uncle Gerard always had hunting dogs, and it sounds like Liam's still a dog guy. You know where he lives now?"

"Next to your great-uncle's house, through the woods, with his mother. She's blind."

"Yeah?" Nick signed the chit for his drink, which had just arrived. "That would be the family place, I suppose. The Connerys left the Island when I was nine or ten and I don't recall seeing him again." Nick frowned. "Of course, I had other things to do. And I started spending summers closer to home."

"He was in the air force?"

"So I understand. Fighter pilot. Bosnia, Somalia, some kind of NATO thing—I guess my mother must've told me. Seems the type somehow, doesn't he?"

Charlotte found herself nodding.

Nick gave her a puzzled frown. "Funny it didn't last. Last place I ever thought he'd end up was back here."

Charlotte leaned forward, deciding it was time to change the subject. "And you're a sailor!"

"Yeah." Nick grinned boyishly. "But, hey, I'm also a serious guy. I run an outerwear company, designing and manufacturing sports clothes."

"Oh?"

"That's in the winter. I sail the rest of the year." He raised his glass. "Great life. Can't beat it."

Charlotte wondered if he was married or engaged. She was only interested because she liked Nick and wanted to get a more complete picture of him. He could become a friend. They had a lot in common— the wealthy childhood, the sailing, the education, the travel. But romantically? No way. He wasn't her type.

And, Ms. Charlotte Moore, just what is *your type?* she couldn't help thinking. Once, at all of eleven, she'd thought Liam Connery was her type. So handsome and romantic, so glamorous, being older and a friend of her sister's.

But now? Definitely not. Too rough, too dangerous, too unpredictable. She didn't particularly like the sensation of being on edge, and Liam Connery was a man who made her feel that way. Unsettled, uncertain. She preferred men of another type altogether. Suitably well-established in life, reasonably handsome—certainly men who shaved everyday— gentlemanly, somewhat sophisticated, at least as far as ordering a decent bottle of wine at dinner. And— this was harder to admit—predictable. She liked reliable guys who showed up when they said they would, dressed well, were good drivers. They didn't have to be rich but they had to be confident. Upbeat. Guys who read the funny pages in the Sunday paper and liked dogs, kids and bunny rabbits.

Well, Liam liked dogs. That was about all, as far as she could tell. Plus, he clearly had no interest in her—as a member of the opposite sex, anyway. *Zilch, nada,* none. Which was okay. She wasn't going to get bent out of shape over his attitude, even though she was aware that it was a new experience for her. Most men—old and young—had liked her, responded to her as a woman, were charming, friendly. Flirted with her, even. All harmless fun.

Like Nick.

She wondered what Liam's romantic past was; a man like that had to have one. But she wouldn't ask Nick. He wouldn't know. She'd pried enough; besides, it was more fun to speculate. Was he nursing a broken heart? The victim of a tragic divorce? Jilted at the altar? Had the girl of his dreams died in his arms when they were teenagers and he'd sworn on her rose-covered grave never to love again?

Half an hour later, they moved into the hotel dining room, where Charlotte ate local seafood in a cream sauce, rice pilaf and an excellent mesclun salad with oil-and-vinegar dressing, followed by crème brûlée. What a change from gray roast beef and Jell-O.

Charlotte was glad she and Nick had hit it off. As the family's representative, he could make decisions that needed to be made about the estate—such as what to do with the library contents and whether or not to hire someone to fix up the grounds. As well, he was a lighthearted and good-natured companion, someone who'd be easy to work with.

Living in Charlottetown, with a few amenities, had some appeal. She briefly entertained the idea of booking into the same hotel overnight, just to enjoy some peace and quiet, not to mention a good night's sleep and a luxurious soak in a modern bathtub. But that could be dangerous. There might be talk about her and Nick Deacon spending the night in Charlottetown the very day he'd arrived. She had to be careful about gossip, if for no other reason than to protect her employer, Stanley Busby and Busby Auctions. Small towns were small towns, whether of the talking variety or not.

The drive home wasn't as burdensome as she'd expected, although if she moved to Charlottetown and had to do it twice a day, it could get old fast.

The evening had been very pleasant, all in all. And it had led her to a firm decision: it was time to say goodbye to Mrs. Jenkins's boardinghouse.

THE NEXT DAY was Saturday. Charlotte did her best to sleep in a little, but it wasn't even half-past eight when she finally gave up. She could hear one of the tenants' radios through the wall of her room, tuned to what sounded like a perpetual horse-racing station—*was* there such a thing?—and, from below, the sound of her landlady banging around in the kitchen. Pots and pans crashing, water running, shouts to her enfeebled half-deaf husband, John, in the next room.

It was enough to make Charlotte's head spin. She wanted to go back to the estate and do some cataloging, but first she intended to drive over to the Connerys and pick up Maggie.

She'd just returned from a trip to the common bathroom—another very serious flaw in her accommodation, in her view—when there was a loud knock at her door.

"Visitor for ya." Clara Jenkins stood outside in the dark hallway, wearing an apron and with a wooden spoon in one hand. She eyed Charlotte's dressing gown with disapproval. "Missed breakfast, eh?" Breakfast, Charlotte knew, was at seven o'clock, "not a minute sooner, not a minute later." "There's leftover porridge sittin' on the stove," Mrs. Jenkins finished, then headed toward the stairs.

Visitor? Charlotte hadn't had the wherewithal to ask who. Surely it was too early in the day for Nick Deacon. He hadn't mentioned coming to Cardigan River today.

She made her bed and dressed hurriedly. Gray flannel pants, a matching jacket with plenty of pockets, her favorite, and a lightweight cream-colored sweater underneath. No makeup, no jewelry, but then she hadn't bothered with either since she'd arrived. A quick comb-through and she was ready. Who could be downstairs—Cyril Rush? She hoped there wasn't a problem at the Rathbone place.

Forget porridge, she thought as she grabbed her handbag and her laptop. She'd deal with Cyril, or whoever it was, have a quick breakfast at the store, and then continue with her day.

But it wasn't Cyril Rush waiting for her in the foyer. It was Liam Connery.

"Oh!" Charlotte was so startled, she actually came out with an "oh!" before she could stop herself. He looked much the same, only bigger somehow. She decided it must be the combination of Clara Jenkins's narrow hallway, festooned as it was with flocked wallpaper and polyester lace curtains bunched at the small window, that made him appear larger than life. Still the usual jeans, but this time with a black pullover and brown wool jacket.

"D—did you want to see me?" she managed to say. He'd frightened her, she decided. Her heart was pounding like crazy. "Is anything wrong...with Maggie?"

"Maggie's fine. She's in the truck. You ready?" He put one hand on the fake brass doorknob behind him.

Charlotte shook her head, bewildered. "Ready for—what?"

"I thought I'd take you out to that sale at Three Corners. Easier than explaining how to get there."

"Sale? Oh, the *sale!*" Now she remembered. The yard or estate sale or something he'd mentioned on Tuesday when she'd visited Ada. "Well, okay." She shrugged. "I guess that's a good idea. Sure." Why not?

"You have something else planned?"

"No." Charlotte frowned—had she? Nothing important anyway.

"Well..." He opened the door and held it for her.

"I'd better grab a coat—is it cold today?" She was thoroughly rattled. Why hadn't he phoned? Or offered to take her yesterday, when he'd come over to the Rathbone place with Scout and Cruller?

She didn't wait for him to comment on the weather, just grabbed her fleece jacket, scarf and gloves from the hall closet and followed him out the door. She was glad her landlady hadn't reappeared.

He had two dogs in the back of his pickup, under the fiberglass canopy. Charlotte went around to the tailgate and stuck her hand under the canopy to pat the happy-looking Maggie. The other dog was a Lab, too.

"This is—?"

"Sunny. She's getting close to having her puppies, and I thought an outing like this might be good for her. Better than taking her for a hard run."

"She's having puppies, too?"

"Ten more days."

"Oh, how exciting!" Charlotte had clambered onto the passenger seat of the pickup and stowed her fleece jacket and handbag on the seat between them. Liam put the truck into reverse and backed up, using his side mirror.

He glanced at her, then at the mirror again. "You like puppies?"

"Of course! Who doesn't?" Charlotte felt positively giddy. Being rescued from Clara Jenkins's porridge pot was half of it.

The other half was the sheer surprise of having Liam show up like this, bring her dog, tell her he was taking her somewhere. It reminded her of the day she'd met him. He'd simply assumed she'd cooperate. Then and now.

A couple of miles went by before Charlotte could think of anything to say. They appeared to be heading north, along the same road she'd taken to Souris the week before. The coast was alternately rugged, with waves crashing on the rocky headlands, and pastoral, with beautifully groomed pastures rolling right down to the water's edge. White-painted farmhouses and gray-and-red-painted barns and sheds alternated with high-steepled country churches, each with its accompanying graveyard.

"Is this an estate sale?"

"Farm sale. Family gone out of business and selling off their goods."

"Oh." Charlotte considered. That probably meant a lot of machinery—seeders, harvesters, shovels, lawn tractors, goods that were of no interest to her.

"Household stuff and old furniture. Didn't you say you liked that kind of thing?"

"I did," she said weakly. Saggy recliner chairs, old record players and chipped magazine racks weren't on her acquisition list. Oh well, it was an outing.

He slowed and made a left turn. They were driving now through scrub spruce forest and open fields overgrown with willows and alders. Rocky, marginal pasture rather than rich farmland.

"Do you know the people?"

"Yes. The Macleans. I knew Sandy Maclean fairly well—you heard of him?" He shot her a glance.

"Should I have?"

"He plays hockey for the Boston Bruins," Liam said. "Defence."

"I'm not very sporty, I guess," she admitted, looking out the window. "Nick tells me you were in the air force?"

"Nick's got a big mouth."

She caught her breath. "Well, is it true or not?"

"True."

Liam showed no indication that he was going to continue but Charlotte couldn't resist probing a little. "How long? Where? Why'd you leave?"

He said nothing, just stared grimly ahead at the winding paved road in front of them.

"I know it's none of my business, but we've got to talk about *something,* don't we? We're spending a few hours together. We should talk once in a while."

His eyes searched hers briefly, then he turned back to the road, dismissing her appeal.

"I remember you always wanted to fly, back when you were living in Toronto," she persisted.

"How did you know that?"

"My sister told me. Plus, Rosie McDermott and I heard all kinds of things when we hid in the bushes at Laurel's pool parties."

He smiled. Charlotte felt a sort of relief. It seemed she was always starting with Liam Connery but never actually getting anywhere.

"Somehow I can picture you. Did you have short, wispy hair?"

"Yes." Wispy? She would have called it a pixie cut.

"Freckles?"

"No, that was Rosie."

"A real attitude?"

"Definitely not! And that wasn't Rosie, either. What are you talking about?" Charlotte laughed.

"I seem to recall some kid always popping out of the bushes and telling Laurel off about something. Or threatening to tell your parents if she didn't let you do this or that—ring a bell?"

"Kind of," Charlotte said grudgingly. She *had* been a bossy kid. But no one had ever held it against her. She'd been the adored younger sister, the baby of the family. "What about you? Any sisters or brothers?"

"Nope." Liam shook his head. "Just me. My mother was in her forties when she had me. I guess I came along as a surprise."

"How old is your mother now?"

"I'm thirty-four, and she had me when she was forty-two—I guess that makes her seventy-eight on her next birthday."

"How long has she had trouble with her eyes?" Charlotte asked softly, glad that he was talking at least.

"Nearly ten years. It's come on slowly."

"What's wrong with them? She sometimes acts like she doesn't really think she's blind."

"Macular degeneration. Problems with the retinas. She has a hard time accepting that it isn't going to get any better."

"How long have you been looking after her?"

Charlotte held her breath, amazed at her own audacity.

He turned to her, and Charlotte knew her cheeks had reddened. ''Nosy woman, aren't you. I've been here with her for the past six years, ever since I left the air force. Now I train dogs, fish with my cousin, build boats and carve decoys, do a little carpentry work to pay the bills. That should cover it. Any more questions?''

Charlotte knew she deserved the sarcasm. ''I'm sorry. I know it's none of my business. It's very good of you to bring me here today and, believe me, I do appreciate it.'' She looked defiantly at him. ''But I can't understand why you bothered, since you clearly don't like me at all.''

They were traveling slowly over a rutted dirt lane off the main road. He met her eyes, and Charlotte caught her breath again.

''I haven't made up my mind about you, if I like you or not. I don't think it matters much, do you?''

He didn't wait for her reply or even glance toward her for a response. ''The reason I brought you is that I had the time and this is a hard place to find and because I thought maybe if people knew you were with me, you might get what you want for a better price. A tourist in these parts is fair game for the locals, even in the off-season. I wouldn't like to see people take advantage of you. Not when I have some connection with you, through your sister.''

He put on the brakes as they reached the farmhouse and turned to look at her, finally, as they came to a stop. ''Do you understand what I mean?''

Charlotte nodded, her hand on the door handle. Actually, she didn't have a clue what he was talking about, except the bit about prices, and that was debatable. But she was grateful for his company, reluctant or not, out in this remote backwoods location, which, as he'd said, she would never have found on her own. And he'd brought Maggie with him. That was all that mattered to her. Wasn't it?

CHAPTER NINE

THERE WERE A DOZEN OR SO pickup trucks parked in the grass beside the lane and another dozen or so cars in front of the farmhouse, a weathered two-story affair with hanging shutters and shingles missing from the narrow-split cedar siding. Knots of people walked here and there, and Charlotte noticed several heads swinging their way as Liam parked his vehicle.

"Do you think the owners are here?" she asked. She always felt bad for people forced into an auction of their life's goods through any of the misfortunes that seemed to go hand in hand with sales of this nature—divorce, death, bankruptcy.

"No, the place has been empty for a while. The old couple died and no one wants to take over the farm," Liam said. "The land will eventually be sold, too."

Charlotte stood by the truck, while Liam let the eager dogs out. They both ran straight to the trees at the edge of the lane, squatted briefly, then came running back to Liam and Charlotte.

"Maggie!" Charlotte went down on her knees to hug the Labrador properly. She buried her face in Maggie's dark coat. What a dog!

"And Sunny," she said, to be fair, reaching out

to pat the other dog. She glanced up at Liam, who regarded her from the distance of a few feet, an odd expression on his face. "Aren't they both gorgeous? Look at them, a perfectly matched pair!"

"Well, not quite," Liam returned dryly. "One's a champion retriever from a long line of top gun dogs and about to have her second litter, and one's a show dog."

"Oh, listen to him!" she said to the dogs, making a face. "You're both pets, aren't you, sweethearts."

Liam laughed. He actually *laughed,* which astonished Charlotte. "If that was Scout you were talking to, I'd have to agree. But Sunny's all business, just like her dad."

"The famous Old Jimbo, I suppose," Charlotte tossed over her shoulder. "I can hardly wait to meet this legend."

Liam ordered both dogs to heel and they fell in beside him. "You will. One of these days."

The sun was bright overhead and the wind was brisk. Charlotte buttoned her flannel jacket, wishing she'd put on the fleece one, too. Her stomach was growling. She was starving but she couldn't wait to see what that group of men by one of the outbuildings was examining.

"Come on!" She hurried farther ahead of Liam, who strolled along with the dogs, hands in his pockets, as though he had all the time in the world.

Two farmers wearing feed hats and overalls gave her curious looks, but made way as she edged into the crowd. She peeked over a short man's shoulder. Disappointing. The men were inspecting angle iron of various kinds, steel drums, chain, some rusty tools and an old-fashioned cream separator, an early electric model.

She might bid on the cream separator—although it would take up a lot of room in the Suburban. Better not. She had most of the fall sale season ahead of her, and unless she was prepared to rent a trailer to haul her treasures back to Ontario—which occasionally she'd done in the past—she'd better stick to smaller, higher-value items. If it had been hand-operated, perhaps…

Liam joined her. "Interested?" He was being sarcastic.

"Maybe," she said. She moved into the shed. On the wall was a collection of antique gardening tools—bulb planters, trowels, cast-iron row markers, hand rakes. She took a notebook out of her handbag and began to jot down the details. She'd definitely make a bid on that lot.

"Tools?" Liam was at her shoulder.

She turned her head. "Yes. They're very hot right now. Anything to do with gardening is hot."

"I see," he muttered. "Latest big-city trend, dabbling in the earth like the common man."

"That's it," she agreed, arching one eyebrow Liam was looking for an argument and she wasn't going to be drawn into one. She didn't care if decorating cakes or potting petunias was the current craze; it was her business to seek out decorative items to satisfy those trends as they came along.

Of course, some things, like quilts, never went out

of fashion. Quilts, folk art, hooked mats, naive paintings.

"Are they selling stuff from the house, too?" It
was dim in the shed and she was standing very close
to Liam. She couldn't see his eyes clearly in the
gloom, but she was sure he was laughing at her.

"Everything goes, I understand. You want to take
a look?"

"Sure." She pushed her way past him, grabbing
at the weathered doorframe to steady herself on the
uneven earthen floor. "Ouch!"

He reached for her wrist. "What happened?"

"A splinter, I think," she said, tugging her hand
away. He wasn't letting go.

He inspected her palm carefully. "I don't see anything. The light's not great in here."

"Just a scratch, I guess," she said, hurriedly putting her hand in her pocket. "It's fine now." He was
only trying to help, she told herself severely. It was
just that she really didn't want him touching her—
holding her hand, running his thumb lightly over her
palm. Not even looking for a splinter.

"I'm going to go poke through the house a bit.
What time does the actual sale start?" They had arrived during the inspection phase, when people
looked items over and decided what they might bid
on.

"Not sure. Noon, I think." Liam nodded toward
the men gathered by the barn. "I'll take the dogs
with me and check things out over there. See you
later."

Charlotte found a few treasures in the old farmhouse. There were a dozen quilts, at least, some in better condition than others. There were four oil lamps she wouldn't mind bidding on, plus a fairly rare Aladdin lamp that had, unfortunately, been converted to electricity at some point. But its tall, slender glass shade was intact, which was a huge find.

Some kitchen utensils were of interest—particularly handmade wooden rolling pins, and some wooden spatulas and spoons and a salt box. A sugar bowl was definitely old Delft, in perfect condition, and there was one plain-looking bowl sitting on the kitchen table that she was quite sure had been made by an historic Prince Edward Island pottery. She'd read about the archeological excavations at the Charlottetown Pottery site before she'd come to the Island and recalled that some unusual items, such as cream-skimming bowls with a white slip-glazed inner surface, had been dug up there. A shallow bowl on the table was made of red clay and it had that white inner surface, and although it had a crack that ran across the bottom, on the outside, Charlotte decided she wanted it, on the off chance it was from the long-defunct pottery.

These were the kinds of exciting discoveries that made all the poking through trash worthwhile.

Several other women, as well as two men, were perusing the contents of the house, most of which was laid out in the kitchen and what had been the parlor. Even the parlor stove was for sale, a sheet-metal oil heater of no particular distinction.

"Good morning, miss."

"Fine day, isn't it?"

Charlotte nodded and returned greetings as she met people in different rooms of the house. Everyone regarded her with bald curiosity, but she was getting used to that.

The bowl was on her mind. When Liam entered the parlor, where Charlotte happened to be leafing through a stack of old knitting patterns, she couldn't contain her enthusiasm—dangerous, she knew, when there were potential competing bidders within earshot.

"Liam!" She went straight toward him and put her hand on his elbow. "I've got something to show you."

He followed her into the kitchen.

"Look!" She held up the shallow, earthenware bowl.

He regarded it with mock solemnity. "Okay. I've looked. What is it?"

"It's a terrific bowl!" she whispered.

"I'll take your word for it," he said dryly, a smile hovering on his mouth.

"No, I'm serious. I think this is an antique bowl from the Charlottetown Pottery," she whispered, glancing around to see if anyone overheard. "It's historic. A museum would love this. I'm going to bid on it and I don't want anyone else to know."

"I see." He watched as she put it back on the table.

She felt a little silly that she'd gotten so carried away over her find. "So, uh, where are the dogs?"

"Outside. I told them to stay and I have every

confidence that they will. I'll admit your sister did a good job training Maggie.''

Charlotte gave him an I-told-you-so look. ''Want to come upstairs? I'm going to see if there's anything there.''

Liam followed her up the narrow stairs. When she reached the landing, she almost wished she hadn't asked him to accompany her. The stairs were so narrowly built under the eaves that he had to bend his head on the landing to keep from hitting the low roof. Upstairs were two bedrooms, both very utilitarian. Charlotte went into the one on the left, Liam behind her.

Sun streamed in the bare windows. It was depressing. The curtains had been taken down and were heaped in a corner. The square-patterned linoleum floors were dusty and bare, and the wallpaper showed streaks of damp in the corners. Everything smelled of mouse. The bed, a painted tubular-steel type, very common even in rural Ontario, had only a cheap mattress.

''Isn't it sad?'' she whispered. She had no idea why she was whispering. It was just that the entire house seemed so empty, so neglected. The place was probably a hundred years old. She had the sense that generations of family ghosts observed them forlornly from the corners.

''Sad?''

''You know—'' Charlotte turned to him, then made a gesture toward the bed and the empty room. ''So much history here. All gone. Finished. Just think of the people who lived here, who were born here, died here under this very roof.''

Liam cleared his throat and didn't say anything. Charlotte was instantly, hotly aware of the bed— worn and rickety. *All the babies who were conceived there...*

''Nothing in this room,'' she said firmly. ''Let's try the other one.''

It was a little larger but much the same. This bed-room contained a small closet door built under the eaves and fastened with a hand-carved wooden peg, secured with an iron screw. Charlotte opened the door and peeked in.

''Whew!'' She shut it hurriedly. Spiders, mouse droppings, a couple of mismatched shoes, tufts of stuffing from the mattress, a limp dress on a rusted wire hanger.

''No treasures?'' Liam went to the window that looked out onto the frozen empty pasture.

''This bedstead is worth bidding on,'' Charlotte said, rocking the headboard a little to see how solid it was. ''Painted iron-and-brass, probably dating from the thirties or forties. I don't have any way of getting it home, though, unless I ship it.'' She glanced at his back. ''I can hardly ask you to drag it away in your truck.''

He shrugged and turned. ''No problem to me, if you want it.'' He looked at the bed, which, Charlotte had to admit, wasn't very appealing with the rusted spring frame holding up another cheap mattress. But she could see the bedstead transformed, sitting in some Toronto loft, piled high with polished Egyptian cotton linens and luxurious down pillows, its brass polished, its paint carefully restored.

"And where would I put it, anyway? In Mrs. Jenkins's garage? Forget it." Charlotte abandoned that idea. She was busy enough with the Rathbone estate; there was no way she wanted to spend time hunting for storage space to house the pieces she found and acquired for her own business.

"If you want it, I'll take it for you," Liam repeated.

Charlotte smiled. "I probably won't bid on it. I'm just getting carried away, that's all."

The bidding started at half-past twelve. Fortunately, the household items sold first, and Charlotte missed out on the Delft sugar bowl, which a local woman seemed to want desperately, but she acquired the woodenware, three of the best quilts, some knitting patterns from the fifties, the Aladdin lamp and three of the oil lamps, plus a hooked mat she hadn't seen on her foray through the house. Liam put in a surprise bid on the bedstead, and that made her jump in and eventually get it for a song. She opened the bidding on the slipware bowl at twenty dollars and there were no other bids. Charlotte was quite sure everyone thought she was out of her mind, offering such a price for a lumpy old bowl with a crack in it.

She was so excited, she could barely stand it. If she'd been with Nick Deacon, she would have hugged him. Instead, she hugged Maggie and fussed over her when they went outside. As Liam had predicted, both dogs had patiently awaited their return.

Liam carried her purchases out to the truck and

stowed them at the front of the box, near the cab. She wrapped the oil lamps in newspaper that the auctioneers had supplied and positioned the quilts around them, so nothing would roll around. The bedstead, taken apart, fit along the side.

"I don't know why you bid on that," she said, hands on her hips. She was pleased, of course, that he had. Because now it was hers.

"I thought you wanted it, and I figured you couldn't stand it if you thought I might get it," he said, smiling slightly. "Am I right?"

"Yes. But now I've got to think of something to do with it. Someplace to store it."

"I'll put it in one of the sheds until you decide. You want to stay around and bid for the gardening tools?"

"Oh, no!" Charlotte dusted her hands on her pants. "Let's not bother. Actually—" she smiled wryly and put one hand on her stomach "—I'm starving. I haven't had breakfast and it's nearly two o'clock."

"Well, why didn't you tell me?" Liam loaded the dogs into the back and slammed the tailgate shut. "We could've picked up something on the way." He sounded irritated.

"I guess I just forgot," Charlotte muttered. What could she say? She'd had her mind on the sale.

"I know a place in Souris where we could get some chowder and a plate of mussels," Liam said as he started the truck. "Twenty minutes from here. That suit you?"

"Perfectly." Charlotte ran her fingers through her

hair and tilted her head this way and that, trying to glimpse her reflection in the side mirror as he drove. She wanted to hunt through her handbag for her brush but felt strange about doing it in Liam's truck, with him watching. She was a lot more comfortable with him now than she'd been when they started out, but there was something so...so intimate about brushing your hair in front of a man.

She decided she'd repair whatever damage there was when they got to the restaurant. That bowl! She couldn't believe her luck. She cast a quick sideways glance at Liam's forbidding profile. He'd dragged her off to this sale because she'd expressed an interest, and now he was dragging her off to get something to eat because she'd missed breakfast and lunch.

She was beginning to agree with Ada: her son's bark was quite a lot worse than his bite.

The surprises weren't over for the day. After a large bowl of fish chowder, accompanied by a plate of steamed mussels and several thick-cut slices of homemade sourdough bread, Charlotte felt a lot better. Liam had a clam roll, french fries and a salad, and explained to her about fishing licenses, clam digging, mussel farming and the price of lobster. He introduced her to the waitress—who clearly knew him—as a friend of his mother's, visiting from Toronto, which struck Charlotte as a bit odd, but then, it was true. She felt she *was* a friend of Ada's, even though she'd only met her a week before.

In general, he seemed unusually relaxed, which had a positive effect on her nerves. Maybe she could relax, too. His earlier outright antagonism toward her and Maggie seemed to have disappeared. Maybe once she'd given up on Laurel's plan to breed Maggie to one of his Labs, he'd backed off. He struck her as very private, very territorial. Looking after his mother like that, making sure she—Charlotte—had something to eat, protecting his dogs from being "contaminated" by the likes of Maggie, teaching Jamie to carve decoys...

Of course, she hadn't *really* given up on Laurel's plan. Maybe by the time Maggie came into heat—if she did—he'd have relaxed about that, as well.

She could hope.

Her impressions today added up to a different man than the one she'd met on the beach a week ago. Only a week! She could hardly believe it.

During the course of their lunch, Charlotte couldn't help contrasting the plain, tasty fare with the sophisticated meal she'd had the evening before with Nick in Charlottetown. Which reminded her of last night's decision. She casually mentioned that she was going to be leaving Clara Jenkins's place, after all, even if she had to stay in Charlottetown and drive out everyday.

"By the way," she added, deciding she might as well be hung for a sheep as a lamb, "why didn't you call about the auction? It was kind of a surprise this morning."

"It was?" He frowned. "I talked to Clara last night. Just before ten."

"I was out."

"So she said. With Nick Deacon." His eyes

searched hers briefly. "I thought she'd pass on my message, but maybe you came in too late."

Charlotte studiously avoided his eyes, trying to hide her smile. So...Mr. Connery could fish a little himself. No way was she telling him what time she'd come in from her dinner with Nick Deacon!

Liam was quiet on the drive back to Petty Cove. Charlotte didn't mind. She turned on the radio for company, feeling full of good food, a little sleepy and definitely somewhat weary after the excitement of the auction sale. Plus, she had her new acquisitions to think about, especially the red earthenware bowl.

When they reached Clara Jenkins's house, Liam stopped the truck, flicked off the radio and turned to face her. His expression was serious.

"I have something I'd like to say to you."

"Yes?" He sounded so formal!

"My mother is a lonely woman, as you may have guessed. She's taken quite a liking to you." His expression implied that the feeling was all on his mother's side. *Here we go...back to square one.*

"I like her very much, too," Charlotte said carefully.

"She wants you to come and live in the house while you're working here. With her. That is, if you're going to leave Clara's, anyway."

"With *her*?" And where would *he* be?

"With us, I guess." He looked very uncomfortable. "I'm asking as a special favor to my mother, you understand. If you agree—" he had his door open already "—I'll move your stuff over tomorrow afternoon. If not, just say so." He got out and so did she.

"Monday would be better," she blurted out, following him to the back of the truck, where he had his hand on the tailgate.

His eyes met hers. "Does that mean you will?"

Charlotte felt hot and out of breath, felt like fanning herself with her scarf. "I guess it does. This is all very sudden, but I— I don't know…it *does* seem like a good idea, doesn't it?"

He shrugged and unfastened the tailgate.

"It's convenient. Maggie's there. I wouldn't be any trouble, I'd do all my own laundry, cooking, whatever."

"That's between you and Ma. She's been after me to ask you. The Rathbone place is ten minutes through the woods."

Charlotte could tell he hadn't been keen on the idea himself. But what did that matter? "And I could take Maggie to work with me."

"That's right."

Charlotte suddenly felt very light. She saw the curtains at Clara Jenkins's lounge window move and knew that either the despicable Freddie Burns or the landlady herself was watching them. She could imagine the gossip that would be flying down at Bonnie Bristol's store tomorrow morning. She didn't care. The prospect of leaving the Jenkins household was exhilarating. "Then, there's no need, I guess, to take my things out of your truck."

He slammed the tailgate shut.

"Monday?"

"No." His eyes were hard, unrevealing. As though he'd withdrawn a million miles. As though today hadn't happened. As though he hadn't just asked her to stay at his mother's house. "Monday I have other plans."

"Okay," she said, feeling the sudden chill in the air. "Tomorrow afternoon it is—and Liam?"

"Yes?" He frowned, his hand on the door frame, one foot already back inside the truck. He couldn't wait to leave.

"Thanks for taking me to Three Corners. I had a lovely day." She smiled sweetly, as much to annoy him as anything, she realized. He didn't like *pleases* and *thank-yous*. He didn't subscribe to the normal polite back-and-forth exchanges between two human beings—conversation, civility, chitchat. He just... *did* things.

He growled something she couldn't make out in the rising wind and nodded. Then he slammed the door and drove off.

Charlotte threw her gloves into the air, caught them in one hand, and then glanced toward the curtain, which snapped shut. She laughed out loud.

CHAPTER TEN

THE DIRECTOR of the St. Agnes Nursing Home watched the man with the forbidding expression come through the front door and start down the long polished hallway. She'd watched him arrive a hundred—two hundred—times before, every Monday, at exactly that hour, the minute the doors opened at half-past eight.

"How is she?" he asked as he passed the front desk. Always the same question, always the same tortured look in those dark eyes.

"Same as usual, Liam," she answered. "Resting peacefully." No matter how many pretty nurses were on duty, Liam Connery never spared them a glance. Marjorie had often noticed that. Liam Connery was a handsome man. Although many of the staff had tried to flirt with him over the years, he never responded. He never smiled.

He'd disappear into the room at the end of the corridor, and when she'd come in half an hour later, the scene that would greet her was always the same. Liam Connery in the chair pulled up to the bedside, holding Dorrie Connery's hand. Her left hand would be in his right hand, his left hand covering hers.

He'd be staring straight ahead, seeing nothing.

He'd stay there until noon, three-and-a-half hours, and then he'd leave. She didn't know where he went afterward, but she'd realized once when Ada had phoned asking for him that he didn't go home. Next Monday would be exactly the same.

Marjorie Williams didn't know all the details. She hadn't been on staff when Dorrie was admitted six years ago, after spending four months in Charlottetown Memorial Hospital, much of it in intensive care. They could do nothing more for her there; there was nothing that could be done for her here. It was a question of waiting. A question of time.

Until she died.

Marjorie didn't like to think about that. She cared for all her patients, those as grievously injured as Dorrie Connery and those with more ordinary frailties. But it hurt the woman in her to see a man like Liam with his life on hold, his marriage frozen, forever reduced to these weekly visits.

And yet she'd never heard a word to fault him. He didn't see any other women, as far as she knew, although he must—a healthy, virile man in his prime. If so, he was discreet. He lived a hermit's life with his blind mother out there on the eastern shore, doing this and that to keep body and soul together. She'd never asked him directly; he was a man with too much pride.

This time, when she walked into the room to adjust the curtains and see if she could do anything, she was surprised to see that he wasn't staring straight ahead, as usual. He was twisting and turning the wedding band on his wife's bony finger.

"It's so loose, Marjorie," he said in a low voice. He sounded hurt, astonished. *Afraid.*

"I've been thinking that, Liam," she began lightly. "You know, she really doesn't need to wear the ring—"

"I don't want it to come off," he interrupted hoarsely. "Not until—not *ever!*"

"But one of these days it'll just fall off and get lost. Maybe a jeweler could resize it for you. Or perhaps we could put it in her night table. It'd be safe there," she encouraged him.

"It's not coming off, Marjorie." He looked directly at her then, and she nearly gasped at the pain she saw. Something had happened. Something was different. The pain she'd glimpsed before had been dull, resigned. This pain was raw and fierce. The fresh pain of a man overcome, yet again, by a grief too hard to bear. And something else—an anger she'd never seen.

"Can I get you anything, Liam? Coffee? Tea?" She knew he'd refuse. He always refused.

He shook his head. He slipped the ring off and looked at it lying in his work-hardened palm—thin, golden, perfectly round. Then he put it back and bent Dorrie's fingers around it, encasing her small limp fist in his large hand.

Marjorie blinked back tears as she left.

Was there no tomorrow for this man? Three months ago, the doctors had convinced him that they should remove the breathing apparatus. Dorrie Connery had been in a complete vegetative state since her terrible accident. She'd had surgery to repair limbs and ribs and spine, but nothing had ever brought her back to life. Not real life. She'd had help breathing for all those years, and the doctors had gently put it to Liam that perhaps it would be best if she was allowed to slip away. Nothing more could be done for her. Perhaps if they removed the breathing device, nature would take its course.

But that hadn't happened. Dorrie Connery had surprised them all. She'd continued breathing on her own, in and out, night and day.

Now she was alive but she was no longer being kept alive, in the view of the medical experts. She could live for years, possibly. But how long could a man be held hostage to a marriage that was no marriage? To a wife who was no wife? To a woman who would never, ever wake up from this terrible sleep? As long as she lived, he was her husband. Her life was over; did that mean his life was over, too?

Liam Connery wouldn't abandon her, although there wasn't a person alive who would blame him if he did. Just as he hadn't deserted his mother when she'd gone blind, he hadn't deserted the woman he'd married when she'd left the world in every way but the beat of her heart and the breath of her body.

Just before noon, Marjorie returned to the room at the end of the hall. She was surprised to see that Liam had taken off the wedding ring again and pushed it onto his own little finger, halfway. As she watched, he sighed deeply, slipped it back on his wife's slack third finger, placed her hand gently at her side, and then stood,

"I'll be going now. Let me know if there's any change. For the worse or for the better."

"I will, Liam. Say hello to your mother for me." Marjorie Williams had never noticed until now how the words he spoke each week were the reversal of the marriage vows "for better or for worse."

"I will." He bent to kiss his wife's bone-white cheek, then left the room without looking back. He always walked faster when he left than when he arrived.

...and that's how I ended up at Liam and Ada's!

Charlotte chewed the end of her pen, glancing out the second-floor bedroom window as she did. Gusts of wind blew the leaves across the bare yard. She'd felt a little under the weather this afternoon, so she'd come back to Petty Cove early.

She resumed her letter to Lydia.

Ada loves to cook, but now that she's blind, it takes her all afternoon to prepare a meal. I have to be careful to put everything back exactly the way it was in the kitchen, or she gets confused. I cook, too—already made my famous couscous and lamb stew, which everyone seemed to like, or at least they ate it. Liam does breakfasts sometimes.

Liam had made breakfast twice since Charlotte had moved in just over a week ago. Pancakes once,

and sausages and scrambled eggs the other time. Ada
was not an early riser, so it'd been an awkward meal,
just the two of them at the kitchen table. Charlotte
had suspected he was only cooking breakfast because she was a guest, and after the second strained
meal, she'd suggested they skip breakfast or each
make their own. Liam had readily agreed.

Seriously, I've hardly seen Liam. He disappears
on Mondays, I've discovered, who-knows
where. It's all very hush-hush and mysterious.
(Maybe he's got a secret lover.) Our bedrooms
are both upstairs, but I haven't even seen him
passing in the hall.

Nick's still here. He decided to stay a bit
longer, and he's hired Liam and that rather useless watchman, Cyril Rush, to do some work on
the grounds. I've been busy. Talk about a mish-
mash of good things and junk! Stanley Busby
is making noises about holding the sale in the
spring, when the bulbs are up. And Nick says
they'll probably sell the house then, too. New
puppies coming soon—one of Liam's ''cham-
pions'' is going to have a litter. I'm looking
forward to that.

Charlotte didn't know how much she should go
on about the trivia of life at the Petty Cove Bed-and-
Breakfast. Trouble was, not much happened in rural
P.E.I. and you tended to obsess about the minor
things, like a dog having pups, or what the weather
was like from day to day. She didn't know when

she'd commented more on the weather, or heard more comments about it from other people.

Time to finish up and maybe take Maggie for a walk. Clear her head. She was being careful to keep Maggie and Scout separated, since they'd had a little scrap yesterday. Nothing serious, but when Scout had done his usual sniffing around, Maggie for once wasn't having any of it and had sent him packing. Jamie had laughed, but Charlotte was worried. She didn't want either dog getting hurt. Nor did she want Liam to have an excuse to send her away with Maggie.

That Zoey! I'm delighted to hear she's finalized her plans to go west. I'll call her one of these evenings, before she leaves. Isn't British Columbia where her so-called first love is from? Somebody better warn that cowboy that Zoey Phillips is on her way! I can hardly wait until we get together again to share all our amazing adventures. Yours, too. I'll bet you're up to all kinds of things back there at home.

Me? No more "first love" foolishness for me. Liam didn't know I was alive back then and to tell you the truth, I don't think he knows I'm alive now.

Write to me here, and call sometime—you have my cell number. I'll see you soon!

Love,
Charlotte

Charlotte sealed the letter and pasted a stamp on it. She felt a little guilty. She hadn't been completely honest with Lydia, who was, after all, one of her two best friends in the whole world. It was true that Liam didn't seem to know she was alive, but it wasn't true that she didn't care. Since she'd moved into the former bed-and-breakfast, she'd become even more excruciatingly aware of him than she'd been before. In ways that were difficult to understand.

Physically, for instance. She was *horribly* aware of him physically. No matter where he was in the room, even if she had her back to him, she seemed to know every move he made. Once Ada and Liam had played braille dominoes after supper, and Charlotte had had to make an excuse and go upstairs— because her nerves were so on edge, just watching them.

It made no sense. It was as though she were ten or eleven again, an innocent, insecure girl, going through the throes of her first crush.

Sometimes, when she used the shower in the upstairs bathroom—she had only a tub in her own bathroom—she'd think about the fact that he'd just taken a shower, maybe an hour before. Or she'd find herself opening the cabinet and looking at his things, like some kind of peeper. The sandalwood shaving soap, the worn Canadian Forces Base, Greendale, N.S. hairbrush, even the house-brand dental floss.

Then she'd shut the door, despising herself. All those old pre-teen feelings were back—the despair of being in love with someone who didn't know you existed. Girl stuff. And it was so silly—*of course* she wasn't in love with Liam Connery. Far from it.

She was long past such foolish thoughts. Maybe moving here had been a mistake, even though she loved talking with Ada and having Maggie around. But day-to-day living had become very difficult. Somehow it would've been easier if Liam was a flirt, like Nick. Or a joker, like Lydia's older brother, Steve. This way, with him ignoring her, it was too much like before. It brought back all the old hurts and rejections—and all her adolescent reactions. Being tearful, being hopelessly romantic over just about everything...

She reminded herself that she had only two more weeks to go until she was finished with the estate. Surely she could curb her girlish yearnings until then. What she really needed was a good dose of big-city living again. Fun, excitement, activity. There wasn't enough to do here; it was too easy to get bound up in your own thoughts and feelings. She was too isolated from other people, so it was natural that she'd focus too much on the people who were in her immediate sphere.

His indifference hurt, more than she would ever have guessed. Maybe she'd look up an old boyfriend when she got back to Toronto, remind herself that she *was* desirable. That she was someone who deserved and commanded respect and attention—from some men.

And then she'd think, *Don't be stupid, Charlotte. There are good reasons you're no longer seeing Edward Sly or Peter Robichaud or Luke Proudfoot. Very, very good reasons.*

Nice men, all of them. But not for you.

Charlotte glanced outside again. She saw Jamie walk from the house to one of the sheds. That meant it was after four o'clock. No Liam, of course. It was Monday, and Liam always disappeared on Mondays, or so she'd gathered from Ada, who'd mumbled and muttered and hadn't answered any of Charlotte's questions directly.

Men. Sometimes she wondered if she'd ever meet a man who would love her the way she'd always dreamed of being loved. The way Mr. Rochester had loved Jane Eyre. The way Rhett had loved Scarlett in *Gone With the Wind*. Only, Charlotte would love him back, as the selfish Scarlett never had.

Or maybe it wouldn't happen and she'd spend her days stalking bits and pieces of other people's personal history in garage sales: this ivory dresser set, inscribed from a lover; that handknit sweater, created for just one darling child. Imagining this, imagining that—dreaming of strangers' lives. Never really having a life of her own, at least not the kind of life she longed for. She'd end up loving Laurel's children, being the kind, generous "auntie" to Zoey and Lydia's children one day. She'd be someone who came to visit, who never stayed. Who had dozens of men friends, but no beloved.

How depressing.

Charlotte sighed and stood up. This wasn't like her at all, these morbid thoughts. Time for a change. She'd go down to the shore with Maggie. Anything to clear her head. Anything to drive Liam Connery from her mind.

WHEN SHE RETURNED an hour later with Maggie on her leash, Charlotte was surprised to see Liam's pickup parked by the kennels and lights in a long, low building she hadn't really noticed before, to the east and behind the kennels in a copse of poplars.

She recalled that he'd offered to let Jamie use his workshop and wondered if this was the workshop. Surely, if Jamie was in there and using power tools, Liam would be with him. She thought of going in, then changed her mind. It was none of her business.

At just five-thirty, it was quite dark already. Ada would be preparing the evening meal, and Charlotte intended to go in and help.

She glanced at the lighted windows of the low building again. None of her business or not, she'd just peer in and see if Jamie was there alone, or if he was being supervised by an adult.

She stepped up to a window on the tree side of the shed. The long grass bent under her boots and she stumbled a little when her foot inadvertently came down on a depression in the ground. Maggie watched her, ears cocked, clearly wondering what she could possibly be doing.

Charlotte wondered herself. She stepped close to the window and cautiously peeked in. She couldn't see Jamie but she saw Liam behind a wooden work-table, doing something with a hand plane, one of those old-fashioned wood-smoothing tools. Charlotte recognized it because she'd bought and sold plenty of them over the past few years.

He was totally absorbed in his task, all his atten-tion on the plank of wood before him. Hanging up in the rafters she could see bits and pieces of wooden ribbing, skeletons that looked like they might become boats one day. Small boats, like yacht tenders or peapods, a slim, deft boat that was favored by many rowing enthusiasts. Lined up on a shelf were duck and goose decoys, in various stages of completion.

Her heart froze in her throat. She was glad she hadn't rapped on the door and gone in. Liam was in another world. A solitary world of his own creation. A world that excluded everything but what he was doing at that precise moment: smoothing a plank to be used, presumably, in his boat-building. Bear, his loyal Chesapeake Bay retriever, was slumped on the floor beside him, snoozing, although the Chessie's ears had started twitching, which told her the dog could sense her and Maggie. The last thing she wanted was to be discovered in this unquestionably compromising position.

She slipped away into the gloom. She'd never seen anything so intense, so beautiful.

Or so desperately lonely.

CHAPTER ELEVEN

CHARLOTTE SPENT THE MORNING sorting through the Rathbone parlor. She'd started it two days earlier and expected to finish up before lunch. Nick was in the house somewhere, most likely in the library with the expert from Halifax, who'd come out to give him a bid. The dealer, a specialist in rare books, reported that the library contained a large number of turn-of-the-century mariners' journals and first editions from the 1800s, which were of definite interest. If Nick sold him the contents, he'd be removing everything and transporting it to his Halifax shop, except for the used paperbacks and other volumes of little value, which he'd send to a Charlottetown secondhand bookstore.

In the parlor, where she was working, she'd already found two Louis XV armchairs in excellent condition and a stunningly beautiful French side table, marble-topped, gilded and dating from the early eighteenth century. There was a gilt mirror, probably American, from about a hundred years ago, and two early twentieth-century paintings by the Nova Scotia seascape painter, Jeremiah Alsop, that would bring top dollar at the right sale of Canadiana.

The bric-a-brac alone was astonishing, and she

just kept hauling it out of cupboards and drawers and more cupboards. She doubted that Gerard Rathbone had been a collector. But someone—perhaps a woman, she liked to think, maybe the same one who'd laid out the gardens—had spent much time and money assembling rare porcelain and other knickknacks, from both east and west. There wasn't much rhyme or reason to the collection; however, everything that had been acquired, from Wedgwood and Minton china figures to oddities like the intricately carved box made from rhinoceros horn, was of exceptional quality.

Funny, Charlotte mused, gently removing yet another dust-caked Wedgwood shepherdess from a dark corner, how the male history was always well-known in a house like this—the shipping, the mercantile interests, prominent member of this or that club. But the women's roles, beyond that of childbearing, were rarely known. Maybe Nick's mother, Gerard's niece, knew more of the family history. Maybe not.

At any rate, everything was to be sold. All of it, including the house and grounds. The end of an era.

Oh, my aching body, she thought, standing and pushing her fists into the small of her back. She'd been on her knees all morning. She stepped to the big windows overlooking the gardens. Liam and Cyril had already worked wonders, clearing away debris and digging up flower beds. A heap of something that looked suspiciously like seaweed, eelgrass, had been dumped in a pile by the rose garden. As she watched, Liam walked across the line of lilacs by the stone fence, a dog by his side. Bear, of course.

He hadn't shown up for dinner the evening before, although Jamie had appeared from somewhere and worked his way steadily through a large plate of roast chicken, mashed potatoes, gravy and peas, followed by the blueberry cobbler Charlotte had baked when she'd come in to give Ada a hand. Charlotte had mentioned that she'd noticed Liam's truck in the yard, and Ada had seemed surprised, then mumbled something about him going his own way. Being stubborn, contrary, independent-minded—or words to that effect. And that if he wanted his dinner, he'd have to warm it up himself.

Jamie's father, Davy Macdonald, a rugged handsome man of medium build and bright eyes, had come for the boy about eight o'clock. As he stood waiting for Jamie to get his books and coat, he'd inspected her carefully while pretending to glance around the room. Charlotte knew her presence in the house was unusual. She didn't mind the inspection. Besides, she'd realized that all Islanders—from the folks she'd met in the diner her first day to Liam's cousin tonight—were curious about everyone From Away, especially someone showing up in the off-season, as she had done. Now that she'd been on the island for a couple of weeks, she found herself wondering about anyone who drove by, too!

Wherever Liam had been last night, he was on the job today, helping Cyril get the grounds ready for the sale, which was planned for spring.

Charlotte walked to the kitchen and checked the

contents of the refrigerator. Since Nick's arrival, it had been full of treats, although it was a little bare today. Once he'd brought fresh oysters and they'd had a happy feast on the south patio, wearing fleece jackets and shucking oysters over a newspaper. Plus, there was usually a bottle of wine or two, which Charlotte wouldn't have stocked.

Nick was used to the so-called good life. That was partly why he had no interest in keeping the Rathbone estate. The family was small—Nick had a sister, a brother and two cousins, all Americans—and no one wanted to be bothered with the ancestral home way off in Prince Edward Island. In a way, Charlotte was glad. The house and grounds had been terribly neglected. At least a new owner would bring fresh enthusiasm and plans.

Charlotte fixed a platter of tuna sandwiches and heated up two tins of tomato soup. She carried the food out to the derelict cast-iron table on the sunny veranda. It was cool, but she usually tried to have her lunch outside, weather permitting, to take in a few lungfuls of fresh air in the middle of her day. She was looking forward to starting the second floor this afternoon. Maybe it wasn't quite as musty as the main floor, where Gerard Rathbone and his dogs had spent most of their time.

She waved toward Liam and Cecil in the garden. "Lunch?" There was plenty for everyone, and she could get more mugs of soup from the kitchen. Liam shook his head.

"The wife packed my lunch bucket today!" Cyril yelled.

"Okay!" she called back, and set the tray down on the rickety table before going into the house to find Nick and the book expert.

It was hard not to think that Liam was avoiding her. He hadn't had dinner with them the night before, nor was he around for breakfast this morning. As far as she knew, he hadn't even slept in the house. But why? Where did he go? More and more she was coming to the conclusion that he had some secret life he kept from his mother. A girlfriend? But why wouldn't he be straightforward about that? Who would care?

Forget Liam Connery, Charlotte thought irritably. She hadn't expected him—or Cyril—to join her. Nearly everyday, Liam went back through the woods to his own place for lunch. And Cyril—well, you never knew what Cyril was going to do.

Nick and Dallas Longhurst joined her on the veranda. They were entertaining company. The book dealer was excited about his discoveries in the Rathbone library and Nick seemed pleased with the bid he'd submitted.

"Are you all finished, then?" Charlotte asked, offering the men a cookie from the plate she'd fetched from the kitchen. Store cookies, lemon creams, but pretty good. The sandwiches and soup had disappeared rapidly.

"All done. Nick's taking me back this afternoon," the dealer said, glancing at his host and then at his watch.

"Actually, I forgot to mention—I'm going to Halifax with Dallas, Charlotte," Nick said. "I have some business I need to do and then I'll head up to Rustico for the weekend, go sailing with a friend. You'll manage without me?''

"Oh, I suppose I will," Charlotte playfully shot back. "I've got Cyril taking good care of me here."

"And Liam."

Charlotte pondered that comment for a few seconds.

"The grounds are coming along, aren't they," Nick continued.

They all looked out onto the garden. Liam was digging up one of the flower beds near the rose garden.

"I think they're putting in tons of daffodils and tulips. Isn't that the idea, Nick?" As she watched, Liam stuck his spade into the ground and walked over to where Cyril Rush was spreading seaweed. Charlotte felt like Lady Chatterley, secretly admiring the gardener while he worked.

"Just like a coat of cheap paint on a duplex!" Nick laughed. "Spruce up the old place for a buyer, eh, Dallas?"

"You'll get a buyer, no question," the book dealer said, gazing around with a speculative eye. "Tulips or no tulips. This is an impressive place, Nick. I'd be interested myself if it wasn't so darn far from anywhere."

"Petty Cove—" Charlotte leaned forward and tapped him on the knee "—is *somewhere,* Mr. Longhurst."

"Oh, yes," he said. "I forgot." He giggled unexpectedly. "Maybe it is, if you're trying to disappear off the face of the earth.'' He pushed back his chair and stood, smiling. ''Well, thank you for the lunch, my dear.'' He leaned forward to kiss the air by her cheek. ''And congratulations on all your work here. I know Nick and his family are going to be pleased with the proceeds, whatever Busby decides.''

Stanley Busby, Charlotte had found out from Nick, was now thinking that the sale of the house's contents might be better conducted from Halifax, where they could be assured of attracting the right buyers. Charlotte had agreed it made more sense to transport the valuable inventory to Halifax, rather than trying to bring serious buyers to Cardigan River.

''Goodbye, Mr. Longhurst.'' Charlotte picked up the platter of empty mugs and sandwich crumbs. ''Goodbye, Nick.''

To her surprise, Nick kissed her cheek, as well, with a wink that told her it was a comment on Dallas Longhurst's gallant style. ''Bye, Charlotte. Hold down the fort, will you?''

''I'll do my best.'' Just as she'd been doing before he arrived. She wished she had Maggie, though. After Maggie's scrap with Scout, someone—Liam or Jamie—had moved her out of the house. This morning, when Charlotte went to the kitchen to get the dog, she wasn't there. Charlotte meant to ask Liam what had happened, but he was so unapproachable, she wondered when she'd ever get the chance.

She was looking forward to this afternoon. Beyond a quick preliminary survey, she hadn't tackled anything yet in the six large bedrooms upstairs.

LIAM WALKED through the woods, swinging the secateurs he'd brought from home. The Rathbone place had all the tools anyone would need, but many were rusted and dull. Bringing them from Petty Cove saved time.

He came out of the trees at the end of the garden and stopped, narrowing his eyes in the bright afternoon sun. It had been cloudy that morning, but the clouds had cleared away by noon. He glanced over at the pile of seaweed Cyril Rush had been spreading earlier. It had dwindled considerably.

He strode toward the house. A quick look showed that they'd left the veranda—Charlotte, Nick and the visitor.

He picked up his spade from where he'd left it stuck in the earth and began loosening the hard-packed soil. These were beds his father had groomed and maintained for years, off and on. Any bulbs they'd once held had long been eaten by rodents or killed by frost.

He stood and stared up at the sky. Bear's amber eyes glowed as the dog caught sight of the long, strung out *V* of a flock of Canada geese heading south. It was that time of year—soon the snow would be coming, heralding another long winter with nothing to do but play cards and look after the dogs.

Liam set his spade firmly in the earth and began walking again. He paused by the scant pile of eelgrass, then went around to the driveway at the front of the house.

He stopped short. The pickup was gone. And so was the car Nick Deacon drove, the rental Blazer. A kingbird called from a nearby tree, a white pine that had once been struck by lightning and was shattered and mangled and mostly dead, ready to be taken down.

Liam started up the front steps and walked around to the veranda. A few cookie crumbs on the painted cast-iron table were all that remained of the earlier meal. He tried the door that led to the parlor; it opened easily, with a squeal of rusty hinges.

The room was empty. An open book on the mantel held neat columns of handwriting, with items and prices noted in appropriate columns. A sharpened pencil lay beside the book.

''Charlotte?''

No answer. Liam went into the kitchen, a depressing place with worn floors, scarred countertops and poor-quality replacement cabinets. Recently washed dishes had been piled on the drainboard. Liam ran a finger over a platter. Still damp.

''Charlotte?'' He stood at the foot of the winding stairs that led to the second story. And beyond, to the third floor.

The house was deeply silent. The wind gusted and rattled loose shingles on the roof. Through the hall window, treetops bent and straightened, sending a flurry of leaves scuttling to the ground. Somewhere on the main floor, a broken shutter rapped madly against a window.

Liam began to climb the stairs, first one slow step, then another. When he reached the landing, he suddenly moved faster, taking the last flight of stairs two at a time.

The sun shone through the stained-glass window at the end of the second-floor hall, like a benediction. Seven doors lined the hallway, all of them shut.

"Charlotte!" His voice echoed down the long hall. Someone called from a room at the far end, the voice muffled, distant.

"In here!"

He twisted the brass knob of the last door, opened it abruptly and stepped inside. The dull crystal teardrops in the chandelier overhead, half the lightbulbs burned out, jangled slightly, a thin, cheap sound.

"Oh!" Charlotte was half hidden behind a vast mahogany wardrobe. The doors were ajar, revealing old clothes inside. Her hair was pulled back in a loose ponytail and there was a smudge of dirt or dust on one cheek.

"I'm here." Her eyes were very wide. "D-did you want me?"

HE SLAMMED THE DOOR behind him and looked at her as though he'd never seen her before. His eyes were all over her.

"Are you all right?"

Charlotte managed a weak laugh. He sounded so—so *serious.* "Of course, I'm all right. What did you *think* had happened?"

"I couldn't find you downstairs. No one seems to be around."

"Nick's gone. He drove the book guy back to Halifax." Charlotte took a step forward and looked up at the wardrobe. "I'm glad you're here. You can help me move this. I was just thinking I'd go find you or Cyril." She looked up at him again. "What did you want me for?" she repeated.

He stepped forward. "I had to put Maggie in a kennel last night. I wanted to tell you that."

"Why?"

"Jamie told me she and Scout got into a scrap. It's for her own good. I think she's going into heat—"

"That's how she shows it?" Charlotte said. "By getting into a fight with him?"

"It's early still. She won't be interested for another few days, maybe a week. She'll make him keep his distance until then."

"Of course, nothing's going to happen, right?" Charlotte closed the wardrobe doors securely and put her shoulder tentatively to the corner. "You're not going to allow it."

"Right." He came all the way across the room and stood beside her. "Where do you want this?"

"I noticed it was covering a little door here and I wanted to move it so I could get in behind. See what treasures are hidden away."

Liam put his arms around the wardrobe, at chest height, and began to inch it across the floor, using his thigh and knee as a lever to help maneuver the unwieldy piece of furniture. Charlotte had been delighted to discover a whole rack of dresses from the thirties and forties inside, looking as though they hadn't been touched in over half a century. What didn't go to the dump could be sent to a drama society or a theater troupe somewhere, locally or elsewhere. Or perhaps a vintage clothing store would be interested.

"Okay?" Liam's voice was strained with exertion. He was a strong man to have moved that huge wardrobe basically on his own, with only her pathetic help.

"Fine." Charlotte let go of the corner she'd been pushing. She straightened and dusted off her hands. "What a job!" She felt strange. Hot. Anxious. She was trapped, more or less, in a small area between the wall and the wardrobe...and Liam.

He was close. *Too close.*

She tried to avoid his eyes but the instant she glanced up, she was sunk. Her gaze fastened on his; she couldn't look away. His eyes shifted to her cheek, and he reached out one hand but didn't touch her.

"Your face."

"Dirt?" She laughed self-consciously and bent to scrub her cheek with the hem of her shirt.

"Other side." His voice was hoarse, and this time he didn't look away, either. He touched her cheek with the side of his thumb, traced what must be the smudge. Her skin burned. Her eyes watered.

"Charlotte." His voice was raw. Cracked.

Her knees practically buckled. She'd never heard her name spoken just that way.

His eyes dropped to her cheek again, and she felt his thumb move lightly against her skin, trace the streak of dirt and then stop. She felt him open his hand, cup her cheek, move his hand against her jaw. She shut her eyes.

''Charlotte!'' He slid his hand behind her neck, under her hair, and pulled her against him. Startled, she opened her eyes and raised her hands, placing them on his chest.

She couldn't think. She could only *feel* the strain in his muscles, the trembling, the tension in his body. As he folded her into his arms. As he held her tight and buried his face against her throat, her collar. She heard him mutter something, something feverish. Unintelligible.

Then his mouth was on hers. Hot, demanding...

CHAPTER TWELVE

CHARLOTTE WAS THRILLED to her soul. No man had ever kissed her like this…*ever.* So passionately.

As though he were starving and had been offered food. Dying of thirst and had found water…

His mouth possessed hers. She gave herself up totally to the sudden, searing, exotic pleasure.

Liam pressed her against the wall, and she felt panic for a split second. This man was strong, powerful. He wanted her. Then she melted in his arms again—he'd never hurt her. She *knew* that. She'd swear any oath that could be imagined: Liam Connery would never, ever hurt her.

He wrenched his mouth away and suddenly pulled back. His breathing matched hers—ragged, harsh. Her heart wanted to burst from the cage of her ribs, take flight. Her cheeks felt hot. Her whole body was incredibly hot.

His eyes were tortured. "God, I—I'm sorry, Charlotte. I—I don't know what came over me." He shook his head, like a man clearing his ears, his brain. Like a boxer reeling, stunned from an unexpected blow.

"Don't! Don't say you're sorry."

"It's not right, Charlotte. I shouldn't have touched you." She closed her eyes for a few seconds, trying to control the emotion that was skittering away from her, to shut out the image of his face.

"Why not?" She stared at him. "Why is it—this wrong? It's *not* wrong."

"It's wrong. You're a guest in my house. A guest in my mother's house." His hand brushed the hair from her temple tenderly. She closed her eyes again, wanting to capture the feel of him forever. "I've wanted to do this—touch you like this—ever since the first moment I met you...."

"No!" Her eyes flew open again. "That's not true. You didn't even like me."

"I lusted for you, Charlotte." She flinched at the word he'd chosen. "That's putting it crudely, but it's the honest-to-God truth. I've never wanted any woman the way I have you these past weeks. It's taken every ounce of strength I've had to resist. Do you understand?"

He adjusted his stance. "It's been torture to be in the same house," he whispered into her ear, "eating at the same table, knowing you were sleeping under my roof just down the hall. I spent last night on my boat. Sleep?" He shook his head. "All I did was think of you. It's been killing me. Over and over— what was I going to do about *you?*"

His voice was hoarse, unsteady, and Charlotte was shivering, melting all over again.

"How many times I've wanted to come into your room..." He buried his face against her throat and began kissing the soft skin, sending shivers and shards of feeling right into her bones. "To do *this*..."

Omigod. Liam. Omigod...touch me. Keep touching me.

He covered her mouth with his again, this time clamping her chin in his right hand, adjusting the angle of their contact so that it was perfect, so perfect....

Charlotte never wanted his kiss to end. She didn't care what happened. She didn't care who came back to the house and found them there, in bed or on the floor, clothed or naked. She only wanted to be with Liam. To fit her body against his. To touch him all over, everywhere. To have him touch her. *To see that terrible look leave his eyes...*

"Believe me—" He shook his head, a gesture of bewilderment. "I never meant for this to happen. When I couldn't find you downstairs, I—" He paused, then finished, whispering against her cheek. "I panicked. I thought something had happened to you. I nearly went mad."

He released her so abruptly she almost fell. Her body felt hot and cold at the same time. Her face was damp with his kisses, and the skin of her throat was aching, on fire.

"Liam!"

His back was to her. He was already at the door, one hand on the doorknob. He half turned at her cry.

"Forgive me," he murmured.

Then he was gone.

Charlotte sagged down onto the bed. Her ears rang. She felt a funny little flutter in her stomach and her legs were weak.

Her hair... Charlotte raised zombie-like hands to

her head. The ponytail had come undone. The ribbon
had disappeared. Her hair was loose, uncombed, all
over the place. She stood and went to the old-
fashioned Austrian pier glass on the wall and studied
herself. Her face was red, her lips looked swollen,
her eyes were huge, brilliant, teary. *Alive.*

Liam had said he was sorry; he'd said it wasn't
right. But it *was* right. It was the rightest thing that
had ever happened to her.

And Charlotte wanted more.

CHARLOTTE WORKED—or tried to work—for the rest
of the afternoon, as usual. She didn't see Liam again,
but when she left the house at half-past four, she
noticed that the eelgrass had been spread over many
of the beds and a fresh pile was heaped near the rose
garden. Liam and Cyril had been busy.

She went straight to the kennel where Maggie was
being kept. The dog whined and pawed at the chain-
link fence that contained her. Several other dogs
barked.

''Shh!'' Charlotte grabbed a lead that was hanging
on a hook inside the door of the kennel building—
this was the Maternity Ward, according to Jamie—
and snapped it onto Maggie's collar.

If Liam was right and Maggie was going into heat,
Charlotte wanted to make sure the dog stayed under
control. Much as Charlotte wished Liam would
change his mind, she wasn't about to do anything to
jeopardize the situation by, for instance, letting Maggie run free when there were so many other dogs
around. On the other hand, after the tumultuous

events of the day, all Charlotte wanted was to spend some time with the happy-go-lucky Labrador. She'd missed Maggie's presence in the Rathbone place today, usually underfoot but always friendly and accepting.

She took the lane that led to Ridge Road. Many of the leaves on the hardwoods had fallen, which gave the forest a tattered, worn appearance. The leaves were leathery underfoot, still red and orange and golden, not yet air-dried to a crisp brown and on their way to eventual dust. Maggie trotted happily at her side, heeling beautifully, as though they were on a crowded city sidewalk instead of what must be a dog's paradise of smells and sounds.

Charlotte thought suddenly of Springer, the beagle she and Laurel had had as children. Cute as a bug's ear, her mother had always said, but not meant for a family dog. She was a single-minded tracker. Gone like a shot following her nose the minute she was off the leash, after squirrels, cats, rabbits—whatever struck her as worth chasing, which had been just about anything. Maggie was a much easier dog. Like most retrievers, she focused on her people, not her nose.

But Charlotte couldn't keep her mind on Maggie or her memories of Springer. She kept thinking about Liam. About what had happened that afternoon.

Her first reaction had been shock. She'd been convinced that Liam had no feelings for her whatsoever, that he was totally indifferent, if not a little irritated by her presence. He'd avoided her, particularly since she'd come to live at Petty Cove.

Now she could see that there was another reason behind that behavior. He'd been hiding his true feelings—he wanted her!

That brought joy. Complete and unalloyed, which terrified her, too. She still felt joy, even now, hours later. She'd done her best to convince herself that she couldn't care less about Liam Connery. That the whole first-crush thing was a stupid artifact from her long-ago schooldays—and it was. No wonder it was called a "crush"; it crushed you when you were so young and vulnerable.

And no, he hadn't measured up to her childhood memory.

But the instant he'd touched her, she'd known that she was a fool. She was as attracted to him as she'd ever been. Only, now he was a man and the attraction was real and ten times more powerful, whereas back then it had just been a figment of her fevered imagination.

He'd said he lusted after her. Charlotte knew she should feel a little offended—weren't men supposed to be *in love* with women, not lust after them? But she wasn't the slightest bit offended by what he'd said. She welcomed his words. No man had ever declared such a passion, such a *desire* for her. Lust or love, what did it matter? At least with lust, you knew where you stood, right? And, to be honest, she had to admit that what she'd felt for him today, in that bedroom on the second floor of the Rathbone mansion, was pure unadulterated lust, too. She'd wanted to tear his clothes off and make love with him right there on the faded old Persian carpet!

And she would have, too, if he hadn't left the room so quickly. She was sure of it. Which proved he had more sense than she did.

All of which was something to ponder. She'd completely surprised herself by her reactions to Liam's kisses. She'd never dreamed anything like that would happen, not to her, and when it did, her response had stunned her.

Elemental. Powerful. Passionate.

These were not words Charlotte had ever applied to herself. That wasn't the Charlotte Moore she knew. The Charlotte Moore she knew was cautious and critical in matters of love. Love, because she'd never considered herself—until now—a candidate for lust. She'd been selective—picky, Laurel always said—about the men in her life. Although she'd had plenty of admirers and no shortage of male company, even lovers, she'd wondered why she'd never had a really happy, long-lasting relationship with any of them. Of course, when she got bored, which tended to happen quickly, she'd move on. Always looking, always browsing, always on the outside of other people's lives, peering in. Wishing, hoping, dreaming.

For what? A swift, hot affair with a man of few words and much action? A man who was practically a stranger? A man who, after a couple more weeks, she'd leave and never see again?

The very thought gave her shivers. And it wasn't because she was cold.

WHEN CHARLOTTE PUT Maggie back in the kennel and entered the house, she was surprised to find Liam in the kitchen.

"Liam's cooking tonight," Ada announced with pride. "His specialty. Isn't that a treat?"

"Oh?" Charlotte managed to say. If Liam was going to be ordinary about things, so was she. He was standing at the stove stirring at something in a big casserole pot. He barely glanced at her, but she couldn't help thinking he looked a little strained.

"Chicken paprikash," he said.

"Your *specialty?*"

"I've made it a few times," he admitted, replacing the lid on the casserole and putting down the wooden spoon.

"Chicken paprikash and apple crumble," Ada said. "Those are his two specialities."

"Just two, huh? I see." Charlotte bent to pat Chip's small head. The cat was purring in Ada's lap.

"I sure miss that Maggie," Ada said stoutly. "Liam tells me she has to be out in a kennel for a week or two."

"I know. I miss her too, Ada." Charlotte glanced toward Liam and was stunned to see that he was staring at her, straight at her, no pretense of any kind in his gaze. It took her a few seconds to remember that his mother couldn't see his expression. "I—I just took her out for a ramble, as a matter-of-fact."

"Did you?"

"We went down the lane toward the road. I checked your mailbox. There wasn't any mail."

"Well, well." Ada stroked Chip's back. "We both miss her, don't we, Chippy?"

"Why don't I go change and then I'll come back down and set the table, okay?"

"You do what you like, dear," Ada said noncommittally.

Charlotte hurried off, her nerves screaming. This was going to be difficult. Somehow, in all her musings that afternoon, she hadn't thought much about how things would be between her and Liam now. She hadn't thought much about the fact that life at Petty Cove would go on, that they had to continue to coexist. In the same house. The way he'd looked at her just now—that open, hungry expression...

It took her breath away.

She changed into a clean pair of slacks and a soft, coral-colored sweater. She brushed her hair until it shone and ran a damp washcloth over her face. Cobwebs! There was no end to the dust and grime at the Rathbone mansion. She definitely wouldn't miss that part of the job when she went back to Toronto.

Toronto. Her apartment. Zoey and Lydia. Her parents. Laurel. Ontario and home seemed so far, far away.

The meal was torture. The two of them sat on opposite sides of the table, Jamie beside her and Ada beside him. At least Ada was directly across from her. But she felt Liam's eyes on her constantly. She didn't dare meet his gaze.

"When's Sunny havin' her pups, Liam?" Jamie asked, scooping up a good forkful of the mashed potatoes Liam had served with the paprikash—which, Charlotte had to admit, was very good.

"Any day now, Jamie," Liam said. How could he sound so calm? "We'll check on her before I take you home."

Charlotte decided she had to contribute, if only to show how unrattled she was by Liam's constant scrutiny—hardly the truth. "Did you ever finish your decoy, Jamie? The one you were making for school?"

"I finished carving it," the boy said proudly. "I need to give it some paint now. My teacher says it's real good. It is, isn't it, Liam?"

"It's a fine job for a first effort, Jamie. You'll only get better, the more you work at it."

Charlotte escaped before dessert was served, complaining of a headache. She lay down on the bed in her room and stared at the ceiling, until she heard Liam's truck start up and drive away, which meant he was taking Jamie home. Then she went back downstairs, feeling like a complete fraud.

"You take something for your head, Charlotte?" Ada asked, concern in her voice. "You're working too hard. You need to take some time off. There's no need to go all out like you are over there. What's the hurry? Tomorrow's another day. Find anything interesting?"

Ada always liked to hear about Charlotte's finds. They had developed a small ritual since Charlotte had moved to Petty Cove. Charlotte read out loud to Ada each evening, after she'd told the woman all she could think of about the wonderful discoveries she'd made at Gerard Rathbone's place. Sometimes they just talked, about this and that. Then, around nine o'clock, Charlotte would go upstairs. She had no interest in the television that was in the room next to the kitchen, a sort of den. Ada liked to go to bed by half-past nine; her bedroom was at the back of the house, on the main floor, next to the small downstairs bathroom. She found getting to that room easier than navigating the stairs each night with the arthritis in her hips.

Charlotte would usually read for a while and then go to sleep about eleven o'clock. It was a fairly boring, predictable routine.

Not tonight. She read for a while, but the words were just many bugs dancing in front of her eyes. She was on total, screaming red-hot alert. Every nerve jumped in anticipation of...of what?

Decisions. *What was she going to do about Liam?*

What *could* she do? She knew what she wanted. She wanted to go down to the end of the hall to his bedroom and offer herself to him, body and soul. She wanted to finish what they'd started that afternoon. They were adults. Something was happening between them, something explosive. Why not find out what it was? Take advantage of it while she was here?

Then she'd freeze in utter shock. *What was she thinking?* The Charlotte Moore she knew would *never* do anything like that.

And besides, what if it went wrong? What if he sent her back to her room with a lecture about morals and ethics and right and wrong, and reminders that she was a guest in his mother's house?

What a crock, if he did. But she'd have to accept it just the same.

She heard Liam's truck drive up and then heard voices downstairs. He was talking to Ada. About what? One door slammed somewhere, then another. Charlotte was ready to jump out of her skin. She tiptoed to the window and saw the lights in one of the outbuildings go on. It was too dark to see which one. He was checking his dogs, as he did every evening. The pickup was parked where he usually parked it for the night; she could see it in the glow from the yard lights. He'd be back in half an hour or so and then...

Charlotte's heart was pounding. Her breath hurt her throat.

She had to decide...she had to take a chance. Okay. If it all went wrong, she'd move out. That wasn't such a big deal. She could handle two more weeks commuting from Charlottetown. And Maggie was in a kennel now and couldn't spend as much time with her, anyway.

Charlotte rushed to her suitcase, which she'd stowed in the closet.

"Aha!" She tossed aside some sweaters and blouses and pulled out a pink silk nightie, thigh-length. She'd decided it was too cold to wear in this climate, but now she was glad she'd brought it. If Liam rejected her, at least she'd be wearing something aside from her birthday suit.

She ran a bath in the adjoining bathroom and tossed in a bath cube—jasmine—which turned the water pale green. She got in. *Aah.* Heaven. Plenty of time to change her mind while she had a good soak.

And change her mind she did...repeatedly. She would, she wouldn't, she would, she wouldn't. Yes, do it—no, no, don't do it!

Once Charlotte had washed her hair and dried it and brushed her teeth twice and painted her toenails pearl-pink, strictly a delaying tactic, she'd decided on no...again.

Luckily it took a while for two coats of nail polish to dry. Luckily she'd come to her senses while she was waiting, before she'd made an enormous and irredeemable fool of herself.

She went to bed and turned off the lamp on her bedside table. It was nearly midnight. Several doors had slammed in the house over the course of the past hour. Liam? Ada? Hard to tell.

She couldn't read. She turned onto her side, pulled the feather comforter up close and determinedly began to talk herself into going to sleep.

Sometime after one, she gave up. She couldn't stand it anymore. She pulled on her slippers, shivering, opened the door to her bedroom, and looked down the hall. The whole house was silent. She heard the clock in the kitchen downstairs strike half-past one.

She took a deep breath and walked as quietly as she could down the hallway, which, as she knew very well, had its creaky spots. She paused at the door to Liam's room, took another deep breath, and ever so slowly turned the handle. Her heart would give her away. *Boom-boom-boom.* Surely they could hear it in the next county!

She slipped inside. Liam's room was very plain. Spartan. Very little furniture. The curtains were not closed and the moon shone through the windows, revealing everything. She tiptoed closer to the bed. No turning back now. She was committed—

The bed was empty. It hadn't even been disturbed. Liam wasn't there.

CHAPTER THIRTEEN

"SUNNY HAD NINE PUPPIES last night." Ada smiled and dabbed at her mouth with a napkin. For some reason, Ada was all dressed up. "What do you think of that?"

"Puppies!" Charlotte nearly dropped her fork. She'd straggled down for breakfast late to find both Liam and his mother sitting at the table. Liam set a plate of scrambled eggs and ham in front of her. She mumbled her thanks, not daring to meet his eyes.

"Nine! Five boys and four little girls, wasn't it?"

"That's right." Liam looked as tired as she felt. So *that's* where he'd been last night—playing midwife to his prize Labrador. Not off visiting a girlfriend, after all—although she hadn't really believed he was. "Seven blacks and two chocolates."

"And mother's doing just fine, isn't she, Liam?"

"That's right, Ma. What time is Eleanor coming for you?"

Ada had on a mulberry skirt and matching jacket. "Nine o'clock sharp."

Charlotte wasn't sure how she was going to drag herself over to the Rathbone place today. Maybe she could take a nap this afternoon. She'd barely slept a wink. And she couldn't bear to look at Liam. Even though he had no way of knowing what she'd done last night—*almost* done—she was so ashamed of herself she could cry.

Charlotte had never seen Ada so dressed up. "You look lovely, Ada. Are you off somewhere this morning?"

"My cousin Eleanor is taking me to town. We're going to shop and then we're having lunch at the Avery Arms."

"Isn't that nice!" Charlotte tried to inject some enthusiasm into her voice.

"Yes, isn't it? It's a treat, just the two of us girls. We go once a month." Ada reached over to pat the table by Charlotte's hand. "I'll bring you back some little thing, my dear. I always do for Liam and Jamie. And now you."

"Oh, Ada. That's very thoughtful, but please don't buy me anything."

"Don't you say a word about it! I'll do what I like."

Charlotte smiled. She was very fond of Liam's mother. She liked her spunk in the face of adversity—widowhood, loss of her eyesight, and now, the increasing pain of her arthritic hip.

"Well, I'd better go to work, Ada." Charlotte bent to kiss the older woman's soft cheek. "You have a wonderful day in the city, and I'll see you this evening. Don't worry about supper, I'll cook."

"Now, don't you work too hard! Liam, you make sure this girl takes care of herself. I'm worried about her. She had a headache last night and who knows what-all could happen if she doesn't slow down a little."

Charlotte caught Liam's eye and instantly glanced away. Maybe by this evening, she'd be able to put last night—and yesterday—into perspective. No more creeping around in the middle of the night, looking for a man's bed to land in.

"Charlotte's a big girl, Ma. I'm sure she can decide what's best for herself," Liam said quietly, getting up to take his plate to the counter. He returned to pick up his mother's plate and then reached across the table for Charlotte's.

Charlotte was putting on her jacket, when she heard the dishwasher start its cycle. No sign of Eleanor yet, which suited her perfectly. She didn't want to meet anyone this morning. She didn't want to have to behave civilly when she felt so miserable. She was glad Nick wasn't around so she wouldn't be forced to make small talk with him, either.

The woods were sunny and bright, the morning frost crisp underfoot. She'd come to enjoy the short walk to the Rathbone place in the morning and afternoon. It gave her a chance to clear her head and plan her day. She still had plenty to do in the second-floor bedroom where she'd been working yesterday when Liam interrupted her. Needless to say, he'd completely upset her schedule.

She didn't know if Liam was working at the estate today or just Cyril. She didn't care. A part of her wished yesterday had never happened. Another part of her was wildly happy that it had. But, considering Liam's low-key behavior since, she had a sneaking suspicion she might be making too much of the whole thing. A few kisses—come on! What was the big deal? She had to assume it didn't mean much to him, because he hadn't mentioned it since, and they'd had dinner and breakfast together. Plus, he could've come up to her room if he was really interested, which he obviously wasn't. He'd said he'd made a mistake and she had to accept that.

Okay. She could handle it. Maybe tonight she'd call Lydia or Zoey. She wasn't going to tell all, she was feeling a little too bruised for true confessions, but she needed to hear their voices. Find out about their adventures. Have a few laughs.

Get some perspective.

Stupid as it was, the very fact that Liam hadn't been there when she'd finally gathered the courage to venture to his room made Charlotte feel rejected. She knew now that he'd been busy with Sunny and her puppies all night—nothing to do with her. And yet... Here she was again—a woman this time, not a schoolgirl—nursing a crush on a man who wasn't interested in her, despite all his fine talk of the day before. If he meant what he'd said, all that stuff about how much he *lusted* after her, wouldn't he have followed up? Done something? Made some sign? Hinted? *Said* something? No, he'd just scorched her with his eyes every time he happened to glance at her.

And spent the night with a dog.

Well, she admitted grudgingly as she came in sight of the Rathbone mansion, she could hardly fault him there. In fact, she was dying to see the puppies herself. Maybe in a day or two she'd ask Jamie to show them to her.

As for Liam, she wasn't asking *him* for any favors. She wasn't even talking to him unless she absolutely couldn't avoid it.

CYRIL CAME AND WENT all morning, doing odd jobs. He brought another load of seaweed at one point, and Charlotte walked out to ask him what was being done with it.

"Protection, miss." Cyril pushed back his worn denim cap and squinted his one good eye at her. "Keeps the bulbs from freezin' if we get a bad winter."

"Does it?" *Learn something new everyday,* Charlotte thought. She knew Nick had no intention of putting a huge amount of money into a garden he planned to get rid of in a few months' time, but the work the two men had done in less than a week was already an improvement. It would be a shame if the new bulbs froze before they had a chance to bloom.

"Oh yes, and it makes great fertilizer in the spring."

"I suppose you use it at home, do you?" Charlotte had no idea where Cyril lived, aside from his run-down camper parked north of the house—just that he resided nearby with a woman he referred to as The Missus.

"I do, indeed. On the garden and for bankin' up the house at this time of year."

"What do you mean by that?"

"Bankin' up the house? Why, we put lots of that there eelgrass around the foundation to keep out the wind and catch the snow when it comes. You wouldn't think the snow would keep a house all snug and warm in the winter, would you? But it does, just like a blanket."

Charlotte went back inside, after telling Cyril she'd be leaving at lunch and asking him, if he left, too, to make sure the house was locked up. She'd meant to pack a sandwich today but in the rush of

morning news about puppies and Ada's trip to
"town" and Charlotte's own haste to get away,
she'd forgotten. She decided she'd walk back to
Petty Cove, pick up her vehicle, then drive over to
Bonnie Bristol's store and buy a sandwich, or sit
down and have a burger and a chat at the lunch
counter. There was always something interesting at
Bonnie's, gossip or otherwise.

The bedrooms upstairs, which seemed to have
been sealed off from the rest of the house, certainly
rarely used, weren't as musty as the main floor,
which made the working conditions a lot more comfortable. Mid-morning she called Stanley Busby to
tell him she'd found a complete Limoges chamber
set—chamberpots, basins, water pitchers, toiletry
bottles, toiletries tray, the whole works—at least a
hundred years old. She'd been so excited. Complete
sets were so unusual, especially in perfect condition,
as this one was, that she just had to tell someone
about it. Not everyone would have understood her
enthusiasm, but Stanley Busby did.

It was half-past twelve before her growling stomach reminded her it was time she ate. She closed up
the house, waved cheerily to Cyril, who'd gotten into
his pickup and looked as though he was heading off
for another load of seaweed. Then she started on the
path to Petty Cove.

By now the sun was warm and the frost had
melted. The woods were quiet, with most of the birds
flown south for the winter. Each sudden gust of wind
brought down more leaves that swirled around her
like cornflakes. By the time she left in early November, the woods would be mostly bare, and in another
few weeks there'd be snow. She'd be in the thick of

the pre-Christmas rush in Toronto, decorating her apartment and working long hours to meet the needs of her clients. Although she employed a part-time assistant during the busiest times, Charlotte took pride in knowing her customers' individual needs and was always on the lookout for acquisitions of interest to a particular client. She'd thought of bidding on some of the items she'd turned up here at the Rathbone house, but she wondered if that would be ethical, since she'd prepared the inventory list herself. She'd have to consult Mr. Busby. That Limoges chamber set, for instance—she knew she'd easily find a buyer for that, probably several—

"Charlotte?"

"Oh!" She'd been walking along, head down and hands deep in her pockets, thinking, planning. Trying her best not to think of the man suddenly standing in front of her.

"You headed back already?" Liam wore a dark-brown jacket and was carrying a canvas bag of some sort—a backpack, it looked like—which he held by the handles.

"To get the truck." She dug her hands even deeper into her pockets. "I figured I'd drive over to Bonnie's for a bit."

"I see."

"Uh, you on your way to work?" She had to say something.

"No, I thought I'd bring you some lunch." He held up the bag.

"Me?" Charlotte was so surprised she almost forgot to be on her guard. She smiled. "Cold paprikash, I presume?"

"No, sandwiches. Ham and cheese." He seemed

a little embarrassed. "Nothing much. I just wondered if you'd eaten, that's all."

"I was going to have lunch at Bonnie's."

"Well—here." He handed her the bag and she peeked in. It seemed awfully bulky for just sandwiches. There was a thermos and a plaid fringed blanket.

"What's—all this?" She pulled a corner of the blanket from the bag.

He cleared his throat and frowned. "It's a nice day. I thought you might like to eat outside."

"I usually do," she said softly, unable to look away from him, despite her best intentions. A picnic? Had he had in mind a *picnic*?

"Yes." He shrugged. "I know you do. It's getting cold, though."

He'd noticed. Charlotte felt a surge of warmth. How thoughtful! She wasn't a person who liked to hold a grudge. So they'd had their little, uh, problem yesterday. Today was another day. He seemed ready to reestablish some sort of normalcy between them. "Enough for two in there?"

He hesitated, his eyes on hers. "Could be."

"Then, why don't you join me?" she invited, adding hastily, "that is, if you haven't already eaten."

"Join you?" He looked startled.

"Why not?" She gestured around her with one arm flung wide. "Maybe not a picnic, though." She didn't trust herself *that* alone with him. "It's kind of cold and— Well, how about at the house? I think Cyril's gone for another load and I don't think it's wise to leave the place unattended for long, do you?" She knew she was babbling.

He fell in beside her without answering. From

time to time he dropped behind her on the narrow path, with a few quiet words for Bear, who, of course, accompanied him. Charlotte's brain was in overdrive. Why the lunch? He'd never brought her lunch before, unless Ada had sent it over. A peace offering?

They reached the house and climbed the steps to the area where she usually sat, with the cast-iron garden table and rickety chairs. Liam rummaged around in the sack and laid out several waxpaper-wrapped sandwiches, two apples, the thermos and what looked very much liked a badly wrapped chunk of Ada's pound cake.

"I'll go get cups," Charlotte offered, when she realized there was only the plastic top on the thermos bottle. *Two* apples—had he planned to join her? She fumbled with the key for a few seconds—it always stuck—and went into the kitchen. She couldn't resist a glance at herself in the mirror hanging in the hallway. Hair flying, color high, a gleam in her eye.... *Now, what's that about, Charlotte Moore?* Just nerves, she told herself.

"Here—" She set the cups down on the table and watched as Liam poured a steaming beverage from the thermos.

"Hot chocolate?"

"Coffee, with cream and sugar. I hope that's okay."

"Fine." Charlotte picked up her mug and opened one of the wrapped packages. The sandwich was definitely man-size, with an amazing amount of ham and cheese stuffed between two thick-cut chunks of bread. Half of one of these would do her.

Now…conversation. A remark or two would be a good thing. *Let's see…*

"So, how are the puppies?" Impersonal was good.

Liam nodded. "They're doing great. Strong puppies."

Charlotte waited for him to elaborate, which he didn't, then continued. "How many again?"

"Nine."

"Two chocolate, right?"

He glanced at her, his expression vastly more serious than the subject warranted. "Yes."

Charlotte thought she'd explode. "How much do they sell for?" Ada had told her Bear's puppies sold for upward of a thousand dollars.

"As puppies?"

"Yes." *No, as rhinoceroses…*

"Eight-hundred to a thousand as puppies. More if they're started." He seemed to be avoiding her eyes. She realized it went both ways: she didn't want to look directly at him, either. All she could think of was yesterday, him kissing her upstairs, and then her incredible foolishness of last night—which, luckily, no one need ever know about.

But at least she was trying to be civil. She tried again. "How much if they're fully trained?"

"Several thousand. Sometimes more."

For a man who made part of his living raising and training gun dogs and retrievers, he didn't seem all that interested in the topic. Maybe he felt she was being nosy. Fine. Okay. She didn't really care, anyway. Charlotte decided to shut up and enjoy the view.

Still no sign of Cyril, but then, it hadn't even been half an hour since he left. *Seaweed.*

"How far do you have to go for the seaweed?"

"Black's Cove. About four miles." He reached for another half sandwich.

Okay, Buster. She'd done her best. She wasn't saying another word until he did. If he ever did.

She took a sip of her coffee. *La di da, la di da...*

Charlotte had just broken a piece of pound cake from the chunk Liam had brought, when he suddenly crumpled up the wax paper that had been on the sandwiches, threw it into his canvas bag and stood. He screwed the top on the thermos bottle firmly.

"I'd better go," he said.

"Why?" Charlotte frowned at him. "You're not finished."

"Yes, I am, Goddammit. I'm finished!"

She sat straight in her chair. "What are you talking about? Is—is everything all right?"

"No!" he said violently. "Everything's *not* all right."

He slammed the thermos bottle into his bag so hard Charlotte thought he might well have broken it.

"I came over here to mend fences," he said. "To make up."

"For?"

"For what happened yesterday, what do you think? I saw how beat-up you looked this morning. You didn't sleep. It's my fault. I upset you. I don't know what came over me—"

He ran one hand raggedly through his hair. Charlotte swallowed carefully. Her throat was dry.

"And now all we can talk about is puppies—and goddamn seaweed!"

"You already apologized," she said dully, shrugging. "Remember?"

So he'd made a "mistake," as he called it. Was it *that* big a deal? If only she hadn't run into him in the woods. If only she'd managed to reach Petty Cove and her vehicle and was even now enjoying a burger and fries and a bit of gossip with Bonnie Bristol, whom she'd come to like and admire. If only…

If ifs and ands were pots and pans, her grandmother used to say, *there'd be no work for tinkers.*

"I know," he said, jerking the buckles tight on his bag. "I *know* I said I was sorry."

"And," Charlotte said softly, wondering where her courage had come from, "are you? Really?"

"What?" He looked angry, confused.

"Sorry."

He stared at her. Then he shook his head. "No, as a matter-of-fact, I'm not. I'm not sorry at all."

Charlotte held his gaze for a few seconds that felt like hours. "Neither am I." She could barely hear her own words.

"What's that supposed to mean?" he asked hoarsely.

"Exactly what I said. I'm not sorry. You kissed me upstairs, sure, but I kissed you back—or did you notice?" She was clenching her fists under the table to keep them from shaking.

"Of course I noticed!" He slung the canvas sack onto his shoulder. He was ready to leave.

"Was it true what you said yesterday? That you— *lusted* after me?" Charlotte pushed on, catching her breath. She was in deep, deep water.

"Guilty as charged," he muttered. His eyes burned into hers.

Charlotte stood up. "Well, if you're guilty as charged, then so am I."

"What…are you saying?" he said slowly.

"I'm saying that—" she took a quick breath and plunged on "—that I'm an adult and you're an adult and nobody has to be sorry. I wanted it as much as you did…."

"It?"

"Sex," she whispered. "I wanted you as much as you—"

He took one step toward her, and she heard the canvas bag hit the battered table at the same time as she felt his arms around her, his mouth crushing hers.

Charlotte reached up to put her arms around him. She kissed him back. Her heart beat madly against her chest, against his chest. Her pulse pounded in her ears.

"Oh, Charlotte," he groaned, breaking away from her mouth to kiss her cheeks, her ears, her chin, the corners of her lips again. "Oh, Charlotte—do you really mean it?"

She could only nod.

Somehow they were inside the house. She heard the door slam and the turn of the key in the lock. Then he kissed her once more, his hands on her skin, under the thick fleece of her jacket and the sweater she had on under that. One hand searched, teased, tantalized…. The other clamped her tight against him.

"Upstairs," she gasped. *"Upstairs."*

Liam ignored her plea. He kissed her until her brain swirled, her knees sagged. Then he swept her up and climbed the wide staircase that led to the second floor. To the bedrooms. They had their choice.

Just like Scarlett, she remembered thinking, as he reached the landing with her in his arms and looked up to the top of the second flight...and paused to kiss her again.

So masterful. So perfect.

It was an old, old dream, one she'd nearly forgotten, coming true at last.

CHAPTER FOURTEEN

CHARLOTTE HAD ONLY the slightest shred of sense left by the time Liam had kicked open the door to the same bedroom he'd kissed her in the day before, just enough sense to fold back the embroidered satin coverlet and drape it out of the way over the footboard.

The sheets probably hadn't been changed for twenty years, but she didn't care. Nor, she was absolutely sure, did Liam. He could have made love to her on the floor if he'd wanted, or on the stairs, or outdoors on the veranda—anywhere.

"Charlotte, Charlotte."

He kept repeating her name, sending shivers up and down the back of her legs. His voice was rough, caressing.

"Are you sure about this?"

"I've never been so sure about anything in my life," she whispered back, tearing at the buttons on his shirt. She stood so that he could take off her sweater, over her head. Then she was naked before him, and the look in his eyes overwhelmed her.

He pulled her against him, and her aroused nipples ground against his chest. He had his shirt off, but still wore his jeans. "You're perfect," he whispered, pressing her hips against his. "So small and perfect."

She wound her arms around his neck and raised her face to his. "Kiss me, Liam!"

He groaned and tightened his arms around her, so hard it almost hurt. "Oh, baby, you don't know what you do to me."

Their mouths met and they fell, entwined, onto the old bed, which sagged and protested, the springs creaking. He explored her mouth relentlessly. She wanted him, how she wanted him! She tore at the buckle of his belt, and he raised himself slightly to aid her efforts, never breaking contact with her mouth. Then, when she'd finally succeeded, he stood quickly and stripped off the rest of his clothes.

She scuttled under the top sheet, her entire body a mass of goose bumps. His eyes never left hers as he joined her under the sheet, melting her heart. His skin was hot against hers.

She reached for him, and he began kissing her again, moving to her throat, then her breast. She arched and cried out. His hands were everywhere, teasing, stroking, driving her wild.

"What about—?" He looked deep into her eyes. Charlotte felt she was drowning. Felt there was no other man in the world for her, no other woman in the world for him. "What about—is this a good time for you?"

Was it? She racked her brain, trying to remember when she'd had her last period. She was sure she was due. She nodded and, as she did, she felt him shift, felt his weight press her down into the old mattress, felt his breath hot on her mouth—and then she cried out as he entered her.

More, more...until he was fully inside her. She could barely breathe in anticipation of the endless pleasure she knew was hers. Theirs together.

"You feel so good, Charlotte. I want you so much," he muttered, his breath ragged. "I—I don't think I can hold back—"

"Don't!" She clutched his shoulders, his back, and arched to meet his first tentative thrusts. "Liam! Please!" She wrapped her legs around his.

He rocked against her and she gasped. Then they were together, their rhythm one, their breathing and moans united. Just when she thought she couldn't possibly feel more, she did, and he covered her mouth with his as she cried out and plunged his tongue against hers. She felt him shudder and freeze and then rock against her again.

She clung to him and...disintegrated. Her tautly drawn, suddenly freed emotions trembled, broke. Tears spilled down her cheeks, and he wiped them away with the side of his thumb.

"Charlotte, honey, don't cry. Did I hurt you? Oh, God, I'm so sorry—"

"I'm not crying," she lied, her voice cracking. She was a blubbering fool! It's just that this is so—so wonderful. So crazy! So...unexpected."

He smiled and pulled her close. He kissed her gently, so softly and tenderly that she cried even more. He stroked her shoulder, her hip, the side of her breast. Her cheeks.

"I've been expecting it," he said finally, enigmatically. "I've been expecting it for a long time."

Charlotte nestled against him and shut her eyes. She wouldn't go to sleep; she'd just rest her eyes for a while. It felt so good to be lying in bed with Liam, to feel the strength of his body beside her. It felt good simply to be horizontal, after such a terrible, sleepless night.

Would she tell him what had happened—*almost* happened last night? Maybe one day...

THE NEXT THING Charlotte knew, someone was pinching her toe. Pinching her toe and wiggling it. And whispering her name...

"Charlotte."

She moaned and tried to roll over, but someone had a firm grasp on her toe. She opened her eyes. Liam wasn't beside her. She must have fallen asleep.

She looked toward the end of the bed. Liam was fully dressed and he had her foot in his hand.

"What are you doing?" She covered her face with the pillow and her arm. She was so warm and relaxed. And sleepy. Surely no one could be cruel enough to wake her.

"Time to get up, Charlotte. It's nearly four o'clock."

She sat up, blinking, remembering at the last moment to hold the sheet against her bare breasts. Not that it mattered. "You're dressed," she muttered groggily.

"I thought I'd let you sleep. I worked this afternoon."

"C'mere." She flopped back down and put the pillow over her face. She felt the mattress sag as he sat down beside her. He tugged at the pillow and she opened one eye.

"Where's Cyril?"

"He's gone home. The Missus called and he had to leave for a few hours. He's coming back at six."

"So there's no one here but you and me?"

"And Bear." He grinned. "Why?"

She wagged a forefinger at him, and he bent to take it in his mouth and bite down gently. "Ouch! I've hardly ever seen you smile before, Liam," she said softly, withdrawing her finger. It was true; he was always so serious. So grim.

He ran one finger down the side of her cheek. "I've never had much to smile about before, Charlotte."

"Before?"

"Before I met you."

"Oh, that's the sweetest thing you could have said!" Charlotte forgot all about modesty. She sat up, took Liam's face in both her hands and kissed him on the mouth. She felt his hands on her breasts. Then she realized he was fumbling at the buttons of his shirt again, unbuckling his belt. Seconds later he was beside her.

"We've got just over an hour," he warned, with a gleam in his eye.

"Well, then," she said, resting her chin on his chest and smiling up at him. "Let's not waste any time talking."

THEY LEFT THE HOUSE at just after five, as dusk began to fall. No one saw them. Cyril, who, in his role as watchman, generally spent the night on the grounds, hadn't yet returned.

Charlotte stumbled a little on the uneven path. She'd never taken this route in the dark before, but Liam was there to catch her elbow when she lurched this way or that. It was a wonder she could even walk, she mused. Their lovemaking had been slower, more relaxed and playful, no less wonderful.

Charlotte was tempted to pinch herself. This couldn't be real. This couldn't be happening to *her*. Not Liam Connery. Not the man who'd once been the boy she'd fallen for so very long ago. Everything was different, of course, but still…the serendipity.

As usual, Liam said very little. When they got closer to the house, he turned and pulled her into his arms and kissed the top of her head. "I have a favor to ask, Charlotte."

"What's that?"

"I don't want Ada to know about this. About us. Or Jamie, of course."

Charlotte immediately felt hurt. She and Liam—it was all so fresh and new. She wanted to shout her happiness from the rooftops. She could see that he might not want to say anything to the boy—and she certainly wouldn't—but his mother?

"Why not?"

He held her a little tighter. "I want this to be just between you and me for now, that's all…."

"You're sorry we made love—"

"No! No, that's not it at all. I'm—I'm happy. About you, about us, about everything."

"Then, why not be open about it?" She didn't understand.

"Just—well, just because." He kissed her hair again. "You've got to trust me on this, Charlotte. You've got to do as I ask. For now. Maybe later— well, we'll have to see what happens. Okay?"

Charlotte didn't like it but she agreed. She could see his point, albeit grudgingly. After all, he'd made the same statement earlier, yesterday—was it only yesterday?—saying she was a guest in his house. A guest in his mother's house. Maybe they were fussy about these things in Prince Edward Island. Maybe the sons of innkeepers, or former innkeepers, didn't have affairs with their guests. Maybe it was a big thing, some weird taboo.

That, of course, was silly. People here just worried more about what the neighbors might say than people in the big city. That was probably it. Right now, though, she'd agree to anything he asked. She was too happy to care.

Ada wasn't home yet, so Charlotte raced upstairs for a quick shower while Liam went to find Jamie and check on the dogs. Then she came back down in clean clothes—a pink blouse, cropped chinos and Chinese slippers—to start supper. She put on one of Ada's aprons and looked in the refrigerator, hoping for some inspiration. Ground beef. She set about putting together spaghetti and meatballs, using a jar of sauce she found on the pantry shelf. Along with a salad, it would have to do.

This was just like playing house. If Jamie hadn't been staying for supper, she could've really indulged herself. As it was, she and Liam exchanged smoldering glances across the table, while Jamie regaled them with a story about something that had happened in his geography class that day.

"Your dad coming for you?" Liam asked, while Charlotte was jockeying a tin of fruit cocktail into dessert bowls. Even with her back to him, she could feel his gaze—on her shoulders, the curve of her hip, her bottom. When she turned around, she was sure her face was red, but Jamie didn't seem to notice anything amiss.

"Nope." The boy accepted the bowl Charlotte handed him. "Thanks."

She'd often wondered why Jamie spent so much time at Petty Cove. Of course, part of the reason was that Liam paid him to help take care of the dogs. Plus, Liam was teaching him the finer points of carving decoys.

"I'll run you over later, then," Liam said, with a glance her way. "When you've finished your homework."

Before that happened, Ada arrived, just as Charlotte was putting away the dishes. Her cousin Eleanor, a tall, lean, iron-haired woman with a kindly smile, carried in three or four shopping bags for Ada.

Out of one bag, Ada produced a box of chocolates, locally made in Summerside, for her and one for Jamie. "Now, you share that with your sisters and brother," she told the boy. Ada had told her earlier that Jamie had lots of siblings, so maybe that was

another reason he spent so much time at Petty Cove;
it was a quieter place to do his homework.

"Yes, ma'am," he said, grinning. Liam got a
book. Charlotte didn't see the title.

"Eleanor helped me pick everything out. I got
some new clothes, too, which Eleanor says are perfectly charming on me. Perfectly charming!" Ada
said, looking blankly about her, as if to judge the
astonishment in the room. "Imagine that, will
you?"

She sounded almost girlish, and Chippy showed
about as much life as Charlotte had seen, weaving
himself about his mistress's legs until she bent to pet
him.

"There, there, my Chippy!"

Eleanor left, and Liam took Jamie home shortly
after. Charlotte sat down with Ada at the kitchen
table. "Have you had dinner, Ada?"

"Supper? Oh, yes! We ate in Montague at the
Lobster Shack. We had to stop off there so Eleanor
could get some gas. How did things go today for
you, dear? I hope you didn't work too hard."

"Oh, no. I didn't. And things went very well today." Very well *indeed*.

"Find anything interesting?"

"Not today." She couldn't even remember what
she'd found at the estate today. The events of the
afternoon had pushed everything else from her
mind.

Ada leaned toward her in a confidential manner.
"Liam's gone, ain't he?"

Charlotte looked at Ada in surprise. "Yes, he's taking Jamie home. Why?"

"Well, there's some things I don't want him to hear. I can tell you, though." Ada sat back in her chair and ran her hand over the cat's fur. He'd settled on her lap. "Eleanor took me to visit a place she wants to buy."

"Oh?"

"Yes. It's one of those retirement places, a condo. For old hens like her and me. There's security and nursing staff on call and everything."

"You'll miss her if she moves away."

"Oh, yes!" Ada leaned forward again, a worried expression on her face. "I'll miss her something terrible, but she's set on it. Says it's too much work keeping up her own house and she's been thinking about it for a while. She wants me to go with her. But, oh, no, I couldn't even mention such a thing to Liam."

Charlotte was shocked. She'd always assumed Liam had stayed at Petty Cove because his mother wanted him to stay. Other than his dogs, he didn't seem to take much interest in the place. "I don't understand, Ada. Why wouldn't he want you to do something like that?"

She'd often wondered how Liam could be content stuck out here in the sticks, with so few neighbors and an ailing mother who needed full-time attention. Despite what she'd told Dallas Longhurst, Petty Cove was definitely remote. She frowned, something niggling at her memory....

Ada sighed and went on. "Liam needs me here.

This is my home.'' She waved one hand blindly around the kitchen she could no longer see. ''This is where I grew up and where I raised my son and where my brother and I and my husband once thought we'd keep an inn. Never mind—'' she reached out and Charlotte put her hand in the older woman's ''—we won't talk about it. Have you got a tissue handy, dear?''

Charlotte passed the older woman several tissues and watched as Ada blew her nose vigorously. ''Liam's not had an easy time, you know. He's here now, he's settled in. He's got his dogs and—oh, no, I wouldn't dream of moving to town and leaving him alone.''

Charlotte sat with Ada for another hour, then excused herself and went upstairs. She thought about what Ada had said. What hadn't been ''easy'' for Liam? Leaving the air force? She wanted to ask him about that. It seemed so odd that he'd been a pilot, a very accomplished pilot, and had left it all behind to move back here. As the Halifax book dealer had said, Petty Cove was the kind of place where you were quickly forgotten by the world. Was that Liam's intention—to be forgotten by the world?

She ran a bath. She was going to have a luxurious soak, put on the pink nightie and then creep down the hall again to Liam's bedroom, once the household—namely Ada—was asleep.

But her plans came to naught. After her leisurely bath, during which she nearly fell asleep, she put on the pink silk nightie, and lay down on her bed, under her quilt. She was just planning to rest until she heard Liam come in. Then she'd give him plenty of time to get into his own bed and maybe even fall asleep, and then…she'd surprise him.

Only, she surprised herself. She woke up to find the sun streaming in her window, dogs barking in their kennels, the clock downstairs chiming eight and the scent of coffee wafting deliciously up the stairs.

So much for Charlotte Moore and the art of seduction.

CHARLOTTE SAW LIAM briefly at breakfast—she came down just as he was leaving—and that was about it. She received a call from Stanley Busby shortly after she arrived at the Rathbone mansion, telling her he'd hired a truck, which would be arriving around noon, to transport some of the more valuable furniture to his Halifax showroom for storage and eventual sale. He asked if she could supervise the loading, murmuring, "You know what those moving men are like."

Which was all very well, but there was a great deal to do in the morning to prepare for the van's arrival. She had to select the furniture that would go, then she had to prepare lists, one on which she could check off the furniture as it was loaded, indicating its condition, and one for Mr. Busby or his assistant to use at the other end when the furniture arrived.

It did occur to Charlotte that Liam was acting rather strange. Was he avoiding her again? They'd barely exchanged greetings that morning before he'd disappeared. Then she told herself she was being silly. He had things to do; she had things to do. She reminded herself that sex, even great sex, did not always mean a relationship. Not in today's world. She'd been there often enough herself; she should be able to read the signs. If Liam Connery wanted a real relationship, he'd be in one already. It wasn't as though he wasn't sexy, handsome, unattached and successful in his way. She was probably the most recent in a fairly long line of temporary partners. He obviously wasn't interested in anything more. Why should she think she'd be any different?

Act cool. Modern. Detached. Don't be all over him. Don't expect more than he's ready to give.

But that wasn't how she felt. She wanted him. All of him. She wanted a relationship, an intense, exciting relationship, even if it was only for the two weeks she was here. She wanted him to do more than acknowledge her over the breakfast table. She wanted to talk to him, make love with him, spend time with him. She wanted to know everything about him—what made him laugh, what brought tears. What he cared about, what he hated. His dreams, his regrets, his plans.

Just as though she was really in love with him....

That thought frightened her. It was preposterous. Because she was *not* in love with him. She was happy because she'd wanted this physical relationship—she had, as he put it, *lusted* after him. But she knew it was only an adult version of the desperate longings she'd experienced so many, many years ago. The unrequited love of a young girl. Now...well, now she could choose to live out her fantasies, even if that was all they were.

And, she reminded herself yet again, it was only two weeks she was talking about—two short weeks! She'd never have this chance again. Somehow, she had to make the most of it.

CHAPTER FIFTEEN

FOR THE THIRD TIME, Charlotte fetched the pink silk nightie. She'd rinsed it out that morning—it was getting awfully creased—and hung it from a hanger on the back of her bathroom door to dry.

Good as new, she thought, taking it down and throwing it over her desk chair. Didn't even need ironing. She glanced out the window before she drew the curtains. Nothing to see, on a cold, blowy night. She sighed. She hadn't even had a chance to look at the new puppies today.

The furniture van hadn't left until nearly seven, which meant she was late for dinner. She didn't mind. A warmed-up meal by herself, the comfort of an excellent meat loaf, boiled potatoes and baked squash while sitting at the kitchen table talking to Ada was a welcome, low-key end to a long day. The day's mail had brought a fresh shipment of library audiobooks, and Ada was looking forward to starting a new novel. So was Charlotte, because it meant that tonight Liam's mother wouldn't want her to read aloud.

She'd even been glad that Liam was nowhere in evidence, although she did venture a query.

"Oh, he's gone over to Davy's place, I believe.

They're working on Davy's boat—I don't know what, motor or something.'' Ada had started knitting another mitten and was just reaching the thumb area. It fascinated Charlotte that Ada was such a competent knitter, even though she was now blind. ''When you've knit as many as I have in my time,'' she'd laughed when Charlotte had asked her, ''you'd be able to knit 'em in your sleep!''

The mittens, Charlotte had discovered, went into the monthly collection of clothing and other goods rounded up by the women in Ada's church to be sent to countries that needed them. Charlotte wondered what country—except maybe Canada—would ever need all those woolen mittens.

She'd finished her meal and washed the dishes by hand as she preferred. Afterward, she'd sat for a while with Ada. Finally, when the older woman had her headphones on and was well started on her new ''book,'' Charlotte went upstairs. That was two hours ago. She'd heard Ada go to bed half an hour ago.

Charlotte began a letter to Lydia and then tore it up. She began a letter to Zoey and then, after writing two pages, tore that up, too. She decided to call Laurel, just in case they'd come back from their vacation early, but the phone rang and rang, and when the answering machine kicked in, Charlotte hung up, not bothering to leave a message.

Liam. It had been thirty-two hours since they'd made love, thirty hours since he'd exchanged molten glances with her over the table while Jamie talked about his geography class. She'd seen him for two minutes this morning. And since then? Not so much as a glimpse.

Charlotte just couldn't shake the feeling that he was avoiding her. Why? Surely he hadn't had regrets? Surely it wasn't this nonsense of keeping everything secret from Ada?

Charlotte needed to know. If he'd had second thoughts, wanted nothing more to do with her, fine. She could see that maybe they'd been swept away yesterday afternoon with a case of the hots for each other, and maybe now, upon reflection, he was a little embarrassed. On the other hand, if he wanted to continue from where they'd left off—well, where *was* he?

Liam Connery might be a lot of mysterious things, but one thing she was pretty sure he was not a coward.

She brushed her hair thoroughly and brushed and flossed her teeth. She dug around in her suitcase until she found the diaphragm she'd brought along, for goodness knows what reason. *Don't leave home without it;* she could hear Zoey now. She and Liam had had that one episode—okay, two—of unprotected sex, but with the tiniest smidgen of luck, that would turn out okay. However, there was no need to take any further chances.

Did she want a baby from a two-week—maybe two-day—affair with Liam Connery? Charlotte shocked herself. She realized she didn't really want to answer that question.

She tiptoed down the hall, fully aware that she was getting to know this route a little too well. Surely this time he'd be in his room, in bed...maybe even asleep.

Liam was waiting for her and he wasn't asleep. He smiled when she crept in and closed the door behind her. "I hoped you'd come."

Charlotte stopped, shivers running down her spine. He was lying in bed, his arms crossed behind his head and a lighted candle flickering on his bedside table. "You were expecting me?" She didn't know whether to be pleased or insulted.

"Not expecting." He held out his arms, smiling. "Hoping."

Charlotte stood beside the bed, stopping herself from going instantly into his arms. "You could've said something. You could've told me—"

"I couldn't tell you anything." His eyes were dark and serious. "I didn't know how you really felt. I didn't want to say or do anything that might make you think that—you know, that you had to follow up somehow...."

"You silly man!" Charlotte slid into the bed beside him and he covered her with his quilt. He was naked and warm—so warm! She pressed close to him and his arms went around her. Thank goodness she *had* come to his room. Thank goodness she'd taken the chance.

He ran his hand along her ribs. "What's with this thing you're wearing?"

She angled her head against his chest so she could look up into his eyes. "I wanted to be wearing something in case you sent me back to my room," she said.

"I'd never do that."

"How would I know?"

Charlotte loved to see how a smile transformed his face. How his eyes wrinkled at the corners, how his mouth curved. She loved how it changed his expression, from grim and forbidding to warm and open. Trusting. She loved how he smiled at *her*.

She loved him.

"Kiss me, Liam!" she suddenly begged, fear gripping. "Oh, please, kiss me."

He didn't hesitate to oblige her.

Later, much later, when the candle had burned down to its last sputtering minutes, Charlotte rested, perfectly happy, perfectly content, in her lover's arms. She knew now that she would have this short time with him, all of it.

He held her close, as though he'd never let her go. And she hoped in her heart he never would. As always, his thoughts were a mystery. The serious expression was back on his face, although his eyes, when he regarded her, were soft, warm, *alive*.

"I'm going away this weekend, Charlotte," he said. "I'd like you to come with me."

"Come with you?" She raised her head and leaned on one elbow to look more fully into his eyes. "Where?"

"To the mainland. I'm taking Cruller back to my buddy in Wolfville. I thought we might—" He caressed her neck and smiled, but it was a vulnerable smile. "I thought we might find a small hotel and have a weekend together."

"A dirty weekend?" She managed a lewd wink.

''Something like that.'' He tweaked her nose.

''What about Ada?''

''I've asked Jamie to stay with her.''

''Before I'd even agreed to go with you!''

''No.'' He sealed her lips with his thumb. ''I asked him if he'd mind, just in case you happened to go away, too. Of course, I couldn't expect you to stay with my mother. Jamie knows that.''

''And?''

''He said he would. I need him to take care of the dogs, anyway. I told him I'd pay him double. Dave or Alice will stop in, keep an eye on things. Will you come with me?''

Charlotte nodded, her eyes filling with happy tears. She kissed him quickly. ''You know I will.''

''That's good,'' he said, kissing her back. Gently at first, and then with more intent. ''That's very good, because now that we're together, Charlotte, I don't think I could stand to be without you, not even for a weekend.''

HE WAS EITHER a very good con man or a very experienced and practical lover. Or he was a master of the perfect phrase, the exact words a woman wanted to hear, Charlotte thought, the wind whipping at her scarf as she leaned over the railing of the *M.V. Abegweit,* the ferry to Nova Scotia. Whether the words were true or not.

Or…he really *did* care for her. That was the miracle she wanted. If he truly enjoyed her company, both in bed and out of bed, that was at least something to build on.

And, of course, he *was* a wonderful lover; she'd found that out in the pleasantest way possible. How ironic that she was traveling back to the mainland by the very same ferry she'd taken to the Island only three short weeks before.

"Coffee?" Liam came up behind her and handed her a paper cup.

"Thanks!" She turned so that the wind was at her back. He stood very close to her, as windblown as she was, with one hand on the railing. She took a sip of the hot beverage.

Liam leaned over to look at the dark wake behind them. He looked more relaxed than she'd ever seen him, dressed in black jeans, a fisherman's sweater and a rather scuffed-up leather jacket. Bomber style. With his sunglasses on, she could well imagine him as a fighter pilot. She wondered if he would ever voluntarily mention anything about himself, about his past.

"How's Cruller?" she asked.

Liam had gone down to the vehicle level of the deck to check on the Clumber spaniel. Cruller was in his fiberglass dog crate, in the back of Liam's pickup. Liam had casually suggested that she drive to a friend's place in Montague and park her Suburban for the time they were away. It was part of the elaborate deceit, that she was going away for the weekend and so was he. Only, people were supposed to think they were going to different places.

She'd been hurt. Why couldn't they be honest? Why couldn't she tell Ada? Liam insisted it was premature. Premature! She was leaving in a week and a half.

Maybe that was it—he knew it was just a short-term liaison and didn't want the bother of having to explain the change in their relationship. But that thought chilled her heart. She couldn't bear to think that she'd never see him again after the end of next week. It *couldn't* happen. She wanted to keep in touch—to write, to phone. Maybe one day get to-gether again…

"I gave him some water. He seems content. A good, solid dog. No flash at all. Boring but steady." Liam took a sip of his coffee and grinned at her. "Like me."

Charlotte caught her breath.

"There's nothing boring about you." She closed her eyes, ostensibly against the wind, but really to send up a quick prayer. *Give me this time with this man. Make it a good time. Give me this week, these ten days—to discover more of what's in my heart. And maybe glimpse more of what's in his.*

She crossed the fingers of the hand she had in her pocket and leaned back against Liam's chest, facing the mainland as it grew on the horizon. Shelter in his arms. The shortest time could still be the sweetest.

LIAM'S FRIEND Derek Childers lived on an acreage outside Wolfville with his partner, Miranda Bliss. They had just built a new house and the smell of drywall and paint was still strong.

Cruller was thrilled to be home, and Charlotte had

to laugh to see how his somber, serious face lit up when Liam opened the crate and the dog saw Derek. He couldn't have wagged his stump of a tail harder.

"That's a boy! That's a *good* boy!" Liam's friend said, thumping the spaniel on the ribs and rumpling his heavy ears. "How'd he do, Liam?"

"Great. I took him out after ducks last week up at St. Peters and you should've seen him. Didn't miss a shot." Liam grinned and turned to her. "Derek? This is Charlotte Moore, a good friend of mine."

Good friend of mine. That was a definite improvement over "friend of my mother's." Charlotte stepped forward and offered her hand.

Derek shook it warmly. "Glad to meet you! Come in and I'll introduce you to Miranda." As they walked toward the house, Charlotte noticed that he sent a quizzical look at Liam, which Liam ignored. Charlotte wondered what that was all about.

Miranda was a curvy blond woman of medium height, a psychology professor at the nearby Acadia University. She was wearing a loose T-shirt, and once or twice Charlotte wondered if there was a small bulge underneath. Were they expecting?

"You'll stay for dinner, of course," Miranda invited. "And for the night—now, don't say no, Liam! Derek wants to know every little thing Cruller did while he was over on the Island. He missed that dog something terrible!"

In the end, it was agreed that they would stay. Miranda ushered Charlotte into a large upstairs bedroom furnished in Laura Ashley prints, everything brand-new.

"You'll be our first guests," she said, showing Charlotte the small ensuite. "Are you and Liam—?" She waved one hand from side to side, eyebrows raised.

"Sleeping together? Yes, we are," Charlotte said, a little embarrassed. But she appreciated Miranda's candor.

"Good! I won't need to make up the hide-a-bed. We've been dying to have someone stay in our new guest room."

"No family around?" Charlotte laughed. She felt comfortable with this woman. Beyond the initial curiosity—which was natural, she supposed—Miranda was welcoming and hospitable. "Don't you always find that it's the family who comes to stay?"

"I wish," Miranda said. "I'm from Montreal and I don't have anyone here. Derek's an army brat, so his family's spread all over." She smiled and patted her tummy gently. "When Baby comes, we'll probably have grandmas and grandpas fighting to reserve space. We're making the room next to this a nursery."

"You're having a baby," Charlotte said softly. "How wonderful."

"It's still a bit of a secret," Miranda whispered. "I'm just four months. We haven't told our folks yet."

"Why not?" Charlotte regretted her quick question—it was hardly any of her business—but Miranda didn't seem to mind.

"Superstition, I guess." Miranda rested her hand on her middle and looked pensive. "I lost a baby once, at two months. I wanted to make sure this one was really okay before I told the world. Besides, it's special when it's just among Derek and me and a few friends."

They made their way back to the family room, where Derek had poured beers for himself and Liam. Miranda refused a drink—Charlotte of course knew why—and Charlotte accepted a glass of wine.

She sat down beside Liam and leaned against him, tucking her stockinged feet underneath her. Cruller sprawled out on a love seat covered with a car blanket, heaved a sigh and closed his eyes happily. It was probably his usual place. Quite a cut up from kennel living! Poor Maggie, confined to a kennel because of her hormones.

As she leaned against Liam and he put his arm around her, Charlotte noticed Derek's interest. He seemed to approve; at least, he was smiling. Charlotte turned to the view from the huge plate-glass window. The house was built on a promontory and the Bay of Fundy spread out below them. She took a sip of her perfectly chilled Riesling.

Later, while Miranda and Liam set the table, Charlotte went out onto the deck where Derek was barbecuing steaks, closing the double-glazed sliders behind her. It was cold, but he said he intended to use his new deck until the snow fell. Maybe, he said with a grin, even *after* the snow falls.

"How do you like yours done?" he asked. His new barbecue appeared to have every possible gadget, including a warming oven.

"Medium."

"What about Liam?"

Charlotte laughed. "I have no idea!"

"Rare, I think," Derek muttered under his breath. "If I remember correctly, and I should, since I've known him since we were in boot camp. Rare for me and well-done for Miranda. So!" He checked the temperature of the grill and threw on two steaks. They sizzled and hissed, and Derek and Charlotte stepped back.

"How's your wine—okay?"

Charlotte raised her glass, still a third full. "Fine, thanks."

"You, uh—" He shot her a quick glance, then checked the steaks with renewed interest. "Have you known Liam long?"

"No," she answered truthfully, "just about three weeks. Why do you ask?"

"Love at first sight, huh?"

Charlotte gazed at him, astonished.

Derek chuckled. "He can't take his eyes off you."

Charlotte felt her cheeks warm. "Oh, I wouldn't say that…"

"Come on! Any idiot can see he's crazy about you. I think it's great. He deserves a few breaks, eh? Happy times, like everybody else." He turned one steak over. "It's been quite a while since he's been this relaxed. It's good to see."

This was the second person who'd mentioned that Liam deserved some happiness. His mother and now his good friend, Derek. What was that all about? She couldn't, for the life of her, see what he had to be unhappy about—if he *was* unhappy. She wasn't convinced of that, either. Sure, he was serious and sober. Yes, he was cautious; she thought it was ridiculous, for instance, the way he wanted to keep their relationship under wraps. Yes, he kept to himself out there at Petty Cove and didn't seem to see a lot of people except his cousin Davy, and now this man, but there were probably all kinds of other friends in his life, people she didn't know about…yet.

"They're smelling good!" Charlotte stepped closer to the grill, as Derek threw the other two steaks on. Interested though she was, she refused to discuss her relationship with Liam. But she wouldn't mind getting answers to a few of her questions.

"Just about done." He opened a bottle of barbecue sauce, then changed his mind and screwed the lid back on. "Hey, don't mind me sticking in my two cents' worth. Liam and I go back a long way and nobody knows better than I do that he's a terrific guy. The best."

"Not to mention mysterious," she continued casually. "Every Monday he disappears. Do you have any idea where?" She hoped it sounded lighthearted enough, innocent enough.

"He ever mention going to, you know…see somebody?"

Charlotte shook her head. *Who?*

Derek gave her a piercing look. "Where does he say he goes?"

"He doesn't." Charlotte smiled and raised her hands. "Just disappears. For the whole day."

"I see." Derek turned his full attention back to the grill and frowned as he prodded the meat with a fork. "Mondays, huh? Probably flying. I guess you know he used to be a pilot until—" he looked uncomfortable "—until he, uh, left the air force, six, seven years ago. He's got a pal in Charlottetown with a flying service. I'll bet he goes there, gets in a couple hours of air time every week. Gotta keep up the license, you know."

Charlotte stared at him. She'd never thought of that. It made sense. But why all the mystery? She'd ask Liam; she'd ask him to take her flying someday.

That night, after they'd made love, Liam held her in his arms for a long time. She couldn't fall asleep. She didn't want to fall asleep. She just wanted to feel him and touch him and be close to him. She was so glad she'd decided to come to Nova Scotia.

"I've been thinking, Charlotte," he said slowly.

"Oh?"

"About Maggie."

"About Maggie!" She struggled to raise her head to look at him, gave up and nestled back down against his shoulder. "Don't you ever quit thinking about dogs? What about Maggie?"

"I've been stubborn about breeding her and it's so damn stupid, really."

"Mmm." Well, she could've told him that, ages ago.

"I owe your sister, big-time."

Charlotte wrinkled her nose and resisted sneezing. She made a face, and the urge to sneeze passed. "How's that?"

"If it hadn't been for Laurel's plans to send Maggie with you, I would never have met you."

That was so sweet! Charlotte murmured something unintelligible.

"So, I'm going to change my mind and do what your sister wants. What the hell." He turned and kissed her, gently, lovingly.

"Actually, I have a confession, Liam," Charlotte whispered, when he'd finished kissing her. "I would've met you, anyway."

He frowned. "What do you mean?"

"You remember me telling you that I had a crush on you when I was eleven or twelve?"

He nodded, grinning. "Yeah. Isn't that the craziest thing...."

"Well, I'd made up my mind that I was going to search for you. Just to see what happened, how you turned out. See if you were bald and fat and had fourteen kids." She heard the rumble of laughter deep in his chest. "Bringing Maggie for Laurel was just—well, it was just a ruse to get to meet you again. An excuse."

He was silent for a few seconds and Charlotte held her breath.

"No kidding!" He sounded astonished.

"Really. It's true. Us getting together, it's fate, Liam. What can I say? It was meant to be."

"Well, son of a gun."

Charlotte smiled to herself and shut her eyes again. *Good old Maggie!*

CHAPTER SIXTEEN

Dearest Lydia,

I can't believe it's just a week since I wrote!
So much has changed. Would you believe absolutely *everything?* First of all, I was totally
wrong about Liam. We got back last night from
spending the weekend together in Nova Scotia
and had a wonderful time. (Read between the
lines, my dear!) I know, I know, you want details.

Where to start? Well, I'll start with the
smallest news—and the funniest.

Liam changed his mind about Maggie—it's
a long story—and then he found out when we
got back on Sunday night that the person he'd
left in charge, Jamie, his cousin's son, had had
a few problems, the end result being that Laurel's Maggie is probably expecting pups by one
of Liam's nicest dogs, Scout. I like him, even
if he is a handful and not much of a gun dog,
according to Liam. But he's very handsome
and has a great pedigree, which is what Laurel
cares about. Apparently Scout got away from
Jamie while they were out on a walk, raced
back and managed to get into Maggie's kennel

somehow, apparently through a tunnel he dug
and—bingo!—true love.

Charlotte nearly giggled just thinking about it.
Liam had been so proud that he'd magnanimously
changed his mind—and then to come home and find
it was a done deal. Poor Jamie. Charlotte had felt
sorry for the boy. He was so apologetic and worried.
She, of course, had burst out laughing, and Liam, to
his credit, had been good-humored about it as soon
as he got over his surprise.

Later, Charlotte had sneaked out to the kennel
where Jamie had put the unrepentant Scout, and had
given him an extra dog biscuit, which he practically
inhaled; then he nosed her pockets vigorously looking for more.

Liam's putting Maggie on a plane to Toronto at
the end of the week. Laurel is thrilled to bits, I
can tell you.

Now, about our weekend together... Lydia, I
can't believe this has happened but it has. I'm
in love! Yes, with Liam Connery. I was so
wrong about him. He's wonderful, he's everything I'd hoped and dreamed he would be. He
really, really seems to care about me. Cross my
fingers, I just hope we can work things out. I
couldn't bear to give him up now. I can't wait
to see you and Zoey in person to tell you everything. Our regular New Year's Eve date, for
sure. But I hope I'll see you before then, although I'm not exactly sure when I'll be back.

I know I'd planned to leave P.E.I. right after
I finish up with the Rathbone estate next week,
but

Charlotte didn't quite know what to say. She
hadn't decided what she'd do. She didn't want to
leave. Last night, after they'd returned from Wolfville, they'd had dinner with Ada. Then Liam had
left to see his cousin Davy. She'd gone into his room
later, just after midnight. She had hoped he'd come
to hers, but he hadn't. Why? It irritated her a little.
She could not see the point of pretending anymore.
She wanted to sleep with him last night—and every
night.

He'd made love with an energy and passion that
had stunned her. Overwhelmed, she'd nearly blurted
out her new feelings. She was glad she hadn't. Much
as she knew he truly cared for her, something held
her back. She was afraid that if she said she loved
him, things would change. Maybe he wouldn't be so
keen to continue their relationship if he thought she
wanted more. Like marriage. Like forever.

Maybe that was why other women in his life
hadn't lasted. There *had* to have been other women
in his life—somewhere, sometime. Even Ada,
though, had never spoken of a former girlfriend.
Surely his mother would know. Ada must've hoped
he'd marry one day, give her grandchildren, and yet
she never brought up the topic, certainly never mentioned regrets. People—some people—must know
about Liam's past. His involvements with women. In
small places like Petty Cove and Cardigan River,

secrets, especially that kind of secret, would be impossible to keep.

Not that Liam wasn't continuing to try—at least with her. This business of sneaking around depressed Charlotte. It made her think he expected her to leave as scheduled when her work was finished. That he believed there was nothing more between them than a quick, hot affair and then *sayonara*.

When she'd woken this morning—late, nearly nine—he was gone. It was Monday. He'd never said a word to her, and why hadn't he? How could going off flying for a few hours be such a big, dark secret? It made no sense.

She put the letter aside. She didn't have the heart to finish it right now. Besides, she wanted to walk to the Rathbone place and see what was happening. Stanley Busby had left a message saying he'd be faxing instructions about the remaining furniture today.

Downstairs, she put on the kettle for tea. Ada was happily listening to another of her audiobooks, but she turned off the machine and put the earphones aside when Charlotte came into the room.

"Tea, Ada?"

"That would be very nice, dear. I hope you had a good time away. You needed a weekend off. Did you go to Charlottetown? The Confederation Centre always has things going on. Eleanor and I often drive up to town to a concert there in the winter."

Charlotte didn't think Ada was really asking about her weekend, so she was noncommittal. "I had a lovely time. Did you make these squares?"

She'd noticed that the cookie container was full. Ada enjoyed baking, although it took her forever to accomplish anything. She knew her recipes by heart, but had to locate and measure out ingredients in her carefully laid-out kitchen. As long as things were put back in their exact places—Liam had had to remind Charlotte more than once—Ada was fine.

"Yes. Try one. They're from a new recipe Eleanor gave me. Caramel fruit squares."

The two women had their tea. Ada had finished the mittens she'd been knitting last time Charlotte had sat with her and now had another one started, with a different colored yarn.

"Where's Liam?" Charlotte asked casually.

"Liam? Oh, he's out somewhere or other," Ada mumbled evasively. "Hand me another one of those squares, will you, please? They're quite good, aren't they."

Charlotte passed the cookie plate to the older woman. "Nick Deacon told me Liam was a pilot in the Canadian Forces once."

"Oh, yes, indeed! Liam always wanted to fly. I remember that boy right here in this house, constantly pestering my husband or me to take him to Charlottetown to watch the big airplanes come and go." She shook her head, remembering, beaming with pleasure.

Charlotte realized how intensely Ada loved her son, the only child of her middle years. She'd do anything—even sacrifice her own personal happiness—to protect Liam.

Protect him from what?

"Look in that drawer, the one to the right of the cupboard. There's a picture in there of Liam when he got his wings, as they say. Of him and his father and me. Oh, what a fine day that was! See if you can find it, dear."

Charlotte felt awkward rooting through someone else's drawer full of mementos. There were quite a few pictures, which she'd love to look at in more detail sometime. Pictures of a young, dark-eyed boy who must be Liam. A boy with a dog. More dogs. Several men standing at the back of a fishboat, in their rubber boots. A family of three shielding their eyes from the sun, in front of a car by a white picket fence. A sidewalk photo taken at the Canadian National Exhibition. A girl on a bicycle in front of a lighthouse. Some old Boy Scout badges, report cards, birthday cards.

"It's in a sort of folder—you know, the kind the photographers give you."

Charlotte opened one cream-colored cardboard folder. Inside was a photograph of a blond woman— a girl, really. About seventeen. She had on an academic gown and was smiling sweetly, her arms full of what were obviously fake roses. "Who's this?"

"Liam?"

"No. It's a pretty girl, blond. Looks like a high school graduation picture..."

Ada's expression had changed, become uncertain. "Is that in there? I thought it'd been put away long ago."

"But who is it?" Charlotte persisted, suddenly curious.

"Oh, just someone you don't know. Never mind that—see if you can find the one of Liam in his uniform."

Charlotte peered more closely at the photo before she put it aside to search for the one Ada wanted. She noticed something written in a fine, childish hand over the rose leaves: To Liam, Forever, Dorrie.

An old girlfriend, maybe. Obviously from high school. Why was Ada so disconcerted by her finding it? It was history. Charlotte located the photo of Liam and took it over to Ada, who seemed pleased.

"Ah, there it is!" She couldn't see it, of course, but she smoothed the photograph over and over with her hand, then passed it back to Charlotte. "You see my husband?"

"Yes. He's a fine-looking man," Charlotte said, studying the photo carefully. Liam was so handsome it could break your heart. He appeared to be about twenty-two or twenty-three, bursting with health and youth and vitality, his proud mom and dad at his side, the brand-new flight insignia gleaming on his military cap.

"Ah, yes. All the Connerys are fine-looking men. Liam takes after his father, don't you think?" Ada said. "After the photo was taken, he treated us all to dinner at the King Edward Hotel! Of course, we couldn't really afford it, but my husband was always generous."

Charlotte considered the two men. There were some real similarities, although Liam was a bit taller. So much for the gossip about Gerard Rathbone fathering Liam Connery—along with half of Petty

Cove and Cardigan River, as Nick had suggested. People talked, no question. And how often was the truth told? she wondered. Maybe Liam had good reason for keeping their relationship quiet. Why voluntarily provide grist for the rumor mill?

"Well, I'm off, Ada." Charlotte sighed and replaced the photograph in the drawer.

"Next door?"

"Yes. I have a feeling Mr. Busby will want me to ship out some more furniture today or tomorrow."

"My, my, that old man was hidin' an awful lot of junk, wasn't he?" Ada shook her head and replaced her headphones. "Never know till folks are dead what they were keeping to themselves while they were living, do you."

IT WAS NEARLY ELEVEN when Liam drove into the yard and parked the truck. He got out of the vehicle, closing the door cautiously. There wasn't a sound, not even one of the dogs barking at his arrival.

The house was dark. He looked up at Charlotte's window but it was dark, too.

He entered through the outside door and shut it quietly behind him. A dog yawned and there was the *thump* of a heavy tail on the floor. Liam bent down to pat Bear's broad head in the darkness. "Easy, pal." Since Maggie had been relegated to a kennel, Bear had reclaimed his spot in the boot-and-coat room.

The kitchen door was ajar, and Liam pushed it open. It was pitch-dark inside. He made his way to the refrigerator and opened it. The light was very bright. He pulled out a quart of milk and poured some into a glass.

"Where have you been, son?"

"Ma! You scared me half to death. What are you doing still up?" Liam wheeled and peered into the corner where his mother usually sat.

"Waiting for you."

"Well, damnit, go to bed. I'm home now." He picked up the glass of milk and drained it in two swallows, then said irritably, "You know where I've been." He placed the glass in the sink and switched on a small light over the counter, which barely illuminated the room.

"How is she?" His mother sounded tired.

"She's—" Liam shrugged. "She's not great, Ma." His voice was flat. "She has a cold this week, and they're worried it could get worse."

Ada nodded and sighed. "That could be a good thing, son," she said quietly. "A blessing."

"What?" He turned to her, made a chopping gesture across his own throat. "Let her die of pneumonia after all this time? Let the doctors kill her by not giving her medicine? That's what it would be, wouldn't it?"

"No, it wouldn't. It would be allowing nature to do its job. No one is meant to live forever, Liam. Not me, not you, not Dorrie. They called it the Old Man's Friend when I was young. It came quick, there was no suffering...."

"I couldn't go along with it, Ma," he said, slumping against the counter. "Not after she's been fine on her own without the machines. What do you take me for!''

''I don't take you for anything but what you are. You're a strong man, and I want what's best for you. You've suffered too long. Six years, nearly seven. Dorrie is never coming back, son. She's gone to a better place—she just hasn't stopped breathing, that's all. You know that....''

''I do.'' Liam's voice was anguished. ''But there's nothing that can be done about it, Ma. Nothing! She's alive. I'm her husband.''

''Shh!'' Ada glanced at the ceiling. ''You don't want to wake Charlotte.''

''No,'' he said under his breath. His shoulders fell and he took a ragged breath.

There was a short pause. ''Where else you been, son?''

''Flying.'' He laughed, a short, derisive laugh. ''I went up in one of Geordie's planes. You didn't think I was in a bar, did you? If I could get any relief from a whiskey bottle, I would, but I can't.''

''I wasn't worried about you being in a bar.'' She paused and then continued, her voice firm. ''But I'll tell you something I *am* worried about.''

''What's that?''

''What's going on with you and Charlotte.''

There was silence in the room for a full ten seconds. ''*What's* going on with me and Charlotte?''

''I wasn't born yesterday. I might be blind but I'm not deaf. I heard the two of you upstairs last night. And the other time, too, before you left for Nova

Scotia. She went with you, didn't she? It isn't right, Liam.''

''What's not right—that I'm attracted to her, that she's attracted to me? That we're both adults and we want to be together?''

''Of course you're attracted to her. You know that's not what I mean.''

''What is it, then? This isn't just—just fooling around. I love her, for God's sake, Ma—*I love her!*''

''Oh, Liam. Fooling around's one thing, but you'll break her heart. You're not free to love her.''

''Don't you think I know that? Don't you think I fought against this? I didn't want it to happen.'' He ran his fingers wildly through his hair. ''But it's no use. It happened. I love her. I can't give her up, no matter what....''

''What about her home? Her family?''

''Maybe she'll stay.''

They were both silent for a few minutes. When his mother spoke again, her voice was soft and faded. ''Well, it's done now.''

Liam laughed, a bitter sound. ''It's done now,'' he repeated. ''If I could do it all over again, Ma, I'd do just the same. Charlotte's the woman I've been waiting for all my life. I can't let her go.''

''You've told her about Dorrie?'' The old woman's voice was frail.

''No.'' He held his head in both hands. ''I'm a coward. I just can't tell her. Not yet.''

Ada got up and stood shakily. ''Think over what I've said. If things were different—well, they're not.

I blame myself. I invited her here, put her in your way...."

"Don't blame yourself, Ma. It would've happened, anyway."

"Maybe so. Now, give me a hand, dear. I'm tired."

Liam took his mother's arm and escorted her down the hall. Her bedroom, at the back of the house, was directly under his, an arrangement that was handy if she needed help in the night. She had only to pull on the string they'd rigged up, which ran to a bell outside his window. It had rarely been used.

He left her to get ready for bed, a ritual she was well able to accomplish on her own. He kissed her forehead. "Good night, Ma." He squeezed his mother's hands in his.

"Good night, dear."

Liam left his mother's room and closed the door. He flicked off the light in the kitchen and then stood for a long time looking out the dark, curtainless east window. The sea wasn't visible from this window, not even in daytime. The bare arms of the sumac waved and clawed the darkness in the light of the rising moon. Nearly full—a harvest moon. A time of plenty before the long winter ahead.

Liam went quietly up the stairs and turned to the right, to Charlotte's room. Inside, he stripped and went to the side of the bed. She slept in the middle, half shadowed in the moonlight, her face pressed into a pillow. Her windows, without the shades drawn, looked out toward the kennels and the road.

He slid in beside her. She had on some kind of silly garment. Pajamas. She was so warm and sleepy, so delicate and beautiful. So alive. *And he'd been dead for so long.*

"Liam?" Her voice was almost inaudible, muffled by the pillow.

"I love you, Charlotte. *I love you.*"

CHARLOTTE KNEW she was dreaming. Liam was whispering that he loved her, so it must be a dream. He was kissing her and she was kissing him back.

She wrenched open her eyes. She'd gone to bed late and had resolved that she wasn't going down the hall anymore. She was tired of the subterfuge.

And then, miracle of miracles, he had come to *her!*

"I love you, Charlotte," he whispered in her ear. His voice was uneven. "I love you. I don't want you to leave. I can't bear to lose you. Stay with me. Stay with me forever."

"Oh, Liam!" she breathed. "Do you mean it?" She wound her arms around his neck, arched so she could look into his eyes, dark and mysterious in the thin gray light of the moon.

"I've never meant anything more in my life. I *love* you!"

"Oh, Liam!" She hugged him as tightly as she could. "I love you, too."

CHAPTER SEVENTEEN

THE NEXT MORNING the van arrived at the Rathbone estate to pick up another load of furniture destined for Halifax. Nick drove up about half an hour later. Charlotte hadn't seen him since he'd gone to Halifax the previous Tuesday. *The day her life had changed forever.*

Liam wasn't around. He'd taken several dogs for a training session with Jamie, who had a day off from school. Charlotte was actually relieved. If he was there, she wouldn't get a lick of work done—and she had tons to do. Her inventory was nearly complete, but there was still the question of designating which goods should go to Halifax and which to the highest bid received from two Charlottetown secondhand stores and one Souris store. Stanley Busby had authorized her to make the decision. The valuable paintings had to be properly crated and shipped with the furniture. Nick and his cousins and the rest of the heirs would profit mightily from the obsessions of their Rathbone ancestors, which included everything from rare early Canadian furniture to Oriental bric-a-brac to New England scrimshaw. Charlotte definitely regarded it as a privilege to have had a hand in appraising the unusual estate.

Ada hadn't shown up for breakfast that morning, and Charlotte was nervous about seeing her. Liam had told her that Ada had waited up for him the previous evening. He'd also told her that Ada knew about them.

"She does?" Charlotte was surprised. "I didn't say anything to her."

"She guessed." Liam didn't look happy about it. Even after last night, even after he'd told her how much he loved her, he still wanted to keep their relationship secret. Didn't falling in love mean *doing* something about it? Like making some kind of commitment? She was ready. More than ready. She'd only known him, not counting her childhood crush, for three weeks' and she'd marry him tomorrow, if he asked her.

He wanted her to stay—and she intended to stay, at least until she figured out the next step. Meanwhile, this secrecy had to go. Never mind Ada. He must realize that other people would notice. Bonnie Bristol, Clara Jenkins—all kinds of people knew she was only here to work on the Rathbone estate. When that job was finished, people would naturally expect her to return to Ontario. Or leave the area, anyway.

"Does she know I went to Nova Scotia with you?"

He nodded and loaded some jam onto his toast. Charlotte had made a batch of blueberry muffins, cheese omelets and fried ham for breakfast. She was starving. People talked about living on love, but in her case it was the reverse. Love made her hungry!

"She guessed," he repeated.

"I feel terrible," she said. "She asked me how my weekend was and I let her think I'd gone to Charlottetown or something."

"Never mind. She's not going to hold that against you. She figured it out because she heard us upstairs—"

"Oh, my gosh!" Charlotte knew she'd turned a fiery red. "You mean...*making love?*"

Liam winked and grinned, and she could have thrown her muffin at him. "I guess the old bedsprings were kind of noisy. Sorry about that."

"I'm so embarrassed!"

Which was why she wasn't particularly looking forward to seeing Ada. She didn't know what she was going to say. Liam, not surprisingly, had advised saying nothing at all. When Charlotte thought about it, maybe that *was* the best advice. She was hardly going to divulge intimate details to her lover's mother.

"Hey, Charlotte!" Nick had bounded up the stairs to find her in one of the upstairs bedrooms, carefully wrapping and packing the Limoges. "Whoa, baby! You're looking good."

He kissed her cheek. "What is it? The fun? The food? The sea air?"

He winked, and Charlotte's face grew hot.

Surely, Nick didn't know! What, was it written all over her?

"You're back," she managed to say in a light tone. "Good sailing?"

"Yeah. Water was a little rough, but a great trip." He grinned. "I'm headed home tomorrow."

"Are you?" Charlotte would miss him. "Well, I'm nearly finished here. I'll be done by the weekend, I think."

"And then you're leaving, too?"

Charlotte studied a toiletry bottle that she'd already examined a dozen times and wrapped it carefully in brown paper. "I may go to some other sales. Or stay here for a while. I haven't decided yet."

"Ah."

Charlotte glanced sharply at Nick, but he was looking around the room—thankfully not the one she and Liam had made love in or she would never have been able to keep her composure.

"You could use some help with this stuff, couldn't you?"

"I'm leaving everything where it is. The secondhand stores have staff to move this furniture out. And the moving guys can take care of whatever goes to Mr. Busby."

"Okay. If you need help, though, don't hesitate to ask. I don't want you straining your back. You're such a delicate little thing."

"I'm stronger than I look!" She smiled as Nick left the room, then a sudden, maverick thought bolted through her brain. *Delicate?* Her period! She hadn't had her period, and she'd been sure it was going to start. When? Back when she and Liam had first made love. It seemed like ages ago but it was only—she quickly counted on her fingers—a week. Okay, she could still be getting her period.

A baby. She might be having Liam's baby. Joy— and apprehension—flooded Charlotte's veins. She'd always wanted a baby. Children. And to have Liam's child? She couldn't think of anything more wonderful.

But she could be wrong. She *had* to be wrong. This was not the time to spring something like that on him. They'd barely started to sort out their relationship. And hadn't he asked her if it was okay to make love? He'd been responsible. She was the one who'd assured him that everything was fine.

She could get one of those drugstore pregnancy tests, but didn't you have to be quite far along before they worked? And it'd only been a week since they'd made love without the diaphragm. Of course, even diaphragms weren't a hundred-percent reliable.

She didn't want to think about those details. She just wanted to think about the future they had, the future they could build together.

She had no doubt about what she wanted: marriage. If he preferred to stay here in Petty Cove, she could do that. She'd run her business from the Maritimes, collect folk art and hooked mats and quilts as she'd always done, and ship them to her customers. Or she could keep her assistant in Toronto on a full-time basis. If Liam wanted to move somewhere, fine. If he wanted to take up flying again, be a pilot, Charlotte would be happy. She didn't care what they did, where they went, as long as they were together.

Ada had talked about moving into a seniors' complex with her cousin. Now she could do that if she chose. She wouldn't have to worry about leaving Liam by himself, although Charlotte had never quite figured that one out. Surely Ada knew a mother on the premises could cramp a guy's style—was that why Liam wasn't already involved? Probably not. Elderly parents living with their grown children wasn't that uncommon in Prince Edward Island, she'd discovered. If Ada wanted to live with them, that was okay, too. Charlotte was in love; she felt agreeable about everything.

And then, when children came, as they would… She let her mind drift pleasantly as she packed up the small valuables in the north bedroom. When she'd finished, she wondered why her face felt tight and cramped, and realized it was because she hadn't stopped smiling all afternoon.

THE REST OF THE WEEK swam by in a haze of happiness. Liam was a different man. Smiling more, loving, openly affectionate. There was no question of her going down the hall to his room anymore; he practically moved into hers.

He brought her out to the Maternity Ward kennel to see the new puppies, which were just a week old and turning into little black and brown sausages on their mother's rich milk. Sunny was maternal with her tiny blunt-snouted charges. They wouldn't open their eyes for another three or four days and she kept them near her in a pile of wriggling fur looking worried when Charlotte gently picked one up. Then they looked in on Sammy's litter, which was now a bouncing bunch of nonstop active pups, seven weeks old, all mahogany brown with those startling blue eyes.

''A couple of them will be going to new owners

soon. I like to keep them for eight weeks, give them some strong socialization time with their mother," Liam explained, plucking one rambunctious pup from the grassy enclosure that adjoined Sammy's pen. The pup wriggled and tried to grab Liam's thumb with his sharp white teeth. "Hey-hey, little guy." He put the pup down. "Then they're ready to bond with their new owners."

"Who'll be getting these?" Charlotte asked, bending over to stroke the pup's soft head.

"Mainly hunters."

Charlotte made a negative sound and wrinkled her nose. "Yuck."

"Hey, ducks and pheasants make good eating, you know," he said. "Besides, it's not fair to keep a big, muscular dog like this on a chain in the city. They need a lot of attention from their owners. You notice the way Bear sticks to me like a burr?"

Charlotte laughed. "I sure have!"

"It's characteristic of the breed. Chessies need plenty of exercise, and they eat, sleep and breathe retrieving. That's why I make sure my dogs go to hunters. Definitely to people who understand the breed and know how to handle them."

"Unlike Labs, right? Who can go to any old owner—"

"It's too late for Labs. They've already been split into show and gun dog lines, English and American. Chessies are still working retrievers, front and center. They haven't been turned into family pets and show dogs."

"And, of course, if you have anything to do with

it, they never will,'' she said, linking her arm in his as they went on to see Old Jimbo and Spindle in their kennel. Charlotte had met the old Labrador earlier with both Liam and Jamie, and had to admit she liked him. He had such dignity, with his loyal eyes, clouded now with cataracts, his gray muzzle, his stiff gait. To think that Maggie's puppies would be related to this magnificent black Lab!

"Right."

Charlotte had her camera with her and insisted that Liam pose for a shot with Old Jimbo. "For Laurel," she explained, quickly taking another...and another. "So she can see her puppies' grandpa!"

Liam looked suitably disgusted, and she laughed again. Charlotte realized she laughed about everything these days. Life was wonderful. Love was wonderful.

That night, she told Liam she wanted him to take her flying. He was quiet for a long, long time.

"You know I left the air force because I couldn't fly anymore," he said, his voice tight. "I lost my nerve."

"Ada showed me your picture. She didn't say anything about why you left."

"That was partly why. I had some personal problems at the time." Liam shook his head and held her close. She snuggled against him. "Maybe it was Bosnia. All those bombing raids. You're aiming for strategic targets, radio stations, bridges, but innocent people die. Civilians. It can't be helped. I had terrible dreams about it. I still do."

"Will you take me up? Derek told me you've been flying lately."

"He did?" Liam frowned.

"Yes. He told me when we were in Wolfville. He said that's where you went Mondays. Flying. To keep up your license."

Liam was quiet for a while. Charlotte wondered if he'd forgotten her question.

"He told you that," he said flatly.

"Yes. So, will you?"

"Friday. When we take Maggie to the plane."

By Thursday, most of the estate had been cleared out. Cyril and Liam had finished with the garden the day before, on Wednesday, and Nick had left that evening to catch an eight o'clock flight to Boston. Charlotte was sorry to see him go. She wondered if their paths would cross again. Probably not, unless she started attending sailing regattas, which was extremely unlikely. Liam announced that he was glad Nick was gone, which made Charlotte laugh. Her lover was jealous!

Not a day went by that Liam didn't reaffirm his feelings for her. Not a day went by that her happiness didn't grow. Even Ada seemed resigned to the romance going on under her roof. She made a few remarks about "young people doin' what they liked" and didn't comment further. Charlotte did her best to be discreet, for Ada's sake, but Liam had the audacity to sneak kisses right in the kitchen while his mother's knitting needles clattered away in the corner—which had startled Charlotte, until she remembered that Ada couldn't see.

It was hard to say goodbye to Maggie. Charlotte wiped away a few tears when they put the dog aboard an Air Canada flight to Toronto. In less than three hours, she'd be home with Laurel, who would fuss over her from now until the minute the puppies were born. How lucky for Laurel—pups for Christmas!

Afterward, they drove to the Charlottetown airport, where Liam's friend, Geordie McEachern, had a freight and passenger business, flying prop planes throughout the Maritimes and to the Magdalen Islands in the Gulf of St. Lawrence. Liam checked out a Piper Cherokee, and Charlotte sat enthralled in the passenger seat as he took her up into the wide blue autumn sky. They wheeled out over the gulf, then flew east to Summerside, veered north to Rustico— where Liam pointed out the yacht basin where Nick had told her he'd sailed the previous weekend—then flew over Petty Cove and back to Charlottetown.

When they'd taxied to a stop, Charlotte wrapped her arms around Liam. "That was fantastic! I saw so much. Thank you—"

Liam stopped her words with his kiss, pulling her into his arms as far as he could, considering that they were strapped into bucket seats.

"I should be thanking you, Charlotte," he said, holding her face close to his. His voice was tight with emotion.

"Why's that?" she asked, breathless and bewildered.

"I've always loved flying. It's what I wanted to do all my life. But since—well, for the past two years, ever since I started going up again, I've been afraid to take anyone with me.'' He looked deep into her eyes. ''I thought I was finished, at least with a passenger. Washed up as far as any possible flying career. You've proved me wrong.''

He kissed her again.

''Don't give me any credit, my love,'' she whispered. ''You've proved yourself wrong.''

They had a wonderful romantic dinner at a harbor restaurant before driving back to Petty Cove. If they'd had someone to stay with Ada, Charlotte was sure Liam would have checked into a bed-and-breakfast. This week had been one long glorious honeymoon.

More than once, Charlotte wondered why Liam never spoke of the future. Yes, he said he wanted her to stay with him, not go back to Toronto as she'd planned. But what then? She couldn't just park herself here indefinitely, pretending she was a visitor. She had a business to take care of, decisions to make. She needed a plan. She needed to know what he had in mind. If she was pregnant—a big *if*—that would change everything, at least for her. If Liam had no intention of marrying her, if he was just talking about a drawn-out affair, fine. She would raise his baby by herself in Toronto. It would break her heart, but she could do that. She was a competent, capable woman and she'd have the support of her family and of Zoey and Lydia and all her other friends.

But that option was a poor second best. She wanted it *all*. She wanted Liam, now and forever, which, in her book, meant marriage. And she wanted his baby, too.

ON SATURDAY, Liam took Charlotte to an estate sale on the northwest side of the island, in a small town called Alberton. There she acquired eight coal oil lamps, some garden tools—which made up for losing out on the Three Corners tools—a small, locally made nursing chair and a chest full of handwoven, hand-spun blankets. The blankets, with a linen warp and woolen weft, woven on 22-inch hand looms and pieced in the center, were the real treasure. She knew textile collectors and decorators couldn't get enough of the rapidly disappearing store of pioneer textiles such as these. So many had been washed to rags over the years, or lost to moths, or wear and tear.

The sale whetted her creative appetite, and she began to think about the fall auctions she'd miss if she stayed with Liam. Of course, she could take day trips and overnights here and there, continue to acquire the objects and goods that formed the basis of her livelihood. But if she and Liam were living together, she wouldn't want to be gone more than one or two nights. She'd miss him too much. Nor was it the sort of itinerant lifestyle she could put up with forever; she needed to know where she'd be in a month, in three months, in a year.

If he didn't suggest marriage soon, maybe *she* should broach the question—ask him to marry *her!*

On Sunday, Liam took her out in his launch and they motored over to Small Island, an islet off one of the headlands of Petty Cove. Liam told her that he and Davy and Geordie had spent many a weekend there, drinking beer and smoking cigarettes and bragging about what they'd do when they grew up. Davy had become a fisherman, like his father, Liam had gone into the armed forces and Geordie had started his successful flight business after a disastrous year managing a hardware store in Souris, which had been his father's fondest wish.

Charlotte was gradually getting to know more and more about the man she loved. She could almost picture his early life there, before the family moved to Toronto. She'd known him when he was in high school. Once he'd gone on to military college, Fergus and Ada had moved back to the Island. What had happened then? The facts were sketchy. There was the air force, yes, and there was leaving the air force. When had he come to live with his mother? Why had he not worked on jump-starting another flying career? Military pilots were usually scooped up by commercial airlines. Of course, it was different for Liam. He said he'd lost his nerve. And maybe the life of a commercial pilot, always being away from your family, didn't appeal to him.

On Monday, to her absolute dismay, Charlotte awoke in an empty bed. Liam was gone. Surely he wasn't rushing off to Charlottetown to go flying again? Not after their session on Friday. She felt hurt. Abandoned. When she went downstairs, there was a note on the table in an unfamiliar hand. Eleanor's. Telling her she'd taken Ada to visit a friend at East Point and likely wouldn't be back until afternoon.

Now Charlotte felt even more desolate, foolish as she knew that was. She didn't even have Maggie to commiserate with anymore.

So she went over to the Rathbone place, out of habit. The house was nearly empty. Cleaners were in, scrubbing floors and mopping cobwebs. All the carpets of value had been taken out, the garish sixties and seventies furniture and appliances had been removed by the secondhand furniture store that had won the bid, a Charlottetown firm. The walls showed pale patches where pictures had hung. Cupboards were empty, closets bare. Even the pile of old newspapers that Cyril Rush regularly perused during his kitchen visits was gone. The trees were almost skeletal, and the wind was cold.

She decided to go to the store for lunch. A bowl of Bonnie's homemade Scotch broth and maybe a grilled tomato-and-cheese sandwich would cheer her up. So would Bonnie's company.

As always, Abe manned the cash register. Today he was sitting on his stool reading an Archie comic and barely looked up as Charlotte entered the store.

"Hi, Abe!" she sang out, determined not to infect anyone else with her gloomy mood.

"Hello, miss," Abe answered slowly and nasally, then returned his attention to the pages in front of him. She wondered if he had allergies, although it wasn't the time of year for allergies; he always seemed to be stuffed up.

"Can I pour you a coffee?" asked his mother.

Charlotte slid onto the stool farthest from the cash register. A couple of other people were in the store, one in front of the magazine rack, another in the canned goods section.

"Sure. Why not?" Charlotte rubbed her hands together. "Feels a little like snow, doesn't it?"

"You think so?" Bonnie, Charlotte had noticed over the weeks, was careful not to disagree openly with her customers. Her reaction told Charlotte that, in fact, Bonnie was of the opinion that snow was still a long way off.

"Any of that great Scotch broth on offer today?" Charlotte asked.

She sipped her coffee, as Bonnie turned up the heat on the soup and waited for it to simmer. Two minutes later, she had her brimming bowlful of rich, meaty broth, swimming with vegetables and barley.

"Sandwich?"

"Oh, I don't think I could, Bonnie. I'll be lucky if I get this finished. I'll let you know."

"Any news?"

"No," Charlotte said, blowing lightly on a spoonful of soup. "You?"

"Guess you're finished up at the Rathbone place, eh?"

"Pretty well done, yes. Nick's gone."

"Is he?" Bonnie wiped down the counter to Charlotte's left. "I hear Alice Macdonald's expectin' again."

"Jamie's mom?"

"The very one. What'll this be? I believe it's her fifth. Could be sixth. Could be more. And they ain't even Catholic."

Charlotte laughed softly. It always amused her to

hear comments like that. "Maybe they like kids, Bonnie."

"Maybe."

The bell jangled over the door and Bonnie looked toward the newcomer. "Coffee, Clara? First cup is on the house."

"Oh, in that case, I'll take some."

Charlotte heard a familiar voice and turned. "Hello, Mrs. Jenkins. How are you?" She had only seen her former landlady once or twice since she'd left the boardinghouse.

"You still around?" Clara Jenkins smiled. It was like a crack running through a brick.

Charlotte disregarded Clara's insulting manner; she knew her former landlady had a rather unusual personality, to say the least. "Oh, yes, I'm still around." She spooned up more soup. "I might be around for a while, who knows? How's your husband? I hope he's feeling better."

"John? Harrumph!" Clara dumped several spoonfuls of sugar into her coffee and stirred viciously. "Nothin' makes him feel good. I swear this weather don't help his rheumatism none, either."

"Poor man," Charlotte muttered soothingly. "Give him my best."

"So." Clara Jenkins studied her boldly. "Thinking of hangin' around, are you? I suppose Ada's feedin' you well?"

"Very well, thank you," Charlotte said, then wondered if she should have been so positive. Visions of overdone beef and mashed turnips swimming in pale, fatty gravy floated nauseously in front of her eyes. She resisted the urge to put down her spoon.

"Freddie tells me you've been keepin' company with Ada's boy. Traipsin' all over the Island with him, here and there, goin' to sales and whatnot. Regular pair, you are, he says."

Charlotte remembered that Freddie was one of the odious boarders. She knew she'd colored slightly and wished she wasn't so fair. She managed the barest of responses— "Mmm" —poking down another spoonful of soup to avoid having to answer.

"You got any more cream there, Bonnie? I could use some." Clara continuing staring at Charlotte. It was beginning to annoy her.

Bonnie went to the refrigerator at the back of the store and came back a few seconds later with a carton of cereal cream. She poured some into the cow-shaped ceramic pitcher that stood on the counter.

Clara glanced at Charlotte, then up at Bonnie Bristol. "You suppose anyone's told her, Bonnie?"

"Clara!"

"Me?" Charlotte was surprised at her former landlady's malicious tone—malicious and triumphant. "Told me what?"

"That you won't be squeezin' a wedding ring out of Liam Connery for all you're a fine city gal and better than he's used to, that's—"

"Clara!" Bonnie repeated loudly. "You stay out of it. It's nobody's business!"

Abe put down his comic and glanced at the women with interest.

"What in the world are you talking about?" Charlotte asked weakly, staring from one woman to the other. Bonnie looked worried and grim; Clara Jenkins seemed pleased as punch.

"Liam Connery won't be marrying you, that's what," Clara said, thrusting her face into Charlotte's. "Is that plain enough? He's already got a wife!"

CHAPTER EIGHTEEN

CHARLOTTE FELT THE WORLD go black for an instant, and she grabbed at the counter. Clara Jenkins's words echoed in her head: *He's got a wife! He's got a wife!*

Her instinct was not to let the two women realize how she felt. The world couldn't know—couldn't!—how this news affected her. How it ripped the bottom right out of her life. What could she say, though? She either knew about Liam's so-called wife or she didn't.

"I'm sure Charlotte don't want to be sittin' here listening to your gossip, Clara—"

"Somebody has to tell her, don't they?" Clara shouted.

"—I'm ashamed of you. I wish't I hadn't offered you a coffee. In my own store and for free, yet. You'd think you'd have the good grace to keep your mouth shut about what's none of your business...."

Charlotte waved one hand weakly, struggling for control. "That's good coffee, Bonnie. I'll have another half cup, if you don't mind. Thank you."

Bonnie regarded her with surprise and reached for the coffeepot. Clara's pale blue eyes were all over Charlotte's face, and her shoulders and arms, her breast and belly. She even bent down—what? To see what kind of shoes she had on?

Could this terrible woman see right through her? Right through her heart and soul?

"Well, if that's the way you're going to talk to me, Bonnie, I'll be leaving—and you won't be gettin' much more business from me, neither." She drained her coffee cup, slipped three packets of sugar into her cardigan pocket and slid off her stool.

"You forgot to pay," Abe intoned, as she stormed off.

"And I've had just about enough of that addlepated son of yours, too!" Clara shouted before the door slammed shut. Charlotte noticed an interested face swing toward the lunch counter from the magazine section.

"She forgot to pay, Ma," Abe complained to his mother.

"Oh, shh! Never mind." Bonnie's work-hardened hands were twisting her rag. "It's just coffee."

Abe went back to his comic. Charlotte stared at her soup, eyes swimming with tears.

He had a wife. What did that mean? If he had a wife, where was she? Why hadn't Ada told her? It couldn't be true—it couldn't be!

"How much do I owe you, Bonnie?" She was proud of her voice; it barely trembled.

"Now, you listen here, Charlotte. That Clara Jenkins can be an evil woman. I suppose she's been harboring ill feelin's since you left her place. Don't pay her no mind. She likes to stir things up, that's all she lives for—"

"Three dollars and seventy-five cents," Abe broke in.

Charlotte dug in the pocket of her jeans for the five-dollar bill she knew was there. "Here, Abe. Keep the change. Buy yourself another comic."

"Gee, thanks, miss." Abe's smile covered his whole face. There was nothing addlepated about Abe Bristol. He was a beautiful human being.

"Charlotte—"

"I'm fine, Bonnie. Thanks." Charlotte sniffed. "I was just feeling a bit woozy there. I think I'm catching a cold," she lied. "Don't worry, I'm not going to let anything Clara says bother me. Besides—" she managed a laugh "—Liam and I are just friends, that's all. I don't know where she got any other idea. Thanks for the soup."

She made her way steadily to the door, praying that Clara would have gone by the time she got outside. As the door closed—Clara Jenkins nowhere in sight—she heard Abe's slow serious voice behind her. "She gave me a tip, Ma. I got a *tip*."

Charlotte drove down a narrow, rutted road that she knew led to the shore, and when she arrived, she got out of the Suburban and was sick in the grass by the front fender. She felt a little better afterward. She walked down to the water's edge and washed her face thoroughly.

She'd never, ever have Scotch broth again, as long as she lived.

Then she went back to the truck and sat in the driver's seat. She didn't move for at least ten minutes, her hands gripping the wheel until her knuckles hurt.

There was no sense getting so upset over this—it simply could not be true. It must be something made up by that vicious, unhappy, pathetic woman. Some sort of nasty payback for the fact that Charlotte had left her boardinghouse to move in with a rival.

But why hadn't Bonnie denied it, then? Why didn't Bonnie flat out say that Clara was nuts and she'd never heard anything so ridiculous in her life?

But she hadn't. She'd been disturbed, solicitous, worried about Charlotte's feelings and her reaction to the news. She'd tried to stop Clara from speaking.

She must have known what Clara was going to say.

Charlotte started the engine and put the Suburban into reverse. The back was still loaded with the goods she'd bought at the sale two days ago. Where was the stuff she'd bought at Three Corners?

Why was she thinking about this right now? Should she leave?

No. She had to see Liam and she had to find out the truth. If he wasn't married, they'd both have a good laugh. If he was—

Charlotte didn't know what she'd do.

TO HER SURPRISE, Liam's pickup truck was parked by the dog kennels. It was Monday. His habit on Mondays was not to come back to Petty Cove until late, sometimes after the evening meal.

She braked and tried to think of what she'd say and how she'd say it. Somehow she'd expected more time to prepare. Even to pack her bags, so she'd be ready to leave, if necessary.

As she dithered, she saw him come out of the house, give her vehicle a quick glance and a wave and then disappear around the back. Four or five minutes later, he reappeared, his arms loaded with split firewood. He was filling up the woodbox by Ada's parlor stove. He paused, perhaps a little perplexed to see that she was still sitting in the Suburban, then went inside. When he came out again, he stood staring at her.

She got out slowly. Her heart was flailing about like a wounded bird. Her throat was dry.

His face—his handsome, wonderful face!—was full of doubt and concern.

"You all right?" he asked, as she came a little closer.

She stopped, her arms folded across her chest. "I—I don't know," she said truthfully.

He smiled. "What do you mean, you don't know? You're either all right or you're not."

"It depends." She bit her lower lip until it hurt. "I heard some news today. I wanted to ask you if it was true."

"News?"

Charlotte was pleased that she'd succeeded in keeping her voice steady and unemotional. "Someone told me you were married—that you had a wife—" She stopped, terrified at how his face had gone pale. *It must be true.*

"Who told you that?"

"Never mind who told me! Is it true?" she cried.

"That's all I want to know! Do you have a wife? Are you married?"

He nodded slowly. "Yes. I'm married. Do I have a wife?" he asked, almost as though he was asking himself the question. He shook his head.

Charlotte's world collapsed. "Just what is that supposed to mean? Married is married! A wife is a wife! Liam, how could you do this? How could you do this to me? Why didn't you tell me?"

"If I had, what would you have done? I love you. I want to spend my life with you," he continued harshly. "That's the truth. Isn't that enough?"

"No, damn it! You're *married!* To someone else. There's no way in heaven that I'd come between a man and a woman. Destroy a marriage—"

"What marriage? The marriage is already destroyed."

"Are you separated?" For some ridiculous reason, this idea struck her as brilliant. Why hadn't she thought of that? That must be the case! It was a lifeline thrown to a drowning woman. "You should've told me if you were getting a divorce—"

"I'm not separated. I'm not getting a divorce. I intended to tell you everything. I just didn't know how."

He looked away. Not separated? Her world was dashed to pieces. But why? *Why?*

"Try this! You could've said, 'Charlotte, I'm married. I have a wife.' Period." She turned toward the house. "Don't touch me! Don't touch me ever again!"

"Where are you going?" He'd been moving toward her but stopped when she threw up her arms to ward him off.

"Away."

"Where?"

"I don't know. Just away." When he stepped closer, she broke into a run. "Leave me alone!" Then she whirled to face him. "You've broken my heart, Liam. *Do you know that?* I loved you more than I ever believed I could love anyone. And I believed you loved me back. And now I despise you— I despise you! You're cheating on your wife, whoever she is, wherever she is." Charlotte mopped at the tears on her cheeks. "Who is she?"

"What's the point?" Liam asked, his voice sounding as hopeless as she felt. "Why does it matter who she is?"

"I want to know—I want a name for her. So I can—" She thought wildly. *Why* did she want to know so badly? She was just rubbing salt into her own wounds. "So I can imagine the two of you together! Is she someone from around here? Is she the one you go to see every Monday?"

His eyes were black with emotion. "Yes. Her name is Dorrie."

Dorrie! That girl in the graduation photo, the one she'd assumed was a high school girlfriend. But Liam hadn't gone to high school here; he'd graduated with her sister in Toronto. Charlotte had just assumed that the photo she'd seen had been one of many exchanged among classmates in the same high school graduating class....

She ran into the house. Within fifteen minutes,

she'd packed her bags and thrown them in the Suburban. Liam had disappeared. She couldn't leave, though, without letting Ada know. What could she possibly tell her? And why, oh why, hadn't Ada said something? Warned her?

She finally scribbled a note, which she put in an envelope and left on the table. Liam would have to read it to his mother, or Eleanor, when the two women returned.

Ada, forgive me, I had to leave suddenly. I will be in touch. Don't worry, it's nothing life or death with my family. Thank you for everything. Love, Charlotte

Just life or death with my heart, she thought as she went out to the truck. She could barely see to drive, through the blur of tears. As she left, she glanced in her rearview mirror. Liam stood in the center of the yard, his loyal Bear beside him, staring after her.

Charlotte drove a mile, until she was well away from Petty Cove, and then she pulled onto a side road and cried her eyes out. She didn't feel any better when she was done.

So much for a future with Liam. So much for marriage, a home, children. So much for thinking that finally, finally after all these years, she'd found the man of her dreams. The one man in the world who loved her as passionately as she loved him—as she'd *always* loved him, for as long as she could remember.

He was already married. To someone named Dorrie.

CHARLOTTE WAS AT THE Wood Island ferry terminal by the time she made up her mind to go back to Charlottetown. She couldn't leave yet. She had to finish this. She had to clear her conscience. No matter what the situation, regardless of why Dorrie and Liam weren't living together, this Dorrie was still legally his wife. She had a right to know that there was nothing at all—anymore—going on between her husband and another woman. She must have suspected. Any woman would.

How long had they been married? Did they have children? Oh, there was so much she didn't know, would never know.

She stopped at a pay phone in Murray Harbor and looked through the listings for Connerys in Charlottetown, thinking that maybe she'd find Dorrie Connery. No luck. She decided to call Bonnie.

"Bonnie? Charlotte here." She took a deep breath and put on as bright a tone as she could. "Look, I'm just going into town and I thought I'd look up Liam's wife. Just to say hello and reassure her that Liam and I aren't…"

Bonnie seemed very upset at the idea that Charlotte would look up Liam's wife. "No, seriously, Bonnie, I *do* want to do it. I've just been thinking that if Clara's spreading that kind of rumor around, about Liam and me, I want to be sure the poor woman knows it's just gossip, that's—*what?*"

She closed her eyes and leaned against the door

of the pay phone for support. "St. Agnes Nursing Home? On Prince Street? Thank you, Bonnie. I realize it won't do much good, but I'll pop in, anyway. Thank you so much."

Charlotte hung up the phone and staggered out into the sun, which had appeared from behind the clouds. Bright as it was, it held no warmth. *Dorrie Connery was in a nursing home. She'd been in a coma for years.*

OH, DEAR LORD...

Dorrie Connery was nothing like Charlotte had expected. She was tiny and frail and connected up to all kinds of tubes. She couldn't weigh more than seventy pounds. Her hair—the only part of her that was even faintly recognizable from the photo Charlotte had seen—was cut short. It was still blond, if lank and lifeless. Her face was narrow and heavily scarred. Her jaw was misshapen. She was wearing a white cotton gown, and her thin arms, just bone and veins, lay over the coverlet, her fingers splayed loosely against the cloth. On her left hand shone a gold ring—Liam's ring!—but the band was so large that it hung on the webbed skin that joined her fingers.

"Can I get you some tea, miss?"

Charlotte glanced at the woman who'd come into the room and was adjusting the blinds. It was the nurse she'd spoken to at the desk, when she'd arrived ten minutes before, enquiring after Dorrie Connery. The nurse had told Charlotte that Dorrie couldn't have any visitors, but she'd relented when Charlotte had pleaded that she was catching a ferry that evening and had to see Dorrie before she went.

"No, thank you."

"Coffee?"

Charlotte shook her head. "Thanks, but I don't want anything."

"Is this your first visit?" the nurse continued pleasantly. Charlotte had the idea that she knew a good deal about the woman who lay before them both.

"Yes. I'm—I'm a friend of her husband's, actually," she muttered. She reached forward and took Dorrie's hand in hers. It was dry and featherweight. There was no response whatsoever to the little squeeze Charlotte gave. "What's actually wrong with her, can you tell me?"

The nurse made a gesture and Charlotte followed her into the hall. "She's dying, I guess you could say. She's been dying for a long, long time. Since before I started here, and that's four years ago. They tell me her injuries were caused by a terrible car accident. I know she had a lot of surgery before she ever came here. That's about it." They went back in, and the woman adjusted the bedsheet over Dorrie's flat breast and wiped spittle from the corner of her mouth. "She's been like this for nearly six years."

"Six years!" Charlotte gasped softly. Poor Liam! Despite herself, despite her grief at Liam's deception, she couldn't help feeling sorry for him. To have someone he loved in this condition...

There was a drip running from a bottle to a vein

in Dorrie's right arm. ''What's that for?'' Charlotte indicated the intravenous equipment.

''She's dehydrated. She's picked up a cold and the doctor thinks it could worsen. It's just a precaution. She's so frail, you know, that she couldn't take an infection of any kind.'' The nurse seemed very tender with her patient; Charlotte was glad to see that.

''Does she suffer?''

''Who knows? She doesn't seem to, although we can't possibly know what goes on inside her head.'' The nurse glanced at her patient, then at Charlotte, putting one finger to her lips. ''The doctors say she's completely vegetative, that there's no brain activity as we know it going on at all,'' she whispered.

''Just—reflex?''

''Yes, just breathing, heart beating, that kind of thing. Are you visiting?''

Charlotte realized she'd been asking too many questions. ''Yes,'' she said, attempting a smile. ''I have been for a few weeks. But I'm leaving today.''

''I see.'' The nurse went to the open door. ''Well, if you need anything, just ring. I can't let you stay with her long. We're going to have to give her some physio soon.''

''Physio?''

''We need to turn her regularly and try to bring up the phlegm in her chest. She can't cough, and there's always the danger of pneumonia if she accumulates too much fluid in her lungs.''

The nurse went out, and Charlotte rested her cheek

on the bedrail, still clasping Dorrie's hand between both of hers.

She was alive, but she was dead.

She—Charlotte—had been fooling around with a grievously ill woman's husband! Not only that, he claimed he loved *her*. He had no right to say such things. She could see that he'd want a relationship, a physical one, with some woman, but to say he *loved* her? And yet, what had he said about Dorrie? That he had a marriage, but no wife.

This was the wife he had.

"Dorrie," she whispered, with a glance at the half-open door. "Can you hear me? Listen to me. I'm sorry, I'm so sorry about Liam and you and everything. Believe me, if I'd known about you, I wouldn't have fallen in love with Liam—" Was that true? Charlotte didn't really know. "I'd definitely have *tried* not to fall in love with him. But I have. I have. I love him terribly."

Tears started to flow down her cheeks and she barely noticed them. "I think I might be—be pregnant with his baby. I don't know what to do. I want you to forgive me. I never meant to hurt you or cause you any harm. And I know he loves you. I know he does! He comes to see you every Monday, and the nurse says he's been doing that for years...."

Of course Liam loved Dorrie. His behavior was evidence. Which meant he didn't love Charlotte. Could he love two women at once? Equally? One who loved him and wanted him in every way—physically, emotionally, spiritually—and one who needed him to watch over her? To watch her die?

But could Charlotte ever love a man who *didn't* act as Liam had done? Who'd dump his wife after something like this? Who'd divorce her because she could no longer fulfill her so-called conjugal duties? It happened. It happened all the time. People were often sympathetic in these cases—after all, it was hopeless. What else could a person do?

On the other hand, Liam was trapped. As long as Dorrie lived, he could never marry, never find happiness with anyone else.

With someone like her.

Charlotte thrust that disloyal thought aside. She was glad she'd come. She'd needed to see Dorrie Connery with her own eyes. Bonnie's warnings hadn't even approached the reality. This was a ghost of a woman. A thin, papery shell of a human being. A husk left behind when the spirit departed. The only thing that seemed half-human, to Charlotte, was the thick, mucousy sound of her breathing, in and out. Evenly, slowly. That must be from the cold the nurse had mentioned.

Charlotte got up when she saw a stream of spittle running down Dorrie's jaw again. She wiped it with a tissue. There was no response. Had Charlotte expected one?

She wondered if Ada ever visited. If this was one of her stops on the monthly trips to Charlottetown with her cousin.

Charlotte checked her watch. She sat down and took Dorrie's hand in hers again. She twisted the wedding ring on the thin finger.

"Please. Dorrie, forgive me," she said in a low

voice. "Just—just forgive me. And trust me. If—if anything ever happens with Liam and me, if—well, down the road, you know—" She leaned closer and whispered in the woman's ear. *"When you are an angel with God."* She held Dorrie's hand tightly, so tightly that the wedding ring pressed into her own hand. "I promise I'll look after him. You can die if you want to. You don't need to hold on anymore. I'll love him with all my heart and I'll take care of him, and you'll never, ever have to worry about him, in case you have been."

Which was silly. Because Charlotte knew—and somehow she believed Dorrie knew—that they were speaking of a time after Dorrie's death.

She bent and cleaned the spittle from the woman's jaw once more and held the thin hand against her cheek. Then she laid it gently on the coverlet and bent and kissed her cheek. It was too warm. As if the blood in her body was the only thing still living.

Charlotte rushed out of the room.

"Everything okay?" the nurse asked, as Charlotte hurried by the reception desk.

"Yes, thanks," Charlotte said, looking up. "Everything's okay."

Charlotte didn't care if anyone ever believed her until the day she died: she knew that Dorrie Connery had taken in every word she'd said.

CHAPTER NINETEEN

THE NEXT THREE WEEKS were as bittersweet as the season. Charlotte felt like a homeless person, or a gypsy, traveling in her van from one place to another, as the spirit moved her. When she'd arrive in a small town like St. Andrews-by-the-Sea in New Brunswick, she'd check into a hotel, have a bath and a nice meal and pore over the local paper. She'd mark off sales of interest with her highlighter, then tear out the column and put it in her handbag. She'd talk to people at sales and in stores, as was her habit when she traveled.

But nothing felt the same. What used to feel like fun and independence felt plain lonely now. She missed Ada. She missed Abe and Bonnie Bristol, for heaven's sake! It seemed so long since she'd seen her dearest friends. If anyone could comfort her, it was those two—zany, sensible Zoey and calm, loving Lydia.

And Liam. How she missed him!

Especially now that she had some real news. She was pregnant. She'd purchased a drugstore test kit in New Glasgow and the color indicator had promptly turned. There was no question—she was pregnant. Charlotte was so happy she could have burst. *She was having Liam's baby!* And the next moment she did burst—into tears.

Why, oh why, was this happening to her? She wanted Liam's baby, but she wanted Liam, too. And she was starting to wonder if being married—actually *married,* as in church and wedding—was all it was cracked up to be. Maybe she'd been rash, running off as she'd done, not giving him a chance to explain.

Since she'd visited Dorrie in the nursing home, she no longer felt she'd committed some crime by loving Liam Connery. Love was what mattered. Marriage was a legal thing; love was of the soul and the spirit. Liam couldn't abandon his legal wife— but did that mean he could never love anyone again?

She knew Lydia was probably worrying. She'd sent only a few noncommittal postcards since she'd left Prince Edward Island and, of course, had mentioned nothing about Liam. What could she say? She still needed to sort things out for herself. Even her cell phone had been turned off most of the time.

She didn't want to talk to anyone. She didn't want Laurel or their mother or Mary, her assistant, tracking her down. She just wanted to be alone. To grieve. To heal. To come to grips with her changed condition. To get used to the idea that she was going to be a mother. Come hell or high water, she was having Liam's baby. She needed time to dream a little, a least as far as the baby was concerned.

To agonize about what she'd do next.

Return to Toronto? Right now, she couldn't face going home to all kinds of questions. Hole up somewhere in Nova Scotia or New Brunswick for a month or so? Rent a room or an apartment? No, too cold. The snow had finally arrived.

But she had to be practical, too. The Suburban was getting very full. She had to either deliver her goods to her warehouse or ship them somehow.

Mainly, she tried to keep busy. She drove to St. Mary's on the south shore of Nova Scotia to take in a few parish pre-Christmas sales that looked particularly interesting. Acadian arts and goods. She ate *poutine râpée*. She bought at least a dozen excellent hooked mats and some folk art sculptures by a driftwood artist who lived in a shanty made of driftwood on Digby Neck. Charlotte had no idea how he managed in the wintertime.

Digby Neck wasn't all that far from Wolfville. She thought about Derek and Miranda, how thoughtful and hospitable they'd been a month before. Derek had told her point-blank how pleased he was that Charlotte had come to visit them with Liam. *How Liam couldn't take his eyes off her.*

Miranda would be over five months along by now. Definitely showing. Charlotte felt a powerful need to talk to another pregnant woman. Even though she was in no position to reveal anything about her own pregnancy yet, she wanted to see a friendly face. And she had a lot of questions, too. Questions about Dorrie and Liam that only someone who'd known Liam for so long could answer.

If Derek would talk to her. So many people had protected Liam. His mother. Bonnie Bristol and the other locals—most of whom must have known what

Clara Jenkins had blurted out. Maybe they'd all believed he deserved some happiness, too, as Derek had said. And as Ada had let slip once.

Charlotte knew now why Liam had wanted to keep their relationship secret as long as possible. If they were openly courting, people would start asking questions. They'd say things—as Clara Jenkins had done. They'd see it as warning her. Or reminding Liam of his duty. They'd secretly feel sorry for Liam and tell themselves he deserved a break. They'd tolerate impropriety as long as it was discreet. But when it came out in the open, no one would be for it.

Eventually, Liam would've told her about Dorrie himself. Why hadn't he told her sooner and spared them both all this grief?

And yet, a little voice reminded her, *would you have accepted it? Would you not have done exactly what you did—run away? If he really loved you, how could he risk that?*

"Miranda?" Charlotte was glad she'd gotten through on the third ring. It was a Saturday and she'd hoped to find someone home. Both of them, preferably. "It's Charlotte Moore. Remember me from a month ago, visiting with Liam?"

"Of course we remember you! Are you in the area? You are! Well, you must come and see us."

Miranda gave her detailed directions, which Charlotte was glad of, as she'd forgotten how to get to their house. She drove through a nearly silent world. Snow had begun to fall before she'd placed her call and by the time she pulled into the driveway, the landscape was white.

Miranda hugged her as soon as she opened the door, and Charlotte felt a huge weight fall off her shoulders. *She was among friends.*

"Sit down. Tell me what you've been doing lately. Glass of wine?" Charlotte refused, and Miranda poured her a soft drink. "Derek's out with Cruller. They should be back any time. I'm so glad you came! I made a huge casserole and there's no way the two of us could eat it all. Even the three of us, I'm afraid. Four, actually!" She laughed merrily and patted her belly.

Charlotte noted the round hummock when she smoothed her shirt over it. *Five of us,* Charlotte thought—*if Miranda only knew.*

When Derek arrived, he was as pleased to see Charlotte as Miranda had been. Even Cruller seemed to remember her and sniffed her avidly before leaping up onto his favorite sofa.

"Have you been out hunting with him?" Charlotte asked. It was that time of year.

"No, I'm not a hunter." Derek raised his glass to her. "You two girls just having soda? Okay, well... Cruller? No, we've just been out for a walk. I do lend him to friends who hunt, though. They're always happy to borrow him."

"Liam thinks he's a wonderful dog," Charlotte said simply, then realized that she'd said the magic word. *Liam.* No one had asked her about him, which seemed odd.

"Yes," Derek said, with a thoughtful look at her. "He's told me."

"I think dinner's ready," Miranda announced, and Charlotte couldn't help thinking that they'd deliberately changed the subject. Why? They couldn't know the details of why she'd left the Island. Why were they avoiding any mention of Liam? Had something happened to him? To Ada?

Charlotte was obsessed with those questions throughout dinner and by the time dessert was served, couldn't stand it any longer. "Have you heard from Liam lately?" she asked casually over the delicious custard with blueberries Miranda had brought to the table.

Derek coughed. "Yes. We saw him a couple of weeks ago at the, uh, at the funeral—"

"Funeral!" Charlotte dropped her spoon. "Who died? Oh my goodness, not Ada—"

"No, not Ada." Derek quickly reassured her. "Ada's fit as a fiddle. No, uh—" He turned desperately to his partner, at the other end of the table.

"Did Liam ever tell you about Dorrie?" Miranda asked gently.

"Yes." Charlotte colored. "Not at the beginning of, well, our relationship, but I did find out near the end."

"Dorrie died two weeks ago."

Charlotte stared at Miranda. Then she burst into tears.

"See what you've done now," Derek muttered, getting up from the table and coming around to helplessly pat Charlotte's back.

"Me?" Miranda shot him a dirty look. "We should've told her right away. I didn't know that she'd—"

"Never mind," Charlotte managed to say, dabbing at her eyes with the clean napkin Derek handed her. "It's just—such a shock, that's all. I—I went to see Dorrie before I left. She was very frail, I thought. Of course, I'd never seen her before...."

"The doctors said she had a cold. It turned into pneumonia and there was nothing they could do. It was a blessing, really."

"I—I suppose so!" Charlotte began to cry again, the tears flowing freely. Miranda put one arm around her and led her to the sofa in the family room. A fire blazed in the stone fireplace. It was a warm and cozy room, with framed pictures, and photographs of family members, graduates in caps and gowns, dogs, and even someone posing with a gigantic pumpkin.

Charlotte blew her nose. "I'm so sorry. I find that I'm just so—" she looked at them and laughed, but her laugh had a sob at the end "—so *emotional* these days."

The two of them exchanged glances.

"Liam and I had a falling out. I admit, it was over Dorrie," Charlotte confessed, with a look of appeal to both of them. "He hadn't told me about her, and when I found out I—I was very upset. I left. I couldn't be with him anymore. I felt betrayed. Humiliated." She blew her nose again. "Shocked. It was terrible finding out the way I did, from a stranger...." Her voice trailed off, and she stared at the fire for a few minutes.

"And now?" Miranda prompted.

"Now I wish I'd given him another chance." She lifted her head and met Miranda's candid gaze. "I'm sure there were good reasons he wasn't frank with me but—" Charlotte ran her hand over her face "—I was so stunned to find out that he was married, that he had a *wife* when I—well, I don't mind admitting I had some hopes in that direction myself...."

Derek leaned forward and put his hand on her knee. "Dorrie goes back a long way in Liam's life, Charlotte. A long, long way. Would you like to hear what I know of the situation? I'm one of Liam's oldest friends, but he hasn't told me everything." He sat back. "I'll tell you what I can, if you think it would help."

"I'd like it very much if you told me what you could, Derek. I'd hoped you would. To be honest, I don't know who else to ask."

Derek got up to put another log on the fire, then he sat down in his armchair again. He looked directly at Charlotte. She was grateful for the compassion she saw in his expression. "Dorrie McLeod was a fair bit younger than Liam. I guess she'd be about your age, Charlotte. She was from the other side of the Island, Campbell's Pond, but she had cousins in the area and she was always around Cardigan River and Petty Cove. She and Liam used to fool around a little, the way kids do, but I don't think he was ever serious about her.

"What he was serious about was flying. Not girls. Anyway, the family settled down in Toronto—"

"Where he went to school with my sister, Laurel."

"He did?" Derek seemed surprised. "I didn't know that. Well, after graduation and after Liam had finished his military training, he came back to the Island one summer. He'd be about twenty-three or -four at the time. He and Davy and their pal, Geordie, had a hell of a summer, I guess. Nonstop party. Dorrie really went after him—maybe she saw him as her ticket out, I have no idea—and first thing I knew, they were getting married. Liam told me Dorrie was having a baby and it was probably his, and he intended to do the right thing by her.

"That was it." Derek held up his hands in a gesture of finality. "That's Liam. Well, the upshot was, she never had any baby. I'm not sure she was even pregnant—" He glanced at Miranda, who made a protesting sound. "I'm serious, Miranda. When I knew her, Dorrie was the kind of girl who'd say black was white if she thought it would get her a new lipstick or a ticket to the movies."

He turned back to Charlotte. "Maybe I'm being too tough on her. Liam was my friend. Naturally, I worried about him. Anyway, there was no baby. They moved to CFB Shearwater, to married quarters on the base, and Liam started going on missions here and there. They argued a lot, and Liam used to drink some. He hasn't done that for years. The drinking and the fighting seemed to go together. Finally, Liam went off on a NATO mission overseas and left Dorrie expecting. This time she really was pregnant."

Charlotte's heart was beating so loudly, she was sure the others could hear.

"She had the baby while he was away, a little boy, and when he was two months old he died—"

"No!" Charlotte covered her mouth with her hand.

"SIDS. Crib death." Derek got up to poke the fire. Sparks shot up the chimney and brightened the softly lit room. "Liam was devastated. It was a terrible shock to everyone, of course. He'd never even seen his son, so I guess he figured he should've been there when the baby was born, for Dorrie as much as anything. He was back about a month after the baby died, compassionate leave, and then he left again."

Derek stared into the fire and sighed.

"Six months later, Dorrie snapped. She tried to take her own life."

"Suicide? The nurse told me she'd been in a car accident."

Derek threw her a skeptical look. "That's what it appeared to be. That's what everyone said it was, even the cops, I think, who investigated the accident."

"So? Then, it was." Charlotte shook her head. "I don't understand."

"Liam knows it wasn't. He got a letter forwarded to him from the military after he came home. He showed it to me. I don't know if he ever told anyone else—maybe Davy. Dorrie had written, telling him she was going to end it all, she was going to drive their car off a bridge—which is exactly what happened—and the reason she was doing it was that she couldn't go on. She was so lonely, he'd never been there for her, he'd never loved her, blah-blah, and the baby's death had sent her right over the edge.''

Derek shrugged. ''It's a very sad story. She was unstable. She came from a family with a lot of unstable people in it. Davy Macdonald can tell you better than I can.''

''So—so Liam blamed himself,'' Charlotte said slowly. ''He felt it was his fault. If he'd been here with Dorrie and the baby, not off in Bosnia...''

''Something like that.'' Derek poked the fire again. ''By then Fergus had died, and so had Liam's uncle who was trying to make a go of the bed-and-breakfast thing with Ada. Ada was losing her eyesight. Everything fell on Liam. He took over the care of his mother. He said he'd lost his nerve, he couldn't fly anymore. I don't know if that's true or not, but I do know he was honorably discharged from the air force. It's been a tough six years, that's for damn sure.''

Derek smiled at her. ''That's why we were so pleased when Liam met you. I could tell right away that you were different. I could see the way he looked at you. He loved you. All those years, the son of a bitch wouldn't look at a woman. He felt like he owed it to Dorrie or something, I don't know.

''Not to speak ill of the dead—'' he looked at Miranda, who scowled ''—but I don't believe she'd have done the same for him. Sad to say, but she wasn't the type to waste her youth and good looks reading a book at home while her man was away fighting wars in foreign—''

''Derek!''

''Oops. I meant to say she was an angel, a perfect angel—''

''Derek!'' Miranda got up from her chair and came over to kiss her husband lightly on the cheek. ''You're a scoundrel, you are. A scoundrel and a misogynist.''

''That's what they always say,'' he complained, smiling at her and reaching out to pull her close. ''So, Charlotte. What do you think of that?''

''I don't know what to think. Except that I'm so sorry for what Liam's gone through. And what Dorrie went through. I can't agree with you, Derek. I got a strong, strong feeling when I visited her. She loved Liam. She really did. No matter what had happened in their lives together, she loved him.''

''Well, I suppose a woman would know. I sure never had that impression. And I don't believe Liam ever really loved her. He stood by her, he was loyal, he did his duty—that's the kind of man Liam is. But love? I don't think so.'' He got up and stretched. Cruller hopped off the sofa and went over to him, wagging his tail. Derek bent down to fondle the Clumber's ears. ''Tea, anyone?''

After another half hour around the fire, Charlotte took a cup of Ovaltine up to bed with her. She was exhausted. All the driving, not to mention the huge emotional load of what Derek had told her, had taken its toll. She wanted to think everything over and try to get a good night's sleep.

Then, tomorrow, she was going to take the ferry back to Prince Edward Island. She had some unfinished business.

But before she turned out the light, she decided to call Lydia and tell her the news—all the news.

She didn't have a chance, because Lydia erupted at her.

"Charlotte, where *are* you, for heaven's sake? We've had all hell break loose here in Toronto! Not to mention a man who was here ten days ago, making a nuisance of himself, looking for you—"

"A man?"

"Yes! A handsome tough-looking man in aviator sunglasses and a bomber jacket, tearing up your warehouse—"

"*What?*" Charlotte gripped the phone more tightly. Liam?

"Your assistant called me. Mary What's-her-name. She was scared to death. Said some man was there and he wasn't leaving your place until he got some answers. I took a cab straight over and convinced him Mary didn't know where you were, I didn't know where you were, no one knew where you were—"

"Did he leave then?"

"I think he went to see Laurel."

"Oh, no!" Charlotte wanted to laugh. Liam had gone all the way to Toronto looking for her? That must mean he was willing to forgive her for running away. That he was ready to start again, as she was.

"Oh, yes! Now, tell me, is that the first-crush guy

you were looking for out there among the dead sticks and swamp marshes of Prince Edward Island?''

Charlotte giggled. ''One and the same. What do you think?''

''I think you'd better snap him up before someone else does. If you don't, I get second kick at the can.''

''No way!''

''Just kidding, of course.''

''Any other news? Or dare I ask?''

''I'm having his baby. In July. Which should make our reunion next spring at Jasper Park Lodge interesting.'' Charlotte didn't believe that Lydia heard everything she'd said because she'd started screaming at the mention of *baby*.

''Do I get to be godmother? Do I? Do I?''

''You *and* Zoey.''

''Well, you'd better marry him, Char. You know what your mother'll say if you don't....''

''I'll do my best. I promise.'' She crossed her fingers. If only she could believe that Liam was as amenable to the idea as she was.

''Drag him here for the wedding. I'll cook. I'll arrange flowers. I'll do your hair. We all want to see him—again.''

Charlotte was laughing when she finally said goodbye. But had she been premature with her good news?

She turned out the light and tried to sleep. At first she thought she'd never be able to doze off. Her mind was spinning—Dorrie, Liam, Ada, Zoey and Lydia, a winter wedding, baby layettes, a special gift for her assistant, Mary, who'd had to put up with a lot...

She heard a rap on her door and sat bolt upright. She looked at the clock on the bedside table. Two in the morning!

"Yes?" She called softly. "Miranda, is that you?"

"It's me. Can I come in?"

Liam!

CHAPTER TWENTY

CHARLOTTE SCRAMBLED out of bed and opened the door. "Liam!"

He stood there dressed in the same bomber jacket Lydia had described, holding something in his hand. Something pink and lacy. Her silk nightie!

"Forget this?"

"Oh, Liam!" She threw her arms around his neck and then gasped slightly as he wrapped his leather-clad arms around her. His jacket was snowy and cold and she was so warm.

He kissed her with such enthusiasm that she nearly squealed, then remembered where they were.

"Shh. Come in here." He went inside the room with her, and she shut the door behind him as quietly as she could. Then a thought struck her. "How did you get in? And how did you know I was here?"

"Derek, on both counts." He took off his jacket and dropped it on a chair. "He called me this afternoon. After you'd arrived. He thought I'd want to know."

"And did you?" she teased, then sobered, thinking of Dorrie. "Oh, Liam. Derek told me about Dorrie. I know it must have been a terrible shock, even though you'd been expecting it."

"For years," he said flatly. "I hear you went to see her."

"Oh?" She hadn't told Derek she'd seen Dorrie until after dinner this evening.

"Marjorie Williams. The head nurse there. She told me you'd been in. She said Dorrie died very peacefully. I—I wasn't there. I should have been," he said heavily.

"Oh, Liam. Don't say that. You couldn't have known. And you went to see her regularly. She must have known how much you loved her...."

He gave her a strange look. "Is that how you see it, Charlotte?" he asked softly. He took off his shirt, then stepped toward her and pulled her into his arms. "You're the only woman I've ever loved."

"Liam!" She searched his steady gaze. "That can't be true!"

"It's true. Dorrie and I were a couple of kids when we got married. I'd just turned twenty-four and she was eighteen. It was a case of lust, not love, and it didn't last long. Maybe a few months, on my part. I always felt bad about that. I never felt I'd done the right thing, marrying her when I didn't love her."

"Derek said—"

"Derek's another one with a big mouth." He smiled wryly. "Believe me, I married her because I thought I should. I didn't think love meant a whole lot, and if it did, it would come later. That never happened. We fought. We never got along after the first year or so. Then—"

Liam sighed deeply and leaned his forehead against hers. "There are some things I regret deeply in my life, Charlotte, and that is one of them. I should've been there when my son was born. I should've been there for Dorrie, no matter what I felt about her. To hell with love! I owed her. I was her husband, I should've been there. I lost something precious. My son's birth and then—then my son.'' He was silent, his jaw clenched. He continued softly. "I never even saw him. I think that's why I've always been so close to Davy's boy, Jamie—hey!"

Charlotte had taken Liam's hand and placed it against the cotton flannel covering the flatness of her belly. She was wearing a long-sleeved, high-necked nightgown suitable for sleeping alone on cold nights. "You'll have another chance, my love."

He stood stock-still. *Stunned* was the description that came to mind, Charlotte thought, not quite sure if she'd done the right thing herself. Hadn't Dorrie claimed she was pregnant, too? But this was different—so different!

"A *baby?*"

She nodded.

"You're having *my baby?*"

"No one else's."

"When?" His voice was hoarse.

"In July."

"You mean—" She could see that he was rapidly calculating.

She nodded again. "The very first time. By my reckoning. In Mr. Rathbone's house. I think it's very fitting, don't you? Considering the old man's reputation?"

"But, honey—" he still sounded stunned...but happy "—you said it was a safe time for you."

"I guess it wasn't," she said, and giggled. "But it was a very *good* time."

Liam laughed, the sound she loved to hear. Then he stripped out of his clothes, picked her up in his arms and carried her to the bed.

"I guess I'll have to make an honest woman of you, won't I?" He growled and buried his face in her neck.

"I *am* an honest woman," she managed breathlessly. "But, yes, I think it would be very nice if you married me, if that's what you're getting at."

"I am." He kissed her, and she wound her arms around his neck.

"If you don't want to get married again, I understand. I'm happy just to be with you," she whispered. "I love you, Liam."

"And I love you, Charlotte. And we're getting married. That's that. Ada would kill us if we didn't."

THEY WERE MARRIED on the last day of December in Toronto's City Hall. That way, said the ever-practical Charlotte—not showing yet under her Donna Karan wedding dress, a smart, knee-length sheath in wool and silk—she'd be a tax deduction for him.

And that way, said the always-romantic Liam—who was married in a very stylish suit picked out for him by his bride—they'd be starting out the New Year right.

Laurel was there with her husband. Their parents

were there, her mother weepy, her father looking proud, Ada beaming. Ada's cousin Eleanor was there, and Ada told her that the two of them had purchased a seniors' condo in Charlottetown and were looking forward to moving in mid-January.

Lydia was there, accompanied by a young girl whose name Charlotte didn't catch and a very handsome man, the girl's father, Charlotte believed. Dear, sentimental Lydia was weeping delicately at absolutely everything—the flowers, the speeches, the gifts. She'd always been such a softhearted and wonderful friend.

Davy and Alice and their family had surprised her and Liam, arriving the day before. Davy told them they were expecting another baby, and, of course, Liam and Charlotte had the same news. When they worked it out, it looked as though their children would be coming along at almost the same time.

The Macdonalds were moving into Ada's house, which made sense, Ada said, because they had so many children and they could certainly use the extra room. Liam had sold some of his dogs, and Jamie was taking over the kennel business, under Liam's guidance, and the two of them were going to continue training a few gun dogs in their spare time.

Of course, Old Jimbo and Bear would be living with Charlotte and Liam in the grand old Victorian house they'd bought in Charlottetown. They were moving in after their honeymoon to Bermuda—their second honeymoon, Charlotte said. Liam planned to take up his new career in the spring, teaching in a regional aviation school he and Geordie had started.

All the people who mattered to Charlotte and Liam were there, including Zoey and the cowboy she'd lassoed for herself in the wilds of British Columbia. She'd astonished both Lydia and Charlotte by bringing him back with her to meet everyone.

"My, we've been busy, haven't we?" Charlotte said to Zoey when they had a photograph taken of the three of them. They stood by the punch bowl in the midst of the lively after-ceremony party at the King William Hotel. The three girlfriends had kept their annual New Year's Eve date, with a difference!

Charlotte and Zoey turned to Lydia and intoned, in unison, "Two down, one to go, Lydia. You're next."

Which, Lydia said, was the most romantic thing she'd ever heard, and she began to weep beautifully all over again.

* * * * *

*The third girlfriend, Lydia Lane,
doesn't need to travel far afield
to meet her first (and last?) love!
Turn the page for an excerpt from*

LYDIA LANE,

*coming from Superromance
next month!*

CHAPTER ONE

"AMBER!" Sam slapped the pizza box onto the coffee table in the family room, pushing aside the week's accumulation of newspapers and comic books. "Mommy's show is on and the pizza's here."

He flicked the channels on the big-screen television to TownTV, Channel 14, and the familiar opening calypso medley of his ex's snoozer of a show.

"Yippee!" His daughter raced into the room with her best friend, Tania Jackson, right behind her. The two girls, both eight, were practically joined at the hip, and now they skidded to a stop as one, grabbed a slice of pizza—the two largest—and scrambled onto the oversize recliner in one corner of the room. No napkins, he noted. The whole room was due for a steam clean.

"Who's Mommy got on today?" Amber said, her mouth already stuffed with a slice of Hawaiian. Sam was so sick of Hawaiian, he could scream. What he wouldn't give for an adult pizza...

"Don't know, honey." Sam dropped a couple of paper towels on the arm of the girls' chair and then settled into the other recliner. Watching his ex's late-afternoon show with his daughter was a ritual Sam tried not to miss. Amber lived with him. Watching

Candace's show on television three times a week was supposedly one way of maintaining maternal contact. Candace's idea, naturally.

What kind of world was that—where you had to catch your mother on TV if you wanted to see her?

Sam shook his head and told himself to pay attention. He leaned forward. Hey, he'd seen that woman before, Candace's guest....

"Homemaking means just that, making a home. There can be a lot of satisfaction in knowing that the people you love are being taken care of—"

"I'll take your word for it!"

"Seriously, many homemaking arts have been lost. In the past, these skills were passed down from mother to daughter, but since the sixties, our mothers have been too busy forging careers outside the home to worry too much about housekeeping skills and techniques. As a result, a lot of know-how has disappeared. And often there's no one to ask. That's where my company, Domestica, comes in. We teach you the skills that'll turn your home into a sanctuary in a hectic world, a place the people you love look forward to returning to at the end of the day."

"Literally turn a house into a home, as they say?"

Sam glanced around the family room. It looked like a tornado had been through it. It always looked like a tornado had been through it when his mother was out of town, which she was, or he'd lost another cleaning lady, which he had, just before Christmas. He could go for some of that sanctuary business....

"That's right." The woman on the screen gave his ex a cool look—one that was very appealing,

Sam thought—and slowly crossed her legs. Long, slim, very nice legs, he noted, a pizza slice halfway between his plate and his mouth. *He definitely knew this woman from somewhere.* A client? No way!

"Homemaking skills are a sadly undervalued art in our world today. They can even affect your health. For instance, did you know that a well-made bed contributes to a good night's sleep? And wouldn't a good night's rest make a stressed-out day a little easier? Science proves—"

"You mean you don't just toss a duvet over the sheets, grab a coffee and race out the door? That's what *I* call making the bed!"

Sam was sure Candace thought she was speaking for the entire civilized world. He was intrigued. A well-made bed...

"Lydia Lane!"

"What, Daddy?"

"Lydia Lane," Sam repeated, feeling a little rush of blood to his knees that he hadn't felt for quite a while. It was the *well-made bed* that had done it. He'd pictured this tawny goddess sprawled out on that bed.... "Daddy knows that lady on Mommy's show, Amber. Remember my friend Steve Lane? We went fishing with him and Uncle Avie last summer and Uncle Avie accidentally caught that mud turtle?"

"Oh, yeah. Yuck." She turned to her friend. "We let him go back in the water."

"Yeah, well, that's Steve's sister Mommy's talking to." *That* was it....

Sam looked around the room again. The carpet

and upholstery needed cleaning. Amber's jeans had holes in the knee—why didn't she put on a new pair or tell him if she needed to buy some? The fridge was empty—again. The Christmas tree had turned brown; Sam had forgotten to put water in the receptacle. The last housekeeper had left before the holidays and Sam hadn't had the heart to look for another one yet. How many did that make this year? Three? Four? *Five?*

He ran his hands through his hair, then got up and grabbed the empty pizza box to carry it through to the kitchen, which was another kind of disaster. Taking care of a house was a hell of a bigger job than he'd thought, and he had renewed respect for women like his mother, who always seemed to know exactly what needed to be done.

Man, this single-parenting stuff—it never ended! Look at his place! It was exactly like this woman said on television: he didn't have the skills. And he didn't have the faintest idea where to start.

LYDIA CHECKED in her purse for a bus token. The minivan was acting up again and causing alarm bells to go off in her head. She couldn't afford repairs right now, not on top of her new mortgage payments—

"Oh, there you are!" Candace Downing slipped into the cloakroom, closing the door behind her. "I was hoping you hadn't gone yet. Did you watch the rest of the show?" She looked excited; her eyes sparkled, her hands fluttered.

Lydia nodded as she smoothed on her gloves.

"You wanted to see me?" Kid leather, soft as butter and bright, bright red. To match her knock-down cashmere beret from Holt's, an after-Christmas present to herself. Her mother had always worn gloves, still did; Lydia's high school friends had said how classy they thought it was. At sixteen, Lydia had scoffed. Now she knew how right they were. There was something so—so forties about gloves.

"Nice gloves," Candace said.

"Thank you." Lydia smiled.

"Listen, have you got time for a coffee?" Candace glanced at her watch. She was a small woman, much more petite than she appeared on television. Dark hair, blue eyes, very pretty.

"Sure. Why?" Lydia was mystified.

"Let's go down to the caf," Candace said, opening the door again. "Come on. I've been thinking about what you said on the show. I may have a client for you."

They both ordered lattes in the cafeteria that served the building and the neighborhood and took a seat by the window.

"You ever do longer jobs—you know, a couple of months if necessary?" Candace stirred her coffee vigorously. Lydia had the impression that Candace did everything at full tilt.

"No, but I've been looking around for something like that," Lydia said. "A longer job would give me a chance to see if the things I do would make a real difference to a real family." She eyed her companion over the rim of her coffee cup. "Depends what it is, of course."

"I'm thinking of my ex."

"Your ex?"

Candace's blue gaze met hers steadily. "Yes. His life is a mess. He's one of those guys who's never done anything domestic. Mama did it all. Ironed his shirts, picked up his socks, cooked his breakfast, tied his ties. Since our divorce four years ago, he's gone straight downhill. Don't get me wrong. *I* was never a great housekeeper—"

Candace laughed, looking thoroughly pleased to acknowledge her shortcomings in that department, which irritated Lydia. But she'd seen the attitude a million times before, especially with career women like Candace.

"—but it didn't matter. I hired people to do the nitty-gritty. But now, since he's been working out of the house—whew!"

"Where exactly would Domestica fit in?"

"Everywhere!" Candace gave her an encouraging smile. "Don't you see? You could start with the cleaning thing, get that house of his sanitized. That's number one. Then you could organize *him.* He's totally helpless. He sends all their clothes to a laundry, even Amber's pajamas. They can't keep a maid. No one will stay. I don't blame those women. They can get all the work they want at easier places."

Lydia bit her lip. Sounded bad. "It would be a challenge."

"You could do it, I know you could. You're smart, you're organized, you know what you're doing. Charge him as much as you want—he's got the money! He's a lawyer—did I tell you? After you get his house sorted out, teach him how to shop. Sam can't cook. They live on cornflakes, pizzas, deli, Chinese take-out, Swiss Chalet. Or his mother brings food over.''

She must have read Lydia's thoughts. ''Don't let me give you the wrong impression—he's a wonderful father. A natural. Amber adores him. He's stable, reliable and he's always there for her. It's just the chaos in his house, that's all.''

Lydia wondered why Candace had split with such a prize. Obviously she wasn't telling all.

''What do you think? Will you consider it— *please?*''

Lydia smiled. She liked Candace, one of those pretty women who were an inch deep and a mile wide and didn't care who knew. ''Sure. Of course, I'll need to talk to your ex—what's his name again?''

''Sam.'' Candace scooped up the bill. ''Sampson T. Pereira. And you know what he always tells people the 'T' stands for?''

''What?''

''Trouble!''

HARLEQUIN *Super*ROMANCE®

Old friends, best friends…
Girlfriends
Your friends are an important part of your life. You confide in them, laugh with them, cry with them….

Girlfriends

Three new novels by Judith Bowen

Zoey Phillips. Charlotte Moore. Lydia Lane.
They've been best friends for ten years, ever since the summer they all worked together at a lodge. At their last reunion, they all accepted a challenge: *look up your first love.* Find out what happened to him, how he turned out….

Join Zoey, Charlotte and Lydia as they rediscover old loves and find new ones.

Read all the *Girlfriends* books! Watch for *Zoey Phillips* in November, *Charlotte Moore* in December and *Lydia Lane* in January.

HARLEQUIN®
Makes any time special ®

*Together for the first time
in one Collector's Edition!*

New York Times bestselling authors

Barbara Delinsky

Catherine Coulter

Linda Howard

Forever Yours

**A special trade-size volume containing three
complete novels that showcase the passion,
imagination and stunning power that these
talented authors are famous for.**

Coming to your favorite retail outlet in December 2001.

HARLEQUIN®
Makes any time special®

Visit us at www.eHarlequin.com   PHFY

TRUEBLOOD, TEXAS

Coming in January 2002...

THE BEST MAN IN TEXAS

by

Kelsey Roberts

Lost:

One heiress. Sara Pierce wants to disappear permanently and so assumes another woman's identity. She hadn't counted on losing her memory....

Found:

One knight in shining armor. Dr. Justin Dale finds himself falling in love with his new patient...a woman who knows less about herself than he does.

Can the past be overcome, so that Sara and Justin may have a future together?

Finders Keepers: bringing families together

HARLEQUIN®

Makes any time special ®